10/21/87

To The Olive Garden Trainers,

It's been, pleasant, hectic, but interesting, fascinating and a learning experience. Thank you-all for your efforts and friendship and professionalism.

Guido Levett

Class #27

A RETURN TO YESTERDAY

by

Guido C. Levetto

A Geneva Book

Carlton Press, Inc.   New York, N.Y.

To the memory of my father, who left before
this book could be completed.

MARIO J. LEVETTO

March 6, 1908-January 6, 1985

"A courtly gentleman, whose word was
his bond"— Art Hamilton.

A RETURN TO YESTERDAY

1

The protective cloak of darkness covered Cutler Garnett as he lowered himself among the reeds of the lazy stream. The lukewarm water penetrated his clothing and relieved the stings of the many insect bites. As he cautiously lowered himself into the stream, his eyes scanned the facing distant horizon. Seeing no movements, he slowly began paddling toward the distant shore. The thin sliver of moon left little reflection on the ripples of brackish water and the horizon melted into the hardly distinguishable distant tree line.

For almost an hour, he swam quietly toward the distant shore. Finally, the weight of his soaked clothes and knife at his waist tired him, so he rested while treading water. As Garnett rested with only his head above water, he noticed a dark form detach itself from the distant shore and grow larger as it approached. The creak of oar locks and scrape of oars against a wooden hull drifted towards him across the water.

A suspicion of having been seen or betrayed caused a knot to tighten in the swimmer's stomach. The boat moved closer, so he lowered himself as much as possible into the water and cautiously paddled downstream, hoping to pass as some floating debris, if spotted.

As Cutler moved downstream, it became apparent that the occupants of the boat had not spotted him, for the boat did not deviate from its original course and passed a scant twenty feet upstream from his floating head.

With a sigh of relief, Private Cutler Garnett felt his feet touch the soft, spongy bottom of the stream. The mosquitoes attacked him as he wound himself through the reeds at the stream's edge toward firmer ground. Ignoring these, he continued noiselessly through the thick underbrush until he reached a thick stand of scrub oak. As he listened for hostile sounds, he removed his clothing, squeezed out as much water as he could, and dressed. He smiled to himself as he sat on a log. Old Sergeant Knolls would have had him hauling horseshit for a week if he had seen him this sloppy, not to mention wearing moccasins and leggings, instead of boots. Knolls had been harrassing him from the first day he had ridden into camp for training. The grizzled old veteran of the Seminole campaigns and General Zachary Taylor's Mexican Army had no use for, as he put it, "spoiled rich kids." Samuel Garnett didn't raise any "spoiled" kids; rich, yes, but certainly not spoiled! The new properties near Mellonville needed serious-minded overseeing, sweat and hard work. Sam Garnett didn't put up with anything less, especially from his son. He had always drilled into his son's head: "Remember, you can do anything anyone else can do, only better."

In April of that year, 1862, it had been an unspoken under-standing that on his 18th birthday, Cutler Garnett would go to Ft. Lee, near Gainesville, and join the Florida Brigade. With controlled emotion, Sam had shaken his son's hand, told him to behave, and trying to be bold, said: "Come back in one piece. There's a lot of work to do here and I'll have to do your work and mine while you're marching in parades and playing with girls, while wearing that pretty new gray uniform."

Although Cutler had proved he was no dandy, Sergeant Knolls had intensified the harrassment of the young soldier. He had made up his mind to prove to himself and the other recruits that he was never wrong, and that the young Floridian would eventu-ally run home to daddy. Instead, the opposite happened. Cutler could out-ride, out-shoot, and out-fight any of the new sol-diers....and some of the veterans. Hunting and camping in the Florida swamps and woods either makes you or breaks you, and Sam Garnett would not have tolerated less than the best! Being in his early 40's, Sam was no slouch himself.

When Captain Teague asked for a volunteer, familiar with the North Florida terrain, to deliver messages, Sergeant Knolls "volunteered" the rich kid. Everybody was happy! Sergeant Knolls got his little kingdom back by getting Garnett and his stoic attitude out of camp, with a good possibility of not returning. Captain Teague could go back to making his white lightning, knowing his embellished messages were on their way to headquarters, and Private Cutler Garnett was away from the routine of camp life and daily aggravation from the sergeant.

The hoot of a night owl on a nearby branch snapped him out of his trance. Slowly standing, he sniffed the night air, listened carefully, and slipped from the stand of trees toward the marsh in the direction from which the boat had come.

After traveling some two hundred yards, Cutler sank down and waited in the muck. The sounds of boots sucking mud and shuffling in the rotten vegetation in front of his position became more audible. He silently slipped the long keen blade from its sheath. With the familiar deer-horned handle secure in his grasp, he slowly squirmed through the thick undergrowth toward the hostile sounds. It took him a full ten minutes to move thirty feet. When he stopped again, he was less than six feet from the back of a shadowy figure. The strong pungent odors of sweat and tobacco were repugnant to his nose. Barely breathing, Cutler drew himself up into a crouch and waited. The shadow shuffled, then slapped a mosquito on his neck and mumbled: "Damn mosquitoes, what a miserable asshole place." He slowly turned and faced Cutler, peering down into the darkness at him. As if shot from a cannon, the crouching figure sprung! His left hand grabbed the rifle upward, while his right hand, firmly gripped around the knife handle, swung a deep arc across the throat of the alarmed sentry.

With a shocked look of surprise, the sentry dropped to his knees and fell over on his left side, a gurgling sound coming from the slice that had been a throat. Still grasping the rifle with his right hand, he pulled his attacker down over him. As the sentry's fingers slowly released the rifle, the corpse emptied its bowels.

Cutler sprang up, still holding the rifle and the dripping knife as a voice on the other side of the bushes said, "What the hell you doin', Frank?" Cutler hesitated, and trying to imitate the voice of the dead sentry managed a muffled, "You and this whole

9

damn stinkin' country can go to hell!" With relief, Cutler heard a chuckle as an answer.

Feeling remorse, he quickly took the rifle, belt, cartridge box, bayonet and cap from the bloody body. After a moment's hesitation, he unbuttoned the blue tunic from the warm body and tucked it in his belt behind him. After rolling the still form under a bush, he lowered himself to the ground and crawled toward the other voice.

Cutler spotted the outline of a figure leaning against the rough bark, under a large live oak. Waiting to see if the figure was alone, Cutler opened the cartridge box and removed a little lead ball. Keeping his eyes on the figure he continued his crawl, moving slightly to his right. He stopped and slowly stood as he reached the opposite side of the tree where the sentry was leaning. The leaning form was barely three feet to his left. Holding the muzzle of the rifle with his right hand, Cutler lobbed the lead ball with his left hand. As the figure suddenly turned to look toward where the lead ball landed, the stock of a rifle hit him full force in the stomach. Falling to his knees, a second blow on the head enveloped him into darkness.

Cutler quickly took these weapons and tunic, relieved he hadn't had to kill this second man. Wrapping the second set of weapons and ammunition in the tunic, he fastened them all with the guard's belt, and began walking northward, away from the river.

2

Gratefully, Cutler watched the lightening of the sky in the east. His tired muscles and common sense made him realize that with the coming of daylight, he needed to find a place to hide and rest. Speeding his pace, Cutler knew where he was going. He had hunted in this area three years ago with old Deep Waters, his friend, the Seminole. The Indian had simply moved into an abandoned lean-to at the edge of his father's lands. Deep Waters has lost his left hand during the war. He never said so, but it had been rumored that one of Andy Jackson's men had chopped it off when he had been captured and taken to Saint Augustine prison with Osceola. Sam Cutler had marveled how the old Indian could do anything any normal man could do. In fact, Sam had joked that the hand had been cut off to bring him down to the level of the rest of us mortals.

As Cutler approached the base of the gentle rise of ground, he dropped suddenly and listened carefully. He smelled smoke, and as he lay among the palmettos, he smelled bacon cooking and heard the sounds of an awakening camp. He planned to reach the line of fallen trees that he knew was on the other side of the low hill. Quietly running at a crouch up the rise, the soldier swiftly reached the crest, dropped down again, and looked at the camp. Through the morning ground fog, Cutler could see a sentry sitting on a log, two men crouched over a fire cooking bacon and coffee, and three more forms sitting up on blankets on the ground.

Keeping his eyes on the camp, Cutler crawled around to the left until he reached the opposite side from where he had come, then with one last look, he backed into a large pile of dead trees and branches. A tornado of years past had torn pines, oaks, and magnolias into an uneven pile of roots and branches over two miles long and a hundred yards wide. Into this tangle of wood, Cutler made himself at home, and except for his thirst and hunger, he was quite content with himself.

He woke in the heat of the afternoon. Sweat soaked him all the way through and his mouth was as dry as cotton. He peeked out between the logs and brush and watched the normal lazy, picket duty, out-camp. Knowing that there was nothing else he could do, he rearranged his bedding and fell back to a fitful sleep until dusk.

The appetizing odor of bacon, beans, hardtack and coffee woke Cutler at dusk, and he knew that he had to get something in his belly before continuing his journey northward. Moving slowly to the left he edged his way toward the food sacks hanging from trees at the edge of camp. The six soldiers were now seated around the fire, eating, talking and joking while Cutler untied one of the the food sacks, threw it over his shoulder, and quietly continued his journey in the fading light.

Stopping at a stream, Cutler drank his fill, then with his

11

pockets full of biscuits, he continued walking and munching, with the spare rifle, ammunition, tunics, and sack of food tied on his back. Avoiding all roads and trails, he continued his journey without incident for two more nights. He broke camp early the next morning, and at midday he arrived at the narrow bridge that led to Saint Augustine. Across a sea of waving saw-grass he saw the coquina and wood buildings of the ancient city.

3

The old city was bustling with activity. Farmers with their produce were everywhere, calling and bargaining. Cattle were being herded in pens, although Cutler noticed they didn't seem as fat as the ones he had seen in the past. The difference in appearances of the soldiers were like a conglomeration of various armies. They varied from the precise, strict, well disciplined formations of patrols, to stinking, unshaven, tattered loungers.

As Cutler headed toward Fort Marion, through the dusty streets, the only attention he attracted was from the harlots openly soliciting. One toothless skinny whore tried to grab him in the crotch and when he pushed her away, without a second glance, she turned toward another soldier.

Rows of tents and lean-tos surrounded the stately old coquina fort, and the thick cloud of choking fine dust and pungent fire smoke, floated in the afternoon heat, reminding Cutler of the cooler shade of the forest. As he approached the first outpost with its moat and bridge to the fort, he heard the harsh commands of close-order drill being given from inside its walls.

Two sentinels, one on each side of the moat bridge, smartly barred the way with their old bayonet-fixed muskets. Cutler fumbled inside his tunic and handed the sentinel on his right the sealed, oil-skin orders. This sentinel called for the Corporal of the Guard who seemed to appear magically with his hand out. The orders were thrust into his hand. All three guards came to rigid attention, saluted, and the Corporal barked, "Follow me, Sir!"

Cutler smiled to himself as he followed the soldier, realizing that with so many variations of uniforms and Companies, these soldiers, not knowing whether he was an officer or not, were playing it safe. By the actions of the sentinels and some of the men in the courtyard, it was obvious that these men had been professional soldiers and had probably recently resigned from the old government army.

The old fort had changed since Cutler had visited it before the war. It was now a well stocked, busy center of military activity. The most noticeable difference, however, was the professional bearing of the soldiers going about their chores and duties. The difference between them and some of the rabble he has seen in town was like comparing thoroughbreds and jackasses.

The Corporal approached one of the doorways in the coquina wall, knocked on the wood door jam, stepped in, saluted, and announced, "Messenger from Captain Teague, Sir." So doing, he disappeared into the darkness.

Cutler followed into the semi-dark room and saluted to the shadowy figure standing behind a large table, and announced, "Private Garnett reporting, Sir." Then after a moment's hesitation, "Excuse the appearance, Sir." Reproving himself, Cutler thought, "I didn't have to say that. Why didn't I keep my mouth shut?"

"When did you leave Fort Lee, soldier?" The officer's voice was non-commital. "Wednesday, Sir," replied Cutler, still rigid at attention and self conscious.

The officer said, "Sit in the chair. That was only four days travel, and I know you couldn't come on horseback past those Federal patrols." Then turning he continued, "Corporal, have some of that fresh beef we had today and cold water brought over...I have some questions and this man must be hungry and thirsty."

"Now, Private Garnett, while I read these messages, you start talking. Tell me everything you know about your trip here. Don't spare even the smallest detail. I'll interrupt you as you go along, and when your food gets here, you just keep talking and eating just like you were telling a story to your folks back home."

After a moment's hesitation, Cutler began his story. As he progressed he began demonstrating by waving his arms. Then after having placed the captured weapons and tunics on the officer's table, he sat down to devour the delicious beef and continued to talk between bites. The officer listened attentively, having laid down the messages, and then occasionally interrupted with questions.

When Cutler finished his story he realized that he was a private in a commanding officer's headquarters, not a country bumpkin at the corner log. Not knowing what to do, he stood up at attention and said quietly, "sorry Sir, I...." "Sit down, soldier. You did fine," the officer murmured. Then he called, "Orderly, bring Major Burns, quickly." Turning again to Cutler, "I want you to sit there and eat and drink. There's some good Tennessee whiskey in that flask in front of you. Take a good swallow. It'll do you good. I want you to calmly repeat to the Major that's coming in everything you just told me. You may have missed something, so I'll listen carefully. Here he is. Just stay seated."

The major was a boy not much older than Cutler. He saluted and then sat at the opposite end of the table. The Commander explained briefly who Cutler was, then he said quietly, "Go ahead, son, tell the Major just what you told me."

As the story unfolded itself for the second time, Cutler studied the Colonel. He was of average height, rugged of appearance, about thirty years of age, with a muscular build, but what really was commanding were his dark flashing eyes. The eyes darted, showed all emotions, and at times seemed to cloud over with a hard cold fury. Cutler was surprised that he hadn't noticed this when he first had come into the Commanding Officer's presence. Occasionally during this second story telling, the two officers would exchange glances, but this time, remembering the questions that had been asked by the Colonel the first time, Cutler told the answers before being asked the questions.

Turning toward the seated Major, the ever pacing Colonel said, "Well, Burns, it seems that if this boy is right, the rivers are being patrolled by unsupported small units. According to those scouts, from you know who, and the messages this boy has brought in, there wasn't supposed to be any penetration by the

Federals on the Saint John River. Either they moved in overland, slipped by our boats and chains, or have been there for awhile under cover. Groups of sympathizers may have been leading small groups without being noticed. We've got a major problem and have to cure it quickly so we can get the beef, salt, and sugar to the ships for the Army. Private Garnett saw no gun-boats other than a rowboat and no cavalry or artillery...plus he saw only small groups of sentinels. Those are tunics are from an Ohio unit and they have been committed to defend Washington, so most of their experienced officers and men must still be up there with minor details down here; probably a few vets and the rest new recruits."

After a silence of a few seconds, the Colonel turned to Cutler and exclaimed while pointing a finger at him, "You, young man, will go wash. My orderly will get you a blanket while your uniform is washed. Then you have exactly four hours to catch up on your sleep. You will then retrace your steps of the last four days." Still facing the seated private, the Colonel continued, "Major, you will follow Private Garnett as officer in charge. You will take with you twenty of the best marksmen and woodsmen of the unit, and, listen carefully, with the advice of Garnett, you will reopen our river again. Draw enough supplies for each man for four days. If you need more, steal from the enemy. You'll have a good helper!"

Major Burns stood up, grinned at Cutler, then turned to the Colonel and saluted. "Yes, Sir," he said, and sounded like he was ready to leave that very minute.

4

The hand on his shoulder startled him from a deep sleep, and looking up, Cutler saw the grin of a young soldier. "Beggin your pardon, Sir, the Major said to call you. Here's your uniform and supplies. I'm to be your point man, so the Major he says, 'You take the spare new rifle, Jacobs,' he says. The Major, he's a good man, he is, yes sir." The young soldier had rambled all these words in one monotone sentence, and then stood waiting.

"Thanks, Jacobs. My name is Cutler Garnett, and I'm a private too, so you can forget the Sir stuff. I'll get dressed in a minute and I'll be with you." Taking the clean uniform, he dressed hurriedly, wrapped his supplies in the blanket, looped this over one shoulder, strapped on his cartridge belt and knife, picked up the rifle, and nodded, "Let's go."

Major Burns was standing with his back towards the two soldiers as they quickly walked up. Facing him was a line of stern-faced, grey-clad infantrymen, rigidly at attention, rifles at their sides, and blanket rolls over one shoulder. Cutler turned to the Major, saluted, and murmured, "Private Garnett reporting, Sir."

Returning the salute, Major Burns said softly, "Stand there." Then, in a louder voice, added, "At ease, men. Group around me. I've got something to tell you, and I don't want the whole world to hear me." At first the men hesitated, then they shuffled into a semi-circle. The Major continued, "This young fellow here is Private Garnett. He will be my advisor and second in command. He will be Acting Sergeant for the duration of this patrol." Cutler glanced at the Major with both surprise and pleasure, and then back at Jacobs, who had patted him on the back and was beaming. The officer continued, "The bluecoats have part of the Saint Johns River and are threatening to cut off our travel route. We're going to take it away from them, and use their supplies to keep it away from them...Now, we don't want to tell them about it until we do it, so, Jacobs, you take seven men and just kind of mosey through town, over the West bridge, and meet us at the old Miller place. As you men are going through town don't say anything about what's going on; those walls have ears. Jacobs, I want you to bellyache about having to stay all night by a stupid bridge swatting skeeters and listening to gators. When you get to the bridge you'll find eight men already there. They are going to stay at the bridge and they know that you will be passing. Don't say anything except 'Uncle Fred makes good shine.' The reply will be, 'There's some by the old Miller place.' You'll go there and wait for the rest of us. Go now!" Jacobs turned and walked quietly past seven of the closest men to him and touched each lightly as he went by. Silently, all eight men disappeared

16

into the gathering darkness through the open gate of the fort. The last signs of their passing were their shadows, reflected by the gate lanterns on ancient coquina walls.

Jacobs and his patrol gone, the Major spoke again, "Sergeant Garnett, you will take eight men with you...Once outside the gate, go North for a couple of miles, then turn West and make your way to the meeting place. The guard at the city gate will ask you for your pass and you reply, 'I burned it.'" With that Major Burns grinned for a moment. "The route that you take will be a little longer, but take your time and make sure you're not followed. If you are...you know what to do! The rest of us will take a small boat on the South side of this fort. We'll row West, then North, and leave the boat at the bridge. Okay, Sergeant, go quietly without any fanfare."

Passing the city gate, Cutler and his men continued northward along the dusty path. The moon was at one quarter, allowing little light for the darting eyes of the alert soldiers. Having traveled almost a mile, Cutler raised his hand and the silent column of single file figures stood still. Cutler motioned to the next man in line to continue forward, then tapped the second man to move into the palmetto scrubs with him. The remainder of the column continued quietly on the same trail while Cutler and the chosen soldier crouched silently by the trail, looking in the direction from which they had come.

As if of one mind, the two men laid their bed rolls, rifles, and cartridge belts down, and with their knives in hand, waited. No word had been spoken.

The only sounds to be heard were the scurrying of little night creatures, the light rustle of a slight breeze at the tops of the trees, and the drone of insects as they began to enjoy the feast of the unmoving figures.

Almost twenty minutes elapsed when Cutler pointed his forefinger toward the trail. Shortly, a scarcely audible padding of footsteps was heard, then two figures emerged from the darkness. Simultaneously, the Confederates sprang and hit the two surprised shadows on the trail.

Cutler hit his man in the belly with his shoulder and as the man fell backward the handle of a big knife smashed him in the temple; this was the last movement the man saw. Cutler turned quickly to his right to assist his comrade, but stopped suddenly, seeing his companion sheathing his knife while bending over a still figure sprawled on the trail.

"Is he dead?" whispered Cutler. "Naw, just sleepin," came the reply. "Good. Let's tie them up. Then you trot back toward town, get some guards to come here and get them. I'm sure that the Colonel will sure like to talk to these two gentlemen."

The two unconscious men were tied securely with their own belts and suspenders, and the soldier picked up his weapons and supplies and quickly turned toward Saint Augustine.

Cutler picked up his weapons, then leaned against a tree and watched his still sleeping prisoners. Both men looked to be in their middle or late thirties, had been armed with the latest rifles, and standard issue Federal equipment, but were dressed as farmers. He doubted that these were amateurs; they had the look of hard-core professional spies or guerrillas. The Colonel would get little information from them.

Twenty minutes later Cutler heard running on the trail, and cautiously he moved back into the bushes. "Garnett, it's me Forselli. The sentries are here...the Colonel is here, too." Cutler stepped out onto the trail.

"Good work. We were expecting this. We were waiting by the gate to hear from you. In fact, if we had not heard from you within the hour, we were going to follow your trail," spoke the Colonel as he returned Cutler's salute. His eyes had flashed with excitement. "I envy you. I sure would like to go along, too. Hurry on now and catch up with the rest of your men. These two are going to wake up in a very surprising place."

Without a word, Cutler and his companion turned northward and sped to join their slow moving patrol. Following the trail, then turning westward through the freshly bent blades of reeds, with just a nod of recognition, the two rejoined their group.

5

"Well, Sergeant, welcome to our little command. Anything new?" asked Major Burns as Cutler and his small band walked into the clearing where the balance of the Southerners were lounging and waiting among the scrub oaks. "Not much, sir. The Colonel has a couple of spies to question tonight." "Colonel Dearing figured so," replied Burns. "You have ten minutes to rest, then be ready to move," continued the officer. He motioned to Cutler to follow him. The two walked over to a fallen log and sat down.

"We have about five hours to sunrise. What do you think?" asked the Major. "Well sir, a couple of nights of travel if we push it, and the sooner we put some distance between the fort and us, the less chance that someone can run across our trail," answered Cutler.

"I agree. You take over. I'll stay right behind you. For now we'll put Jacobs and another as rear guard, just to make sure we're not being followed. How about Forselli?"

"He's very good, sir. He's no city boy either."

Major Burns stood up, motioned the men around him, and when they had grouped around, he turned to Cutler who was now standing beside him and said, "The Sergeant is going to give the orders. Listen carefully."

Cutler looked around the semicircle of serious, young, faces. He was now responsible to get the mission down successfully and to get as many of these men through it alive. "The Major and I will lead, for now. Everybody single file, no talking, no rattling of equipment, no shooting, no eating or drinking while we travel. Keep at least five to six paces distances between you...Randolph, you will be twelfth man in line. Unless you specifically are ordered forward, you will follow the column by no closer than fifty yards. If the front column is attacked, unless the attack comes from the left, you will always circle to the right and come to our aid. That way if we're attacked from both sides, the front, or behind us, we'll always know from what side the friendly fire will come. if we're attacked from the left only, circle left and hit them from behind. We'll counter, and hit them from both sides....Jacobs, you and Forselli will follow Randolph's men as rear guard. You know what to do! We will travel strictly by night for the next two nights, and rest by day. Get all the rest you can when you can. Afterwards, we may go a long time without sleep." After this long speech he turned to the Major and continued, "Sir?" "Carry on Sergeant. You're doing fine," was the reply to the unasked question.

For two nights the twenty-two men continued on their journey, walking all night and resting and eating cold food during daylight. On the third night of the patrol as they approached the spot where Cutler had hidden in the fallen trees, he signaled a halt and advised Major Burn of their position.

"We have to strike quickly and take the whole group!" whispered the Major. "Beg your pardon, sir. I think we should move in, follow, listen for awhile, and then decide. We may find out something more than we think, is goin on," countered Cutler. After a short hesitation, Burns said, "You might be right. We'll do it your way."

Although there were still several hours of darkness, the Southern patrol stopped and rested in the middle of the fallen trees, about three hundred yards from the quiet camp of the Northern soldiers. The men, although relaxing, remained alert. Of course, the customary precaution of placing sentinels was a normal part of the routine.

"What's your next plan?" asked the Major. "Sir, I'd like to use the next few hours and go in close with Jacobs, Forselli, and Randolph. We could go in from four sides and listen. Maybe follow someone coming or going to camp. Unless we're too far away trailing someone, we should be back by dawn," explained Cutler.

"Go ahead. I'd like to go, too, but someone has to stay here," reasoned Burns, with a tone of regret.

Having had a short conference with Private Jacobs, Forselli, and Randolph, the Major listening in without comment, Cutler and the three soldiers slipped into the darkness toward the enemy camp. Traveling two hundred yards, the four dropped to the ground and began to squirm silently in the same general direction, but now they fanned out and shortly were completely out of touch with each other. Each man was in uniform minus cap, and carried only a long knife, all other supplies and equipment having been left with the other men.

Cutler approached the far side of the camp. He knew that by now, the others were in place, moving closer in to listen and observe. He finally spotted the glow of hot coals and the faint odor of smoke drifted to his nostrils. He counted twelve still forms lying around the glowing embers and another nodding while seated on a log on the opposite side of the camp. As he crawled in, he had noticed a narrow trail leading away from camp. Alongside this, he hid, making himself as comfortable as possible under some palmettos. Nothing stirred in the camp for quite awhile and Cutler closed his eyes and rested, relying on his ears.

The sentry stood up once, stretched, paced for a few steps, yawned and sat down again. An hour later he went to one of the sleeping forms and shook it by the shoulder. Cutler heard him say, "Your turn, Gus. Nothing to report. I think a coon tried to get to the food sacks awhile ago but he must have given up." The man then went to his bedroll, put down his weapons, covered them, and laid down. The second man, a very young boy, went to the dying embers and poured himself some coffee from a scorched pot that was sitting nearby. He had his cup that he had taken from his bedroll. After putting a few sticks on the coals, he watched them flare. Cutler could see his dark features in the fire's glow as he stared down into the flames. The boy seemd to be fascinated by the crackling fire and only after the flames had diminished did he stand up again and walk to the log that the other sentinel had sat on before. Sitting down, the young man sipped the hot coffee and stared into the darkness.

Sounds of approaching footsteps and the clink of metal and creak of leather alerted Cutler that an enemy patrol was approaching on the trail to the camp. As the first man walked passed him, even the sentinel heard them, stood up, cocked his rifle, and called out, "Who goes there?"

"Sergeant Crocker and the patrol from the river." The answer came from in front of the hiding Confederate. Eight men walked down the trail into the clearing. The first man wore sergeant stripes on his sleeves. He was followed by two more soldiers. To Cutler's surprise, the next five men also armed, were dressed as sailors!

The new arrivals filed wearily into camp, and all except the Sergeant, were soon wrapped in their blankets. While sipping coffee from the cup he had taken from under his jacket, the Sergeant sat alongside the young sentinel on the log. Cutler could hear them talking but could only distinguish traces of their conversation from their murmurings.

The sky in the East was getting light when the sentinel and the Sergeant went to each man, nudging each with his foot. "Hit it, let's move it. Can't sleep all day you lazy slobs, and for you water bugs, hit the deck!" barked the Sergeant. All the men were quickly on their feet, rolling their bedrolls, while several went to the food sacks and carried them into camp. "Today is the day. Get enough out of those sacks to eat on the way, then split them up to carry. We've got six hours to get back to the boats. They won't wait for us, and I don't know about you, but once we quit all this damn walking and rowin, I'll be happy. Let the paddlewheels do the work," said the Sergeant as he watched the men scurrying with the packing of equipment.

In less than ten minutes, the entire Federal patrol had gone down the path led by the Sergeant; and Cutler was running in the opposite direction towards his comrades.

6

The three other scouts were talking with the Major when Cutler arrived. "They told me what happened. What do you think?" burst the Major. "We've got to get that gunboat or transport. It must have slipped past Jacksonville. Taking just this patrol won't do much good," replied Cutler between gasps. Burns nodded in agreement.

"I think we should ambush this patrol, take their places, capture the boats, then someway get on board the steamship and either capture it or blow it up, sir," said Cutler.

"Good. Explain your plan as we get after them," agreed the young officer, and with that, the Confederates quickly left in the direction the Federal soldiers had taken.

Having traveled at a quick pace for about a mile on the path, the Southerners veered off to the West through a pine forest sparse of underbrush and thick in pine needles; now the column broke into the frontier run, a type a long striding lope that woodsmen can continue for hours, and in good terrain, can eat up five to six miles every hour.

Three hours of traveling through woods, palmetto scrub, and the more difficult marshland began to tell on the perspiring runners. None too soon for any of them, Cutler slowed to a walk and then signaled a halt. "We're about fifty feet from the trail that the Feds are going to pass on. They should be here in about twenty minutes if I guessed their pace right. Major, if you would take five men to the head of the trail like we discussed, I'll try to capture all of them alive. Shoot only if absolutely necessary. If someone tries to get away, try to bring him in quietly. Guns are good, but we can't afford someone hearing us and reporting our presence," continued Cutler. "Jacobs, take two men and hide on this side of the trail. Forselli, you take two and get on the other side. Don't leave any tracks when you cross the trail. Randolph, you get up this pine and stay hidden. Give me that mockingbird imitation you showed me, when the first person comes down the trail. The rest of you come with me. We'll keep anyone from trying to double back and getting away. If they have a rear guard, we'll take care of them, too. Now get!"

The men in grey melted to their assignments, and in less than five minutes not a trace of them remained.

The sound of a mockingbird alerted the tense, hiding troops and shortly a soldier in blue was seen coming down the trail, scanning the underbrush. About thirty feet behind him walked fifteen more, in single file, their rifles also at the ready position. The last five men, comprising the rest of the unit, were yet to be seen.

"You're surrounded by regulars of the Army of the Confederate States. Halt and put down your arms," shouted a voice from the head of the trail. With this signal, the Confederate soldiers all around the path stood up and cocked their rifles. The column in blue hesitated. "Save, your men, Sergeant Crocker. You're surrounded and it would be a shame to commit suicide....,and forget

23

about the rear guard. They should be walking down the trail any minute now as prisoners," continued the Major.

"Lay em down, boys. They got us," barked the Northern Sergeant.

The men in blue laid down their rifles and remained standing where they had halted. As Major Burns and his men moved forward, he motioned to the side. One man from each side of the trail moved up and gathered the weapons lying on the trail. This done, the two men carried the weapons back into the bushes; all the while, the rest of the Confederates remained with weapons pointed. "Major Burns, Florida Brigade," introduced the Major. The surprised Northern Sergeant saluted and said, "Well, you know who I am, Sir. Didn't expect this, especially regulars."

"We have a lot of surprises, Sergeant. Now be so good as to tell your men to remove their cartridge belts, bayonets, and knives. They can keep their bedrolls and food. Here comes your rear guard now," remarked Burns as he look up. Culter was walking down the trail carrying an armful of weapons. He was followed by the rest of the Northern soldiers with sourful expressions. These in turn were followed by more grinning Confederates.

7

Major Burns looked around with satisfaction. The prisoners had been tied securely, each one seated with his back to a tree. The tunics had been taken from the Union soldiers and now, except for the four guards left behind, the rest of the Confederates were wearing blue tunics and five were completely dressed as sailors. The men were carrying their own uniforms in the bedrolls and an extra weapon. "Move them out, Sergeant. Guards, we'll be back to get you and your friends. Watch them closely," and with that, the Major began walking down the trail dressed as a Union Sergeant

The Confederate patrol moved cautiously down the trail for about an hour before reaching the river bank. At the end of the trail two Union guards were standing and talking. Upon the approach of the column, they turned and greeted the arriving men. Not until the column had come within five feet of the guards, was it realized that none of these were familiar faces. With a half dozen rifles pointed at each of them, the hapless sentinels laid down their weapons. At the same time, the balance of the Confederates rushed the dozing sailors, two in each of the three longboats, pulled up on shore. Opening their eyes and staring up into rifle muzzles, subdued the men without a struggle.

"Tie up those two guards. Now you sailors, no tricks. Get in the boats, men, quickly," said the Major. After all the men were firmly seated in the now floating boats, the officer motioned to the captured sailors to row.

The three boats moved slowly into the deep blue waters of the river. Rowing steadily without a word, the sailors brought the three boats in single file towards the middle of the waterway, and then turned slightly to the Southwest. The Saint John's River is one of the few rivers in the world that flows northward. The three small boats continued traveling southward against the current in the bright sunlight of the mid-afternoon. Coming around a gradual bend, the dark stern of a ship was sighted in the center of the river, not two hundred yards away.

As the boats continued on their course towards the large gunboat, Cutler saw no activity on the decks. A thin wisp of smoke was rising lazily from the one stack located amidships. Lines and shrouds hung unmoving from the two dark masts and empty yard arms. The large paddle wheels, one on each side of the great ship, sat motionless in the water. Large dark muzzles of cannon pointed out silently from the gunports of each side of the ship. The long stern gun pointing towards the oncoming boats sent an ominous chill up the young sergeant's back.

Major Burns, in the lead boat pointed toward the starboard side of the gunboat and as the lead boat began to turn to the right, the six rowing sailors dropped their oars, stood up, and dived off the port sides of the little boats. "It's a trap. Grab those oars, and get us alongside and on that tub," exclaimed the officer.

Almost at the same time, a volley of musket and pistol fire erupted from along the entire starboard side of the ship.

Lead balls thudded into the timbers of the little boats, splinters flew and wounded men fell. Gradually, the Southerners returned fire.

"Move it, move it! Get alongside. We've got to board her," yelled the Major. Blood was streaming from a deep wound on his neck. Men scrambled for the oars and with some semblance of order brought the boats under control and moved the few remaining feet to the low, light colored, hull of the gunship. As the boats bumped against the larger ship, the Confederates scrambled up onto the deck of the warship and a fierce hand to hand fight with the Union sailors.

Cutler grabbed hold of one of the rat lines at the stern and swung up to the deck of the ship. As he did, the flash of a cutlass swung toward his face. Ducking, he parried the blade with the barrel of his empty rifle. Then he turned, pulled his long knife, and faced his opponent.

All around, men were fighting, stabbing, shooting, yelling, dying, but Cutler had his complete attention on the thin young sailor with the scared expression facing him and getting ready to swing that awful cutlass again. The Southerner's rifle hit the closed hand gripping the handle of the big blade. At the same time, Cutler brought the sharp point of the long knife forward in an upward thrust between the ribs of the sailor. With a gasp of pain, the sailor stood motionless, his eyes staring upward. Then he fell in a heap as a thin stream of blood seeped through his teeth and flowed passed his lips and down his quivering chin.

Reaching down, Cutler picked up the cutlass with his right hand, shifted the long knife to his left hand, turned, and began yelling and swinging the heavy blade in wide, sweeping arcs.

Rallying around the Sergeant, the remaining Confederates felt as if new breath rejuvenated their powers, and fought with renewed vigor.

When the grey-haired Captain of the ship fell with a bullet through his left eye, the fight ended as quickly as it had started. The sailors stopped fighting, dropped their weapons, and raised their arms.

Looking around, Cutler saw a scene of death, suffering, and destruction. Men lay on the deck, blood was everywhere, some men were holding their wounds. Others were staring blankly, while others were staring in amazement at their gaping wounds and moaning in anguish.

"All right you heroes of Florida, let's get this mess straightened up. Sergeant Garnett, get those boats tied up and give me a count of men ready for action. Jacobs, get the wounded on the stern in the shade. See if there's a doctor on board. Forselli, get the prisoners locked up below decks in the cargo house. Randolph, bring all their officers to me in the Captain's cabin. Carry all the unfortunate to the bow, and cover them up," barked Major Burns, "and," he continued, "get your own uniforms back on."

8

Having fished the sailors out of the river and questioned them, they were locked below with the other prisoners. Cutler realized there were only sixteen men left for action of the original twenty-two, including the four guards left on shore. Two privates were too badly wounded to report for action, and four were lying under the canvas on the bow. Although wounded, two others were going about their duties. Even the Major had a large bandage around his neck. Luckily for everyone on board, the young Navy doctor was knowledgeable and impartial in treating both the Federals and Rebels. Mindful of sabotage, and checking that the fires were still banked and the fire gang watched, Cutler accompanied Private Randolph, two guards, the officers, and the midshipmen, to Major Burns in the Captain's cabin.

The cabin door was open. Cutler knocked and stepped in. "The officers are here, sir. Shall I bring them in?" he said quietly. "Come in and shut the door," was the reply. Doing this and then turning, Cutler said, "We're in trouble, aren't we. I found out how we got shot up. The sailors that we had rowing told me. Actually, they were kind of braggin....All ships have a type of return to the ship code when in enemy waters. The safe way to return on board is to approach broadside with all three boats abreast, stop and backwater, then advance to the hull. They were then to call out for the officer of the deck and ask permission to come aboard. I guess if we were sailors we would have known this, just like they wouldn't know about some of our ways in the woods. While they were braggin about how they almost outsmarted us, one of them slipped up about another shore party. For a ship this size, they do seem a little understrength."

Burns thought for a moment and said, "How many officers are there on board?"

"Countin the dead Captain, four, and three midshipmen."

"We've got to turn this thing around and get the hell out of here. I guess there has to be an officer and midshipman missing. They wouldn't go alone, so there has to be at least eight seamen with them, maybe up to twelve. Do you have any ideas how to get this thing moving, and not run aground?"

"No, sir, but I could figure how to keep it from hitting aground hard by throwin the mark. I've seen it done on some shallow Florida rivers, and I've been on the St. John before."

"All right, we'll try to bluff these officers into thinking that we know what we're doing. Maybe Randolph can get the fire gang to cooperate. After all, if this thing blows up, they're the ones that don't have a chance. Send in the officers and the guards. You talk to Randolph and see if he can get down there and do some talking," murmured the Major softly. Cutler nodded and went out.

"Guards, accompany these gentlemen inside. All right, pilot, let's go," he said as he turned to Private Randolph, and winked. The puzzled, but stoic faced private turned and followed.

"We've got to fool these Feds into thinking we're regular river rats. Get down there with the fire gang and promise them anything to help us, or some boilers may blow up if they don't," whispered Cutler. Calling Forselli, he said, "Get three men, put one up on that platform on the mast as lookout. There's a bunch of blue-bellies missing somewhere. Once we get movin, get with the others and between you figure out how to throw a mark ahead with a weight. When it hits bottom you keep it taut and as we go over it you pull it up and count the knots in the line that were underwater. That's not the exact way to do it but it's close enough for us to figure out how deep the water is. We'll be movin very slowly anyway. When we go around the next bend you make sure to send a heavy guard in the boats to get the prisoners and our boys we left on shore. Got it?" Forselli looked up and nodded. Cutler was satisfied that between this man, Randolph, and Jacobs, he couldn't do much better, and really the rest of the hand picked patrol was pretty sharp, too!

"Sergeant, look what I found." Cutler turned and faced one of the younger Confederates. He was standing grinning holding two pistols by their barrels, one in each hand. "These here, six shots, are the Colt pistols without a topstrap. You know, the Navy 36's," he continued. "There's a mess of them all around this here place."

Cutler took one of the pistols and examined it. "I've heard of these new guns. They're lighter than the Army ones. Load two for every man. Get the rest of them into the Captain's cabin and tell the Major. He'll tell you what to do...Good work, soldier," he said to the beaming boy as he hurried off on his errand. Jacobs had talked all about different types of weapons one night on the trail, and judging by his knowledge, Cutler figured that if anyone knew weapons, he did. In fact, once underway, he would have him look over the heavy armament on the ship so that if necessary the Southerners could give a good account for themselves.

Surveying the damage on the deck, Cutler saw that the men had been picking up weapons and had doused the bloody planks with buckets of river water.

"Men, rest, eat something, but keep a good look out. We don't want to be surprised by any bluecoats. Look around on deck and see if you can figure out how this equipment works. Get with Jacobs about these cannon, too. I'm going below," said Cutler.

Stepping slowly down the steps into the dimly lit interior of the ship, he marveled at how all the equipment was neatly in place, and everyting perfectly spotless. All the lines were perfectly coiled, hammocks tied exactly the same way, and weapons and arms shining and in place. As he came to where the prisoners were, the heavily armed guards barely looked up, as they kept their weapons pointed at the tightly packed, seated and scowling sailors and soldiers.

Talking softly to the guard, he said, "I want each one of those men searched carefully, one by one. Don't push them around, but be thorough. As they're searched put them in those three center storage cabins...empty them first. Divide the prisoners equally; separated they can't cause as much mischief and it won't take as many guards to watch them. Be careful but quick. We could get attacked any time and we've got to get them under control before we get this thing out of here."

"Randolph has three of the boiler gang to work with us. They're getting the fires stoked up now," said Burns. Cutler had returned to the Captain's cabin and reported the progress. There were ten cases of new Colt revolvers in the crowded little cabin and two privates were seated on the floor busily loading them and carrying them out to their comrades with extra powder, balls, grease, and caps. The Major continued, "We should be turning and starting to move north in about thirty minutes. They had one boiler always ready and with a medium head of steam. With experience we could have been moving now, but we've got a lot of learning to go through. We'll put one of our men on the wheel and between you and me we'll get this thing to Jacksonville. The officers are locked in the anchor locker."

The two bow anchors came slowly out of the river mud bottom as the men turned the capstan. Then with the wheel turned all the way to starboard and the huge port paddle wheel slowly turning, the big ship moved sluggishly into the middle of the stream and faced north. The rudder straight, she began moving with the current, both paddle wheels churning.

"Six knots on the rope," sang out the soldier at the bow, "whatever that means."

Cutler turned to Burns, "I understand that we'll hit bottom if we go under four of them knots, so I guess we'll just have to keep in the middle of the river, and if we look like we're going to get more and more shallow, we turn one way or the other until we figure out the deep way. It's going to be slow travel, but it beats walking, and if we make it, Colonel Dearing will probably be so happy that he'll make you a Colonel, too!" Then he turned and grinned at the laughing officer.

"If he does that, then I'll have to make you a Major. You've been my right arm."

Standing by the rail, Cutler Garnett thought, "Boy, if Pa could see me now, he sure would be proud. If that asshole Sergeant Knoll could see me, he's shit coconuts...If I could go back to him as an Officer, he and that drunken, redneck, asshole, Captain

Teague, would probably both shoot themselves....I'd load the damn guns for them." He smiled to himself as he watched the dark water slide by.

"Goin to get our people," said Forselli, as he walked by. Following him were six soldiers. "I'll be back as soon as I can. We have those Colt 36's, so we should be able to take care of any problems we'll have." He climbed over the gunwale and lowered himself into the boat. The rest of the guards followed. The boat loaded, Cutler cast it loose, and with oars flashing in the sunlight, it moved slowly towards the northern shore.

"We'll continue about half a mile around this bend, then stop this thing and wait for them. When we stop, drop a stern anchor. That way we will be facing the right way just in case," Burns told Cutler. Cutler turned to pass the order, but Jacobs, who had been standing nearby watching, motioned with his hand, and said, "Got it," and moved off to carry out the orders.

Cutler was surprised as the Major stood alongside, leaned against the rail, put a hand on his shoulder, and said, "You know, we sure have some good men, Cutler. Tell those three that as of now they're Corporals. We'll worry about elections later. When we get back to Saint Augustine after delivering this gunboat to Jacksonville, we'll be heros. What I'd really like is, once we get her delivered, that they supply her with a crew and take her to St. Augustine to protect that city and the Matanzas Inlet. Between this iron boat, the big Spanish fort, Fort Steele, and the fort at Matanzas near Snake Island, Mister Lincoln's boys will play hell taking Florida." Embarrassed, Cutler turned and nodded. "You're sure right about that, sir," he replied. Looking straight at Burns, he said, "I really think you should have that wound cleaned up again...we need you, so you can't get sick." Hesitating for a moment, but feeling the throb in his neck, Burns murmured, "I'll find the Union doctor and have him look at it. I poured some French Brandy on it before, but it won't hurt to have it looked at again. There's some bottles of that stuff in the cabin. Pass out a half a cup to our people once our patrol gets back, then lock it up for later." With a friendly grin and another pat on the shoulder, the young officer walked off.

Within the hour the lookout called, "Boats leavin the north shore. Looks like ours." The fresh bandage on Major Burns forced

31

him to turn his whole body stiffly, instead of just his neck, as he turned to face the shore. Loud enough to be heard by all his men he said, "Watch those boats. Jacobs, place two men on the other side just in case we get some unwanted visitors from the opposite shore." Jacobs silently pointed to two men, showed them where to watch, and returned to his place.

Without incident the boats pulled alongside, and recognizing Forselli and the guards, Burns motioned everyone up. The Union prisoners still had their hands tied behind them and were assisted on deck, escorted below deck with the other prisoners, and untied.

"Hoist those boats on deck, and let's get movin. We still have a couple of hours of daylight, said the Major. The men, anxious to leave, scrambled to do his bidding.

9

For two hours the U.S.S. Frederick steamed slowly northward, pushing the brackish waters to lap against the swampy shores. The large boat had run aground once, but they had successfully used her powerful engines to put the paddle wheels in reverse and pull her keel off the sandbars. Maneuvering mostly through the center of the two hundred yard wide river, Cutler and Burns soon learned the way to read the ripples of the water to determine the locations of the shallow area, currents, and also the numerous snags and floating underwater logs.

At dusk, the boat stopped and all fires save one were banked. The stern was anchored to keep the ship in mid-stream, facing northward. Sentries were posted, plus one man kept as lookout in the crow's nest, high up on the foremast. The Union cooks prepared dinner for the Rebels and the prisoners. After the guards had taken their turns eating, the prisoners were taken on deck in small groups for their dinners and fifteen minutes to refresh themselves on deck.

The Major went to his cabin and gratefully fell sound asleep on the soft bunk. Cutler checked his sentinels and took the first watch. The waters rippled quietly along the heavy hull with a sporadic slap. The occasional step of a sentinel, the shipboard creaks, and the calls of night birds from the shores were soothing to the ear. The light river breeze, thankfully, kept the mosquitoes away, and the men that were off duty slept soundly on their blankets on the decks.

Cutler listened attentively for sounds that would have been hostile to the peaceful environment. The small, new, Confederate Flag fluttered happily at the stern post and the single large bar shone bright white from the rays of the moon rising behind the blackness of the wall of tall distant trees. The low dark ripples were highlighted in silver and the only changes out of the ordinary were the scattered splashes made by fish as they jumped and their flash slipped back into the dark waters, and the silver beads of spray splattered around the rings they left.

He had been watching a dark form floating with the wind and current towards them and only relaxed when it was seen to be only a palm log, as it slipped past the still ship.

After two hours, Cutler quietly woke Randolph and his shift of guards, then laid down on his blanket as his own shift of men did likewise. They were soon asleep. Randolph's two hours, and then Forselli's, and then Jacobs' turns were all uneventful. Jacobs woke Major Burns and reported in hush tones that nothing had happened and it was about four in the morning.

Burns stretched and yawned, put his feet down on the deck, then still sitting on the bunk, he pulled on his boots, stood up and stretched with arms outspread, yawned again, and said, "Good, go wake my shift and tell your people to go back to sleep for another hour or so. We'll get everybody movin at around five. I haven't slept this well in months." And turned and patted the soft bunk.

Slowly pacing the decks of the gunboat, Burns felt the humid chill of the early pre-dawn morning. The dew-wet rails were cool and slippery under his hands, and the beads of moisture throughout the ship glistened and sparkled from the silver rays of the moon now in the west. Nodding to the sentinels as he made his rounds, he noticed the reduction of river breeze from the south and as he turned to make his return walk towards the stern an irritating odor assailed his nostrils. Running up the last three steps to reach the stern, he noticed a thin wisp of smoke rising from over the side. Gripping the rail and bending over to look down over the side, he saw a mass of smoldering branches and palm fronds wedged against the rudder on a raft of floating palm logs.

"Guards, guards, alarm, watch for an attack," yelled the officer. Turning, he grabbed a fire bucket and splashed the contents into the now beginning to crackle fire. Men were springing from their blankets with rifles and pistols in hand. Grabbing the shoulder of the nearest man, Burns ordered, "Get these buckets emptied on the fire down there. Keep refilling and splashing on the fire until it's out. You there, give this man a hand!"

The men stopped running around and were kneeling with their rifles ready, facing out over the waters, waiting. Sergeant Garnett hurried to Burns, "I checked below decks. The fire didn't come through and I don't think there was any damage. You must have noticed it just in time. Do you think they tried to burn the ship or distract us for something else?" he asked. "It has to be a diversion. Other than an explosion or an intense fire, the metal sides of this ship couldn't catch fire with a pile of sticks and leaves. Either they were testing our alertness, made a mistake, or are doing something else. We'll just have to keep alert," replied the Major. "Get some cold breakfast passed out to the men, keep them alert, and get the boilers ready to turn those wheels," continued the officer. Then looking over the side, he exclaimed, "That's it..." and pointed. "They had us looking over the stern and meanwhile the wooden paddles are burning. Get some men over the side to douse those flames. You others, watch over them with your rifles."

Several soldiers removed their weapons, shirts, and boots, and jumped into the inky waters and started pulling the mass of burning branches from between the paddles on both sides of the gunboat. The sticks and branches had been well wedged into the framework and after being lit, the smoldering hot coals had gone undetectd because of the smoke from the decoy set at the stern. None of the enemy was to be seen, but the men on deck, knowing they were being observed, watched for any movements, other than their own men splashing in the water.

A scattering of flashes from the eastern shore, then a crackle of musketry, and thudding of lead against the hull and rails, brought the realization that the Federals were in good position to harass them with sniper fire, while well protected by the cover of the dark woods at the river's edge.

"Take cover. Stay down and fire at the flashes. Take your time; they'll be shooting at flashes, too," warned Cutler. At the time, one of the men grunted, and fell backward, his rifle clattered to the deck, The hit soldier rolled on one side and said painfully, "I reckon I didn't listen in time, Sarge,...this burns like hell," as he held his stomach.

"Lie still there, son, let me look at that," the Union doctor said to the writhing boy, on the table in the dimly lit cabin below decks. Then looking at the big hole just above his belly, the medical officer, stood straight and looked into the scared face of the Confederate. In the hushed silence below decks, the muffled rifle fire from above and the river banks, sounded like a distant crackling of paper.

"Son, I won't tell you a story. This is serious, but with a little relaxing from you, a little skill from me, and a lot of prayers from both of us, I'm going to make you well enough that you can shoot some more of my men." Then turning to his two assistants, "Let me have that sheet for his wound and my instruments, give him some laudanum."

The aggravating shooting back and forth between the forces continued until the rays of daylight forced the darkness away, and then as suddenly as it had started, the shooting from the shore stopped.

The men waited in the changing from darkness to the gradual misty grayness of the humid steamy morning. Their tenseness was portrayed by the flexing of white knuckles gripping nervously the moist and oily wood of their weapons. The men in gray waited quietly and without complaint as the bright sun rose slowly above the graying tree line in the east.

"Get those men out of the water. Forselli, get down there in the hold, find some lumber to replace those burned out paddle wheels and get some men that know something about carpentry on it. Randolph, get the anchors up and a helmsman to steer this thing with the current moving north away from any grounding. Sergeant Garnett get a couple of sails up the best way you can. Maybe we can get the morning breezes to get us movin northward. Jacobs, find some spars to get the men to use as poles to shove us away from any shallows," ordered Major Burns.

10

The deep impenetrable walls of forest along both banks of the river, slipped slowly by the metal sides of the silent ship. The brackish waters swirled in miniature whirlpools, as the ungainly ship, caught in the powerful, northward current, moved to the will of the wide father of Florida waters. Palms, leaves, and swamp debris, floated alongside the drifting ship. An occasional oath or order among the men on deck, the creak of the wheel, cables and rudder, were the only foreign sounds that disturbed the natural stillness of the warm October morning. The sweep of the current is slow, without hurry or noise. The river is in command, its majesty and supreme control is not to be disputed. Only with cajoling by man, will it yield, and then only slightly, with the control of a condescending parent. The soul of the great river extends past its secret depth into the marshes and stands of live oaks draped with soft delicate moss along its eroding shores.

Turning to Cutler, Major Burns muttered, "Well, Sergeant, it looks like we may have a ship to add to our navy...of course, we have a way to go and those Feds along shore are going to take pot shots at us whenever they can." Still watching the eastern shore, Cutler replied, "I'd sure like to get a scouting party up ahead of this boat so we don't float into a surprise. You know, when the First Florida Volunteers pulled that raid near Pensacola, 'just when everything was about to work out right, and the Feds would have lost everything, a big rope got tangled in the propeller on the Neaffle, and before it was all over Captain Bradford, Sergeant Routh, and four men were lost. That was an accident too, but I'm sure that those men along the river would be more than happy to help us have an accident, too, some way or another. In fact, the way we're travelin, they could go ahead, cut across country, and get to wherever they have other troops."

Thoughtfully, the officer said, "Send someone up to Palatka. We can't be too far from there. Maybe we can get a riverman and some information. You stay here."

"Major, I'll send one of the ship's boats and about eight men. It might be quicker and safer," replied Cutler. Burns nodded assent.

"Everybody ready?" Randolph turned to the seven rebels waiting crouched along the port gunwale. "Make it quick. When that lifeboat hits the water, we get in and row quickly past the next bend of the river. Remember, keep your heads down."

The pulleys on the davits whirred, the lines streamed through them, and as the wheels stopped spinning, the waiting men scrambled over the side, unhooked the lines, tripped and crawled to their benches and frantically placed the ungainly wooden oars in the locks. Once in place, all eyes turned to Randolph, who was seated at the tiller.

"Ready...pull, pull, pull," he began repeating. Slowly, then establishing a rhythm, the flashing oars reached, dipped, and pulled, the boat moved away from the captured gunboat, and began moving northward in the center of the wide river. "Men, we have to get this damn heavy boat past the next turn before the bluecoats can get organized and shoot us out of the water. Speed the rhythm up a little," he said breathlessly. The six soldiers redoubled their efforts and the heavy lifeboat cut deeper into the heart of the might river. The seventh man was seated at the bow, rifle ready.

Watching anxiously from the bow of the drifting gunboat, Major Burns and Sergeant Garnett remained crouched behind the carriage of the bow chaser. "Just another couple hundred yards and they should be around that bend and out of range of the Feds," whispered Cutler. At that time a scattering of shots rang from the eastern shore, and splashes appeared around the little boat. "All right men, fire a volley towards the shore. Shoot at anything that moves," exclaimed Burns. "Jason, over there, under that big pine, see that smoke...quick fire over thee. You too, Piquet, keep them damn Yankees pinned down!" Jacobs put the flames to the touchhole of a starboard cannon, and pieces of metal clipped leaves and trees on the shore as the crash of the cannon echoed across the water.

Flashes from the ship reached out over the side toward the flashes from the eastern shore. A dark figure in the little boat slumped forward, and a limp hand released an oar as it slipped from drooping fingers into the water. The little boat turned sharply to the right and lost momentum, but just as quickly, the rowers reorganized, returned to their original course, and picked up speed again as Randolph in the stern, released the tiller and grabbed the oar that his fallen comrade had dropped, and took his place.

Sporadic shooting from shore continued, but because of the heavy fire from the ship, the shots were inaccurate and unorganized. The little lifeboat became smaller and then, as little more than a glimmering dark hope in the now shimmering waters, it disappeared around the bend of river into the distant thickness of forest. The tenseness of the Confederates on board the gunboat, as they vainly tried to look past the barriers of the turns in the river, was felt throughout the ship.

The humid day and night had passed slowly. Since early afternoon, dark smoke had been spotted moving beyond the trees, moving slowly toward the drifting gunboat. Major Burns and Sergeant Garnett waited in apprehension as the smoke came closer. Friend or foe?

11

"That's about the purtiest, ugly little steamer I ever did see!" expressed the young rebel pointing at the slow moving little cargo boat that had rounded the bend. Smoke was pouring from her single stack amidship and spray and foam was flying in the air from her two sidewheels that were churning slowly and deliberately. "That's the Hattie Brock. My mother's daddy used to ride her with the mail from Welaka when she had a cargo going to Jacksonville," the young soldier continued. "She's owned by Jacob Brock. He's the owner of the Brock House at Enterprise. I'm sure Cap'n Brock would be happy if he knowed his boat was helping against the damn Yankees. They've got him in jail for helpin evacuate Fernandina and they've taken his steamer, the Darlington. His daughter, Hattie, is a purty little dark-eyed gal."

The little steamer continued slowly against the strong current toward the drifting gunboat. A voice echoed across the water from the heavily ladened boat. "What you landlubbers tryin to do? Ram me? Drop a stern and bow anchor afore that rust bucket turns us into splinters!"

The soldiers scrambled over each other, but in a short time a splash from the bow and later one from the stern informed everyone that the drifting ship would soon be halted and approachable.

Coming alongside the port side of the gunboat, the little steamer dropped her anchor and halted within thirty yards of the larger vessel. Cheers broke out among the relieved soldiers as they looked down onto the cargo ladened decks of the Hattie Brock and the grinning faces of their companions were spotted among the white and negro rivermen. Among the eight grinning and waving Confederates packed among the boxes and bales, one had a bandage around his chest in place of his grey tunic, but although pale, he was waving weakly.

Up in the paint peeling pilot house, a large figure dressed in dark trousers and a grey vest emerged with a bold and confident step. The heavy, black bearded Captain Velter bellowed, "Well, soldier boys, Captain Velter is ready to help and babysit our protectors of the state."

Stepping near the gunwale, Major Burns saluted and replied, "Major Burns, Third Regiment, Florida Infantry, and are we glad to see you. If you can help us repair and get this thing to Jacksonville, Florida will have a nice new warship."

"Well, young feller, if'n I can get this lazy bunch to lower this here fancy lifeboat in the water, me and Eb will take a look at your troubles." As the Captain turned toward the soldiers on his deck, they hurriedly dragged the boat they had rowed the day before, across the deck and slid it into the water. While they held the little boat, Captain Velter grandiosely stepped from his ladder onto the stern and sat down. He was followed by the blackest, greasiest, little negro man Major Burns had ever seen. "This here is Eb. If he can't fix it, it can't be fixed," shouted the Captain. Eb stepped into the boat and without a word went to the bow and seated himself on the gunwale. Noisily, the young soldiers climbed into the boat, picked up the oars, and with a few swift strokes, brought the little boat up to the side of the waiting warship. Anxious hands held the boat firm against the side while others helpfully reached down and pulled everyone up over the side, and then secured it with one of the many lines on board.

Without a word, Eb slowly edged his way over the side into one, and then the other of the paddle wheel boxes that had been burned. As the soldiers waited, the slender negro inspected, probed, and tapped the blackened wood with his knuckles. He then retraced his steps to Captain Velter, who had been standing with Major Burns. Eb and Velter had a long whispered conversation, with explanatory hand motions.

"We tow you to Palatka to fix. The boards are burned bad enough that if we push too hard one might break and then the whole damn wheel jams and the main rod will break and you will drive this rust bucket in continuing circles," explained the river captain. "I send some of my boys on board. We tow you to Palatka."

In less than twenty minutes, the U.S.S. Frederick was under tow. A negro river man stood at the bow watching the hawser that had been secured to a cleat at his feet. The long thick hemp rope swung in a long downward arc, sometimes dipping into the dark waters, and then climbing high up over the stern of the Hattie Brock to a pair of heavy steel posts behind her wheel house. Another river man, this one was white, if you looked closely, held the wheel of the gunboat and steered her in the center of the wake of the cargo vessel. With the aid of the current, the little vessel pushed northward with its reluctant traveling companion close behind.

Suddenly, with a grunt, the riverman at the wheel grabbed at his right side, grimaced, and slid slowly to the deck as his knees buckled. As the wheel in his hand spun wildly to the right the ungainly ship turned toward the eastern shore. The puff of rifle smoke from the shore drifted lazily among the trees as the sharp crack was heard.

Forselli, who had been standing nearby, grabbed at the spinning wheel and vainly tried to stop its travel, succeeding only to slow it down. "Damn it, give me a hand, someone," he yelled. Two privates came running from the gunwale where they had been standing, daydreaming into the deep water. One reached the wheel and stopped it as the other pitched forward on his face with arms outspread. The sound of another shot was heard from the east bank.

As the two men at the wheel began turning it slowly to the left, the now alert southerners fired a volley into the undergrowth from where the gunsmoke was drifting.

With a ready axe, the negro boatman at the bow neatly severed the now tightening hawser. It fell over the port bow into the water with a loud splash. Dropping the axe, the man fell to the deck with his hands covering his head.

"Keep a steady fire, boys; just enough to keep them honest," ordered the Major.

Cutler ran to the stern from the coil of ropes on which he had been seated. Grabbing the anchor chain release, he jerked it forward, and with a loud rattle the chain slid quickly through the scupper and the anchor hit the water and sank down into the soft mud.

The heavy gunboat had shipped some water through the gunports on the port side and now that she was straight and on an even keel, the water ran back down the decks and over the sides. There had been no danger of capsizing, but the bow had come within five feet of a bough overhanging the river. The stern anchor sank deep into the muck at the bottom of the river, the Frederick halted her forward movement, and slowly swung back into the current of the river, stern pointing into the current.

The Confederates continued a scattering of shooting into the semidarkness of the thick undergrowth and trees, while Cutler and Forselli checked the two men who had been shot.

"Forselli, have Dick carried up forward under the canvas....the riverman looks like he'll live," said the somber-faced Sergeant, as he shook his head sadly at the still form of the young soldier's head in his hands. The boy's eyes were wide-open, and an expression of surprise was still on his face. "I'll take care of him, Sarge," and Forselli reached down and picked up the body of the dead private and carried it forward toward the bow.

Cutler turned to the wounded riverman who was now leaning against the gunwale, holding his right side. A thin trickle of blood seeped between his fingers. "Cap told us there was big skeeters along here. He sure weren't fibbin'," murmured the man between clenched teeth. The Federal doctor walked quickly up to the man, knelt beside him, moved his clutching fingers, and looked into the wound.

"You'll live in spite of the dirt." Then, wrinkling his nose, he continued, "God, don't you ever wash?" Looking up at Cutler, the young doctor said, "Sergeant, I can bandage this man better below deck. Have him brought down. He's not going to like it though but I'm going to have the orderly wash him and change his clothes. These are going over the side." Then turning, as he walked toward the hatch, Doctor Spoons mumbled, "Even a Reb shouldn't smell that bad."

The Hattie Brock hauled in the hawser and turned back upstream toward the anchored gunboat.

Cutler walked up to Major Burns as he was standing by the wheel, watching the approaching steamer. "Beggin your pardon, sir, but we're just a bunch of sitting ducks. Those bluecoats have a couple of sharpshooters in the woods that can keep us here as long as they want, especially now that we're closer to their shore. I'd like to slip overboard and get in there among them. I can't do anything sitting on the boat here." Turning slowly toward the explaining Sergeant, Burns thought for a minute and answered, "I'm sure you're right. Out here depending on being towed slowly, we're exposing ourselves and could lose most of the few men we've got. Go ahead. Do you need anything or want anyone to go with you? We could cover you as you approach the shore."

"No, sir. In fact, I don't want anyone to see me leave, or it may give me away. I'll slip into the water just on the port side of the stern, among floating logs, while everybody is busy hooking the ship back up to be towed. Thank you, sir," he replied. The officer reached over and patted Cutler on the shoulder, then turning, he began barking useless orders to his men.

12

With only his head above water, Cutler watched the stern of
the U.S.S. Frederick as it moved slowly northward, once again
under tow. Turning toward the east bank of the river. Cutler
maneuvered the clump of brush that he had around him, with
the current but also slightly to the right, closer to the shore.

As he felt the muck around his ankles and legs become solid
under his feet, he moved closer to the shore. Suddenly a volley
of rifle fire burst from the shore less than fifty yards north of
him. A similar answering gunfire responded from the ship.
Realizing that the men on shore had moved parallel to the gunboat
and weren't aware of his presence, he quickened his movement
toward the shore. Once under the protection of the low hanging
branches, he shed himself of the floating brush, scrambled up
into the tree branches, and then on to the low shore.

Stooping, the dripping figure ran inland, weaving and leaping
among the trees, logs, and undergrowth for about one hundred
yards. As suddenly as he had started his run, Cutler stopped and
sank to the ground in some high grass. Waiting to see if he had
been spottled, he listened to the crackle of rifle fire. Checking
to see that his knife was still in its sheath, he started moving
quietly toward the shooting. The deer-horn handle had brought
a comforting feeling back to the young soldier. As he moved
forward, his eyes darted left and right of the direction of his
travel. He saw a sturdy pole and picked it up. During one of his
frequent stops to observe and listen, he used the knife and put
a sharp point on one end of the pole.

Cutler stopped suddenly when he heard rifle fire a short distance
in front of his position. Dropping down to the soft ground, he
crawled forward.

Through the trees, a few spots of dark waters could be seen.
Watching for movement, Cutler caught a glimpse of a blue
sleeved arm, and the dark blue metal of a rifle barrel being
lowered in a level position toward the waters.

Only a few seconds passed from the time that the Union soldier
was concentrating on aiming, and he heard running approaching
him from behind. A dark shadow, and flash toward him appeared.

He turned, a sudden pain, unconsciousness, and his heart stopped, pierced by a sharp wooden shaft.

"Sorry, you'd killed me if you could," Cutler mumbled as he quickly picked up the new rifle. With gritted teeth, he pulled out the shaft from the dead man's chest and threw it into the bushes. Reaching back down, he unbuckled the cartridge belt, put it around his waist, and started walking quickly northward, about thirty yards from the river's edge, and parallel to it.

The gunfire moved slowly northward with the river and suddenly increased in intensity and became stationary. Looking over the rifle carefully, the rebel soldier cocked the hammer and moved slower, eyes darting side to side and occasionally turning his head sideways to listen while halting in concealing bushes. Having traveled almost two hundred yards, Cutler cautiously looked around a water-oak toward the west and saw seven men, spaced eight to ten feet apart, lying on the ground, firing and loading as fast as possible toward the gunboat that was now stopped on the river. The captured boat was only about fifty yards from shore, and despite the bullets clipping the bushes and hitting the trees, no damage was being done to the northern men, hidden behind trees, logs, and stumps on the ground.

Cutler quickly aimed and fired at the nearest man. The man was in the process of loading his rifle. The bullet hit him in the back of the head and without a sound he slumped forward, his face into the humid bank.

Opening the breach, Cutler inserted another shell, cocked the rifle, aimed and shot the second man in the back of the neck. This man, a sailor, was just aiming his rifle. As the bullet severed his backbone, his shot went up into the trees, and he, too, fell forward on his face.

Looking toward the next man in line, Cutler was momentarily startled as the sailor happened to look up while loading and spotted him. The sailor yelled, "Watch it, there's some goddam rebels behind us!" He then slammed the breach shut, jumped up on his right knee, cocked and fired the rifle at the Confederate. Cutler had just brought up his rifle when the heavy bullet hit him in the side. He temporarily lost his balance and staggered. Recovering, he quickly brought the rifle back up to the shoulder and shot the man in the chest.

As Cutler jumped behind a large magnolia, two bullets hissed by where he had been standing. "I've got to get the hell out of here," he thought; and, stooping low, he ran as fast as he could toward the east. Two more shots went through the branches over his head as he bobbed and weaved over bushes and through vines and low branches. Having traveled for almost a mile, he turned sharply to the left and ran another half mile before sinking to the soft ground. He was breathing hard, feeling faint, and his right side throbbed painfully.

Reloading and then laying the heavy rifle down on a dead branch, the panting sergeant looked to his wound. Painfully opening the torn tunic, he saw an ugly gash that ran for over six inches along his right side. Blood was oozing out of the dark wound and, dabbing at it carefully, Cutler could see that the bullet had grazed a rib bone and had cracked it. The bone had deflected the lead slug to run its length, cutting his side badly but saving him by keeping the bullet along the bone. Removing his shirt, he tore it into strips, knotted the ends, and bound the long wide strips tightly around himself. Painfully, he slipped the grey tunic back on, and then lay back, closed his eyes and rested.

The rifle fire had stopped once he had run into the thick cover of trees and underbrush, and lying on the ground resting, the only sounds to be heard were the normal noises of the swamps.

Having rested for almost an hour Cutler forced himself slowly to his feet. As the dizziness subsided, he stooped down, picked up his rifle, and moved once again toward the river.

Moving slowly and deliberately, Cutler edged through the underbrush until he could again see the river through the trees. Anchored midstream he saw the outline of the Hattie Brock through the grey moss, drooping from overhanging branches. The sounds of undistinguishable voices carried across the water to him. Finding a clump of cypress he settled behind them.

The Hattie Brock pulled up her anchor, turned and once again headed back toward the Frederick. Checking the rifle, Cutler pointed it upstream, and waited...

Sounds of movements came closer, in different areas of the underbrush. Placing a handful of cartridges by his side, Cutler intently watched the woods for movement.

Simultenously two faces were seen by the hidden Confederate for a few seconds, then they disappeared. Shortly, a man walked cautiously into the clearing, looked around, turned, and called out, "It looks clear, sir." Four men moved into the clearing and joined the young midshipman.

"Keep your weapons ready, men," said a tall slender man. He was dressed in the dark blue of a naval officer. "Those rebels in the woods might be still around. Poor old Simms must have hit one of them pretty bad judging by the blood back there. Let's get ready. They should have the Frederick ready to tow again. Johnson, you keep an eye on the woods behind us."

"Gentlemen, I suggest that you drop your weapons," called out Cutler. "You're surrounded, and don't have a chance."

After a moment's hesitation, the men dropped their rifles, upon seeing their officer's disgusted nod.

"Hold your fire, men!" continued Cutler. "All right you Yanks, put your hands on your heads and start walking into the water...slowly! I'll tell you when to stop."

The Federals stumbled slowly over the rotting vegetation into the muddy river. When they had the water up to their waists Cutler called out for them to halt and not turn around.

Hobbling quickly to the dropped weapons, he gathered the rifles and pistol, and carried them back to his hiding place. Scrambling to a large branch over the river, he perched himself and waited.

As the Hattie Brock moved again northward, towing the crippled gunboat, Captain Velter was surprised to hear a voice call from the bank. "Captain, I've got a present for you. Send over a boat and pick up these bluecoats before they get waterlogged." Looking closely into the shadows of the trees, Velter saw five men in blue standing in the water with their hands on their heads.

"Move it, move it, you heard him. That was the young sergeant. Lower a boat. I'll keep this baby of ours in midstream till you get back," bellowed the Captain.

Cutler watched the men of the little cargo steamer help the northern men into the crowded boat. The men were rowed to the steamer and placed under guard. Then the lifeboat returned for him.

Once he was lifted into the lifeboat, the young man in grey fainted.

13

Not completely aware of his surroundings, Cutler opened his eyes to a young, bearded face looking down at him. Trying to focus, he gradually realized that the features were faintly familiar. The lips were moving and the tone of the voice began to take the shape of words somewhere in the cobwebs of his brain. "Sergeant, can you hear me? Don't move...can you hear me?" The words made sense. Cutler tried to talk, but it was such an effort, no sound came from his lips.

"You'll be fine," murmured the young navy doctor. "Now, just lie there and rest. Your wound is not serious, although you lost a lot of blood. I poured some brandy on it and in you. Once you're bandaged and washed, the orderly will shave you and you'll feel better. Now, shut your eyes."

As if by the command, Cutler drifted back to sleep. The dull pain in his side continued in his dream. His father was telling him to steer the mule straight, keep that furrow straight, but no matter how much he pushed, the mule kept pulling to one side, the wide belt biting into his rib cage.

"Wake up, Sergeant, you're dreaming," and Cutler looked up into the frowning face of Major Burns. "Is he all right, Doctor? He's pouring sweat."

"It's normal. He's sweating out some of that evil Rebel meanness. After the shock and pain wears down a little, he'll sleep like a baby and be around on his feet in a few weeks. I think the brandy is supposed to help it heal quicker. The Captain used to preach for me to use clean bandages and wash all instruments with hot water whenever they were needed; of course, you fellows killed him and I'm saving his killers." The tone of the doctor had become bitter, and he turned away.

Major Burns was silent for a few moments, then turned to Doctor Spoons, "I understand your feelings, doctor. I hope that some Confederate Doctor somewhere is helping one of your boys. Someday our two countries will be at peace again." Turning back to Cutler, he changed his voice to joy, and with a smile said, "Hey, I don't know what you did, but you really saved us from all those pot shots. That Lieutenant was hoppin mad when he realized you tricked him into surrendering all his men, thinking you had a bunch of men hidden in the bushes. I told him he was lucky he surrendered. If he hadn't, he wouldn't have lived to find out what happened. You relax. Acting Sergeant Jacobs will help me until you get on your feet again. Anyway, Captain Velter said we should be in Palatka by dark."

Cutler slept the rest of the day, rocked by the soft swaying motion of the Frederick under tow. The sounds of the creaking ship, the water rippling against her hull, the breeze through her superstructures and lines didn't disturb him. The Southerners on deck dozed and daydreamed. The Northern prisoners sat dejectedly in their hot, close quarters. Only the bow man, the man at the wheel, and Major Burns, were alert on the captured gunboat.

Captain Velter and his crew of riverman on the Hattie Brock settled down to the routine of plodding northward with their ungainly dependent in tow.

The heavy rush of anchor chains woke Cutler into consciousness. Painfully, he tried to raise himself, but the restaining hand of the orderly on his chest held him in place. The man in the white coat shook his head, "Stay down, the doctor will have you and the other wounded carried out at the right time."

Cutler hadn't realized that other men were with him in the ward. Turning his head slowly from side to side, he saw the dim figures lying on cots. The lanterns were burning and swaying slightly, casting alternately, their yellow light and dark shadows. He counted ten figures lying on cots, and wondered how many were his men.

Within the hour the wounded were comfortable on soft beds of straw, quilts, and blankets on the floor in the center of the new wooden church. The benches had been moved out of the way to the sides of the church. The men were lying quietly watching the hustle and bustle of Doctor Spoons and his orderly. The women from town were coming in as they received the news of the victory. Soon, appetizing odors of fresh baked corn bread, fish, deer, fried potatoes, gopher stew, roasted corn, greens, and other goodies, filled the air, as the ladies brought in the dinners that had been intended for their families.

All around the church, boys and girls were on their tip toes, curiously looking into the windows or trying to see past the two stern-faced guards at the door. Men from the town and surrounding areas watched in wonderment, and more than one young man asked of the guards how they, too, could become soldiers.

In the warehouse by the river, eleven bodies lay on the rough floors, and among barrels and sacks of goods, sat the Federal prisoners. Outside, by the doors and windows stood the local militia, proud to have a chance to do something other than parade with old shotguns and brooms. The new Federal rifles were fondled lovingly.

Despite the excitement, the little community settled down for the night after all the soldiers of both sides had been fed and guards posted.

The next morning a slight crispness was in the air as the sun gradually melted the ground fog and threw its yellow rays at the sparkling dew that ran off the larger leaves in the wilderness. The docks of the wharves and decks of the several craft tied to them and anchored offshore were slippery with moisture. The mirror that the boats sat on was disturbed only by the slight ripple of the current and occasional dives of birds into the waters searching for breakfast. A territorial dispute was being argued in a cypress tree at the water's edge. The shrill of the mockingbird and the enraged chatter of a large squirrel were the signs of a gross misunderstanding of housing rights in this vast unoccupied wilderness.

Cutler awoke to the bright beams of sunlight as they displaced the darkness under his eyelids. Lying quietly, he enjoyed the softness of the quilts. As he began to move his muscles, he became conscious of the tight bandage around his chest and the dull ache penetrating his pleasant euphoria. He then realized where he was, and why. The rustling of cloth brought his attention to a young lady that was moving among the beds of straw and slowly looking

49

down at the faces of the sleeping men. As she came closer he was enchanted by her pretty face. She had a look of anxiety and was obviously looking for someone. As she would bend down to look into a sleeping face, her long auburn hair would fall from her shoulders, and when she would stand straight again, she would reach for it impatiently with both hands and toss it back over her shoulders. Cutler thought to himself, "why doesn't she just tie it back there and save a lot of trouble? She really looks nice every time she frowns and pushes that hair back. I guess she better leave it as is! Nice shape, too. A little thin for heavy work or farmin. Hope she comes here. She must be about eighteen; that's a good age...really, I haven't seen a woman in so long, I guess that any age is a good age!"

The young girl finally reached Cutler's blanket and looked down. "Oh my, you're awake. I'm looking for someone," she whispered. Her voice reminded him of velvet. "Do you know Ralph Jacobs? He's...a very dear friend of mine. I heard he had left Saint Augustine on a patrol."

Cutler had to break away from his trance at such a pretty face and smooth voice. He sure was glad the orderly had shaved and washed him after his little excursion into the woods. "Yes, ma'am, Jacobs is now Acting Sergeant. He took my place. He's probably with Major Burns." Cutler didn't know what else to say, but he wanted her to stay. "My name is Cutler Garnett, ma'am. Could you ask Jacobs, Ralph Jacobs, to come see me when he has time? I sure would appreciate it."

"My name is Flora, Flora Gordon. My daddy is Thomas Gordon. He's First Sergeant with the new Marion Light Artillery. We're from Marion County," she said softly. She turned away and whispered with her head down. "I'm betrothed to Ralph."

Cutler's heart sank. "That's nice...I mean, Jacobs is a nice fellow. Congratulations. I hope you find him."

"I'll bring him back. You take care." As she left, her hand touched Cutler's shoulder.

"Shit! Just my luck, the one pretty girl I see in months that talks to me, and she belongs to my friend."

The sounds of the awakening camp brought along the fragrances of breakfast. As one of the ladies of the town propped Cutler up on an enormous feather pillow and placed a large plate on a board on his lap, he forgot all about the girl. The hot corn bread dripping with honey, a thick slice of country ham, a bowl of swamp cabbage covered with fresh butter, some baked sweet potatoes, and a mug of steaming hot coffee, brought a wide grin to his face as the lady said, "You want more, you just holler." The lady was dressed in a long dark plain muslin dress, her sunfaded blue bonnet was tossed carelessly back behind her neck, and her hair was dark with loose strands of grey. Her sunburned face seemed to crack when she smiled. The hard years in the wilderness and fields had caused her hands to be as calloused and rough as a man's. Cutler couldn't grin any more, but he did nod with his mouth full of as much as he could stuff into it.

"Well, sleepy, we're movin out." Cutler opened his eyes. After that delicious breakfast, he had fallen back asleep. Jacobs was standing over him. In his left hand, he held the slender hand of Flora.

"You awright?" he continued. Cutler nodded. "We uns are goin on with the gunboat. Some of that hammerin' you would have heard if you was awake, was the fixin of the paddle wheels. Captain Velter is sending a couple of his men with us to run the thing. You and the rest of the wounded will stay here till you all be ready for duty. The Yanks are stayin', too, and when they're well, the militia will take them to Jacksonville to be exchanged for some of our boys. Doctor Spoons and his orderly volunteered to stay and care for all the wounded and not try to escape. He's a good feller for a Yank. Flora, here, said she'd help him until her sister comes to fetch her back to Ocala. I sure was lucky she was here visitin' her kin for a few days."

Although Jacobs was talking, Cutler's eyes never left the face of the girl. "Don't you go and misbehave," continued Jacobs. With a smile, but a slight hardness in his tone, Jacobs placed his other hand lightly on the wounded man's arm and said, "If you do, the bullet that the bluebelly gave you is goin' to have company."

Then he turned to the girl and said, "Come'on, Flora, here comes the Major, and he said that he wanted to talk to Cutler." Turning again, "You take care of yourself, you hear? I sent word to your pappy, and he'll be here in a couple of days. Forselli, Randolph and the others said they've been mighty proud to serve under you and want you back soon. Me, too!" The friends shook hands and Jacobs and Flora left. Cutler knew he had a friend for life...as long as he didn't try to take Flora. "Well," he thought, "ain't no bit of fluff goin to come between me and any friend of mine. I'll just keep my distance."

Major Burns pulled up a chair, sat down, then reached over and shook hands with Sergeant Garnett. "You get yourself well, quick, friend. We're not transporting any of the wounded. The care here is better than in Saint Augustine or Jacksonville. When you're ready for duty and the men can travel, take some of the militia if you want, or I might be able to send some men, borrow a boat, and get them to get you to Jacksonville. I'll be looking for you. You can trust that Doctor, I'll bet. I'll miss your help, and you can be sure that Colonel Dearing is really going to hear about your actions. Good luck."

"See you soon, sir, and thank you," Cutler said to the departing officer.

For the next two days Cutler did little more than eat and sleep. Occasionally he would wake up to see Flora or the farm lady that continued to bring him meals, but he had somehow lost his appetite. Doctor Spoons and his orderly checked on him twice a day, and changed his dressing daily. On the third day, Cutler opened his eyes to see his father's face bending over him anxiously. He saw his father's lips moving but all he could hear was a loud hum in his ears. His eyes and head hurt terribly.

The next time he opened his eyes he saw the distorted features of Deep Waters and Doctor Spoons face merging into one.

The poultice that Deep Waters placed on Cutler's reopened wound, and the bitter hot drink that was forced down his clenched teeth succeeded totally by the fifth day. The orderly had just finished washing him and wrapping him in a dry blanket, when he woke to see through eyes that were no longer feverish.

In the days following, recovery was rapid. Once able to again get on his feet, Cutler spent his time wandering through the small town with his father and Deep Waters. He told them every detail of his Army life, from the time he had left home, his training, through the patrol, and until he was wounded. Deep Waters had seemed satisfied that his pupil had become a good scout and woodsman. Cutler avoided Flora!

Three weeks from the time that the gunboat had gone north, the blasts from a whistle caused everyone to hurry to the docks. Townspeople, Confederates, militia, and Federal soldiers, all waved excitedly at the cargo boat, Hattie Brock. "Well, Sergeant, that little darlin may be takin us into captivity, but it'll sure beat walkin or rowin, I'm a thinkin," said a Federal sailor standing alongside Cutler. "Aye, she's not much to look at, and in Boston Harbor she'd a been a garbage scow, I'm a thinkin, but right now in this laddie's eyes she's the finest, sleekest, fastest sloop that ever sailed in any man's navy."

Colonel Dearing had sent five men to assist in their return to Jacksonville. The five new recruits were from Company A, Third Florida Infantry, and were anxious to show off that, despite their new uniforms, they could be trusted as seasoned veterans. Cutler, understanding, posted the men in a circle as pickets around the waterfront. The Northern wounded, smiled, but said nothing. Even in the Federal forces, green recruits had to be humored and kept busy.

"Well, my young Sergeant, I see that you look better than when I see you last, yes? You a little skinny, but I think I bring something that will make everybody happy. Come, I show you." Turning, Captain Velter walked up the gangplank onto the deck of his little steamboat.

Down to Velter's luttered cabin, the two went. "How you like? Nice and tender!" the Captain said, as he pointed to the three large pieces of skinned alligator tails on a table. "You want to give this to all of us?" asked Cutler. "Ya," was the answer. "Good. Most of us Florida boys like 'gator tail, but those Yanks are in for a big surprise. We'll get the women to serve this up, and we'll keep it a secret until after they eat," winked the young man.

The Captain let out a loud laugh and held his belly, "Good joke on the bluebellies. We no tell."

That evening the townspeople held a goodbye celebration for the little group of soldiers and prisoners. The weeks spent in such close areas and common pain and recovery had helped to minimize the hostilities among the wounded, prisoners and Confederates.

The large steaming platters of mouthwatering foods were

served on the long benches, set up in the center of the main street. The thick "catfish" steaks were especially popular. Doctor Spoons mentioned that he had heard that freshwater catfish were big, but he never realized they could be that big and tasty. Captain Velter and Cutler exchanged glances, smiled, but didn't reveal their secret.

The following morning, Cutler was standing on the dock as the last of the men were boarding the Hattie Brock. Sam Garnett and Deep Waters were just finishing their goodbyes with the young soldier when a group of ladies approached the three men. "It certainly has been a privilege, serving you and your men, Sergeant. We wish you much fortune and hope that you will return under more pleasant circumstances," spoke the Mayor's wife. "I'm sure my husband would have enjoyed your presence. You may meet him if you come in contact with the Jacksonville Light Infantry under Captain John Oliveros."

Flora moved up to Cutler and said, "It has been a pleasure, Sergeant. I appreciate your concern about everything...I hope that when you see Ralph you will tell him...how much I miss him, and, Sergeant, I want you to meet my sister, Cora." As she spoke, Flora moved to one side and gently pulled the arm of a slender blonde haired girl of about seventeen. Cutler looked down into the pale blue eyes of the suntanned girl.

"Howdy, Ma'am, I sure am pleased to meet you. This is my daddy, Sam Garnett, and here is my friend, Deep Waters," spoke Cutler. He could not take his eyes away from the depth of Cora's blue eyes. Cora held out her hand and shook Cutler's hand and then Sam's. She had a strong grip for her size. She then reached out to shake hands with the Indian, just as she had the two white men.

"Gentlemen, my sister has spoken highly of all of you. Mister Garnett, my daddy is Thomas Gordon. I believe you bought some powder and shot from his store in Ocala a few months ago," continued the young girl. Her voice sounded very much like her sister's.

"Why certainly young lady. I remember you well. You helped me load my wagon. You picked up some lead bags that must have weighed as much as you. How is your father?" answered the older Garnett.

Cutler was still looking at Cora's eyes. Flora was watching him with a slight smile on her face.

Cora smiled at Cutler, then moved closer to his father, and said, "My daddy is fine. He is now in the Marion Light Artillery which has been organized in Ocala. I'm sure he would like to visit with you the next time he is home. We will send word when he arrives and you are welcome to stay with us as our guest." Then as if remembering Cutler, she turned to him and said, "Oh, of course you're welcome, too Sergeant."

The deep low horn of the Hattie Brock was accompanied by the bellow of Captain Velter. "We go today, Sergeant? Kiss all the ladies. We go!"

Cutler looked up, red-faced, and stammered, "Goodbye," and ran up the gangplank to the cheering, and clapping of the laughing soldiers and prisoners lined up along the rail of the little steamboat.

"Thank you, Sergeant. We go now. Cast off bow and stern lines!" With a sly smile, Captain Velter pointed the little craft northward as the large paddle wheels began to slowly bite into the dark waters of the Saint John's River.

In the little cemetary, eleven fresh mounds covered the new pine boxes. Men of blue and grey would lie there side by side through eternity. During the next four years, over six hundred thousand lives would suddenly cease, throughout the country, more fresh mounds would appear.

14

The crisp March breeze from the North filled the brown patched sails of the small schooner. The three men on board the little vessel were heavily bundled against the cool breeze, their weapons and ammunition were wrapped in canvas, protecting these from the ocean spray. Less than a mile off their starboard, foamy breakers rolled over to the glistening white sand of the Florida east coast.

"Captain Steele was sure upset when the Company left Jacksonville. There wasn't much we could do against four gunboats and two transports loaded with Yankees. I never seed so many blue coats; and the size of those cannons....," Lewis Jackery, the youngest of the three, muttered. Leaving the mouth of the Saint Johns River near Jacksonville under cover of darkness, the men had sailed for hours in silence. The little craft steered through the calm waters just beyond the breakers for the past two days and nights, and had not been seen by any of the ships of the Union Blockade Squadron. Had they been sighted, they knew that the water close to shore was too shallow for the large gunboats. Now they had begun to maneuver further from shore as they approached Mosquito Inlet with its treacherous shifting bar and undercurrents.

"Cutler, you're not going to like havin to tell Cap'n Bird that Jacksonville and Saint Augustine are in the hands of the Yanks. That man is really goin to cuss when he finds out that not a shot was fired." John Ponce had spoken with feeling. He was the elder of the three men, with coal black hair and tanned, weather beaten skin. Although Cutler Garnett was now a regular Sergeant, John was the guide for the little expedition.

"We've got about another three, four miles, then we can make the cut into the Inlet. You'll see my house after we turn into the Halifax, and then we'll be only a little way from Smyrna. Tonight you fellers are in for some good eatin. My Pa and brother can sure hunt and fish, and my sister got a garden that just grows if she looks at it, and you ain't tasted nothin till my momma loads up a table. She's a gran Spanish lady deep down, even if the rest of us be backwoods."

The trio continued in silence. Cutler trimmed the sails and John continued steering southward while edging further to the east, from shore. Lewis sat on the deck, crosslegged, leaning against the mast, his eyes closed, and his new grey cap held firmly in his hands. Earlier, the cap had blown off into the water, but it would not happen again!

While at Saint Augustine, Cutler had met Mr. Gibbs, the owner of the old Kingsley Plantation, east of the Yellow Bluff fortifications on the Saint Johns River.

Originally, John McQueen, a Scot, had received the island-plantation in 1791, from Spain. John McIntosh was the next owner from 1804 to 1817. Zeph Kingsley had bought it from McIntosh when it was found out that the present owner was plotting against Spanish rule. Gibbs had intimated that politics, intrigue, and some underhanded dealings, had placed his uncle in a favorable position to purchase the property for next to nothing. Zeph Kingsley had been a shrewd, eccentric, and wealthy owner. He had married a negress slave and had even advocated voting rights for freed negroes. Sam Garnett's father had known him quite well.

His nephew, Gibbs, had bought the plantation through some kind of trading of slaves with his uncle, and had told Cutler all about the 1200 acre plantation. Gibbs was a militia officer at Saint Augustine , and he and Cutler had become quite friendly. Cutler had a standing invitation to visit and spend some time at the plantation...and to bring his bride, when he got one. Cutler wondered and fantasized if Cora....

Standing at the bow and holding tightly to a line secured to the top of the mast, Cutler squinted into the bright sunlight. "I don't know, John, it sure looks like a lot of smoke down there. Is the town that big?"

John examined the smudges against the clear sky the best he could from his seated position by the rudder. "Let's see as we get closer. It could be the pine burnin down at the salt works, or maybe the runners Kate or Cecile gettin up steam to make a run for it out the inlet with the tide, toward a hole in the blockade."

Continuing in silence, the trio scanned the horizon with apprehension.

"Do you see what I see?" exclaimed Lewis. "Looks like a ship, probably a blockader...it's not movin, just sittin there waitin...just clear of the bar. He hasn't spotted us yet, but we sure can't sail past him through that inlet. He'd blow us out of the water."

"Head to shore. We'll try to get by them tonight. Can you get through the breakers without swampin us—" asked Cutler.

"Yup, the tide's right and the breeze is from the north and droppin. We'll go in without canvas."

With sails lowered and mast and yards removed and secured, Cutler and Lewis pulled on the sweeps while John steered them safely through the breakers onto the hard white sand. The boat secured on the beach, the three scrambled up into the dunes, and out of sight of the dark gunboat. In the dunes, they walked parallel to the sea.

"Now that we've rounded the bend of the dunes, let's look over to the town," said Cutler. The men edged to the crest of the highest sand dune and looked out from between the sea oats.

In the distance, past the curve in the river across from New Smyrna, the masts and funnel of a ship could be seen anchored on the calm sparkling blue. The ship they had originally seen was much larger, and anchored in the ocean, just outside the entrance to the inlet.

"Damn, looks like a raiding party. They must have gone down to the salt works by longboat. That's where all the smoke is comin from," said John, bitterly.

"We'll take turns watchin and sleepin. I'll go first, then John, then Lewis, then me again. We'll slip past them in the dark," commanded Cutler.

Cutler sat crosslegged on the sand dune gazing at the ship floating quietly beyond the breakers at the mouth of the inlet.

The dull roar of the breakers muffled any sounds. Several hours had passed since he had seen a longboat depart from the larger ship and pass through the inlet into the Halifax River southward toward the anchored ship in the river across from New Smyrna. The longboat was returning now, and he thought that it now was carrying some officers; probably the Captain and First Officer of the gunboat anchored in the river. Several lights appeared on deck as the sun's rays quickly faded. The dense woods on the far western shore transformed to an uneven line of black. The sleeping figures awoke instantly from the hand on their shoulders. Gathering their belongings, the three men retraced their steps to the beached boat.

They dragged the boat through the shallow water along the beach, and followed the curve of the inlet. Not until well inside the inlet did they row to deeper water and place the mast and raise only the mainsail. The sea breeze was light, pushing the boat slowly through the open water of the inlet into the river, past mangrove islands.

Upon reaching the wide bend of the river, the sail and mast

were lowered and two men rowed slowly and as quietly as possible, as the third figure steered them along the western shore.

A few lanterns swaying lightly and the creaking of a ship, gave the position of the anchored gunboat. The three Rebels manuevered into the dense mangrove vegetation on the western bank, covered their boat with branches on the water side, and made their way with their belongings toward higher ground.

"Ralph, Ralph Jacobs, what the hell you doin down here? Haven't seen you in months!" exclaimed Cutler. The picket they had encountered had just led them into the dark camp by the river. In the dim moonlight, Cutler had recognized Jacobs' voice, joking with some of the other men.

"Why you knock-kneed, pidgeon-toed, bowlegged, pipsqueek. I'm fightin raiders just like you," was the answer.

The two grinning friends shook hands and then proceeded to laugh and pound each other on the back.

"I got attached to the 3rd Florida Infantry, Company E, under Captain Bird. He's not here now. He's with a convoy, takin some munitions we unloaded from the Katie. They're goin to Cabbage Bluff with some of the load, the rest's going to Enterprise...it's really good to see you. How you doin? You look pretty well healed up."

Then with a mischievous note, Ralph Jacobs continued. "Flora said you were a real gentleman, and there was no need to put another lead ball near the one you got from the Yank. Besides, that Cora is a real sparker, ain't she?"

"You know, Ralph, when I first met that little lady on the wharf in Palatka, I immediately got jealous of all the attention she was payin to my father, just like I wasn't there. Well, in January, my father was in Waldo with a wagonload of medicine he brought to our headquarters at Camp Baker. He said he'd been to Ocala and visited with Thomas Gordon who was home with fever. He saw Cora and Flora, and he said that Cora asked how I was doin. In fact; she seemed interested when he talked about how I had grown up, and the things I had done in Mellonville. Tell you the truth, that purty gal has been on my mind a lot. What you grinnin about, you rascal? You planin on us bein brothers in law?"

"Come on, let's get you to meet with Captain Strain, and then the three of you get somethin to eat. We'll talk more about this later before you forget what you sailed down here for."

Captain Strain was seated on an old broken-down kitchen chair, his feet propped up against one of the poles holding up the thatched roof of one of the sheds. Smoke from several of th green wood and moss fires, to discourage the voracious mosquitoes, drifted throughout the area. The young bearded Captain had just finished supper, and was enjoyed his pipe.

"Come on men, heard you arrived. Sit down and give me the news of what's been goin on with the Yankees. With no telegraph here, our only news come by travelers, blockade runners, and occasional couriers. The last newspaper I read was a month old, and after all of us read it several times, it started falling apart and we used it for wipin the other end." Captain Strain hadn't moved except for looking up, as he spoke.

Cutler, John and Lewis sat on a huge live oak log, one of the many scattered throughout the area.

Cutler began, "Captain Oliveros and Lieutenant Butler sent us with the news, Sir. Company A abandoned Fort Steele and spiked the guns when the invading squadron came, four gunboats and two transports loaded with troops. The city was abandoned and most of the men have been sent to Cedar Key. Some went to Waldo. This happened on March 12th. Not a shot was fired. We got most of our equipment and stores out. The day before that, Saint Augustine was surrendered to the Yankees. There was nothing that could have been done, but we heard that the women of the town really got upset, called the men cowards, gave the Yankees a rough time. In fact, they cut the flagpole down; didn't want to soil it with the enemy flag. We had to tell you. Now, this inlet is more important to Florida than ever. Our supplies have two less ports to come into. Matanzas Inlet is watched real close, and once a runner comes through it, he can't turn northward any longer toward Saint Augustine. The Saint John is practically closed. Supplies down here have to come through here. Key West belongs to the Yankees and they're watchin Old Fort Lauderdale and the inlet by Fort Capron by Indian River. Cedar Key is watched and raided once in awhile, and Pensacola is bottled up. Do we have any cannon here?"

The crestfallen Captain replied, "Well, that's bad news...We have one gun that's being brought overland. The last I heard, it was bogged down in the swamps, three, four miles from here. We probably can keep the enemy from landing here, unless they bring in troops, but if they start shelling us, we're up the crick. Now, we're goin to get ready in case those sailors decide to land. Why don't you all get something to eat and some rest. We may need you tomorrow."

The three soldiers stood up, saluted, and left the still seated officer. "Well, I guess we better not go over to my folks. We better stay in the area," said John Ponce.

Jacobs walked over from where he had been standing out of earshot of the conference and said, "Well, fellers, I heard that Mrs. Sheldon would be highly put out if you didn't go to her house for supper, so let's mosey on over. I'm especially fond of her possum pie."

"I'm real hungry. I think my stomach is eatin a hole in my backbone. Hey, have you heard from Major Burns, Forselli, Randolph, and the others?" Cutler said as he placed a hand on his friend's shoulder.

They walked down the sandy path and crossed the old Turnbull Canal, as Ralph talked. "Major Burns up and got married; purty little filly from Jacksonville. Forselli is with Lieutenant J. J. Dickison. Randolph is in Cedar Key with the rest of the old group. I'm planin to go visit Flora next month. You want me to give any messages to the family?" he smirked as he said these last words.

Cutler shoved his friend and answered, "I'll give you a letter."

15

With the coming of morning, the men of Companies E and H waited anxiously along the riverfront behind the improvised breastworks, logs, and trees.

"I know what we need; we need the Virginia here. She'd really do the trick to these damn raiders. Did you hear what she did to the blockaders at Hampton Roads? She really showed em.

Even that new cheesebox, Monitor, couldn't beat her. We'd have em all runnin again. It'd be Manassas all over again." The words came from a young soldier dressed in butternut. The uniform had been sewn by his mother in Pensacola. She was now sewing another for the soldier's younger brother.

Among the Southerners was a grey-haired, grizzled type. Looking over toward the young soldier, he paused, then spoke in a gruff voice. "You look like you're spoilin fer a fight, young feller."

"We're gonna kill those bastards. I hope this war don't end afore I get my share!"

"Well, son, I've done my share a killin. I killed Englishmen with ole Andy Jackson, Injuns with Colonel Dade, Mexicans with Sam Houston, and now I'm gonna be killin Americans with Captain Strain. I'll tell you one thing, killin a man is easy, livin with it, ain't. I can still see the faces of the boys dyin at Orleans, the bodies at Chapultepec, the bloated bodies of men, women, and children, rotting in the swamps. Wait, you'll see and smell sights that you'll remember when you're an ole man...if you live that long. The blood, screams, pain, guts, men scattered in little pieces, men cryin while surgeons cut their limbs off. The sweet stink of rottin flesh. Oh yes, I was the same back in '12, but if you live, you'll remember, and wake up at night sweatin and shakin."

With those words the man turned and spat, then resumed his position behind the large coquina stone.

"Boats comin. Looks like six ships' boats, and they're scattered." The low signal had come from a scout running up the path from the south.

Captain Strain hurried up the path from the sheds and watched the longboats moving slowly in the middle of the river. He whispered, "Pass the word, no one fires until I do."

Pistols and rifles were cocked along the waterfront as the waiting Confederates watched the boats continue on their course. Suddenly, the lead boat turned and began moving toward the shore. Shortly, the second boat turned, and hesitantly, the third followed by the others.

"Steady men, wait till I fire...That's a hell of a stupid way to attack land forces," spoke Captain Strain.

The first boat was within twenty yards of shore when Captain Strain stood up, fired his pistol and yelled, "Fire."

The entire shore erupted in flashes and powder smoke.

The officers and sailors in the lead boat fell in the hail of lead. Men yelled, scrambled for cover, and fell overboard throughout the little flotilla. Oars fell in the water, while others became entangled in the confusion of sailors trying to backwater, while a few grabbed at weapons and fired wildly toward the shore.

A few more shots from shore and the sailors, realizing the futility of their position, jumped overboard and began wading and swimming away toward the opposite mangrove covered shore. Several simply raised their hands to the mercy of their enemies.

The firing ceased, and after a moments hesitation, the Rebels ran into the water and retrieved four of the helpless boats. The others drifted with the tide out of reach. Seven bodies were brought to shore, and ten prisoners were helped to the breastworks.

As the excitement subsided, it was realized the short battle was over.

"Take the prisoners to the sheds, bandage up the wounded, and report our casualties," commanded Captain Strain.

The Confederates had suffered no casualties. The Federals had seven dead, seven wounded, one which was serious, and three other prisoners. One of the prisoners was an escaped negro slave that had been guiding the Federals. With little debate, he was taken to a nearby live oak and hanged. The young soldier who had been so belligerent earlier, went behind some bushes and retched.

Cutler walked up to Captain Strain, "Excuse me, sir, I checked the bodies and talked to the prisoners. Two of the dead are officers. One is Commander Budd of the USS Penguin, the other is Acting Master Mather of the Henry Andrew. The Penguin is the gunboat at the inlet; the ship out there is the Andrew. I understand that the Wabash is expected soon. She's a three masted Man of War. We could be in trouble, although I doubt if she can get through the inlet. I've told the rest of the men to split in two shifts, one to rest and eat while the other watches."

"Good. Captain Bird should be here shortly. I sent a runner for him. That was sure a stupid and strange way to attack a fortified shore," answered Strain, shaking his head.

Throughout the rest of the day and evening, the Rebels kept a tense watch. Captain Bird arrived in the late afternoon, inspected the waterfront, looked at the dead and the prisoners, and then he and Captain Strain sat on the porch of the Sheldon House and conferred for a long time.

Little was said about the battle among the troops. Tomorrow things could change!

During the night several militiamen arrived from Orange Grove, a plantation that had been burned by the Seminoles over twenty-five years earlier. This was a favorite camping and stopover spot, along with the sugar mill, on the long trip between New Smyrna and Saint Augustine.

These men were the only ones anxious for a return of the Federals.

The seriously wounded sailor died during the night and was carried over to join his still comrades under the stained canvas.

The next morning a launch was seen approaching the defenders. A white flag flew on a pole at its bow. Captain Bird walked to the water in full view, a soldier at his side with a white handkerchief tied to the bayonet of his rifle. After a short conference with the officer in the boat, Captain Bird sent his escort to Captain Strain, standing with his men at the earthworks. "Sir, the Cap'n says for us to carry the dead Yankees and the papers belonging to their officers to that there little boat," said the messenger.

The bodies and documents were taken to the waiting sailors, and the boat departed.

A somewhat relieved Captain Bird called his men around him and said, "Men, you did a good job yesterday. Wish I had been here. The Yankees are leaving this time; they've had enough, but you can bet they'll be back again someday. Our job is to keep this inlet open. It won't be this easy the next time. I'm proud of all of you and tonight we're going to open that barrel of rum that the Katie brought in from Nassau."

As he walked away, a cheer arose along the waterfront. The cheer was also heard by the men in the launch moving toward the center of the stream, and many a bitter curse was muttered by the grieving and defeated sailors. They would be back, by damn!

16

It sure felt good sleeping in a real bed, but the yellow warmth of the morning flooded the room through the open window, and the angry calls of mockingbirds echoed throughout the surrounding woods and fields. Cutler stretched, grunted, wiggled his toes, then while pulling himself up into a sitting position on the bed, he smacked his lips and scratched his belly through his nightshirt, while all the time he was gazing around the room.

Pa had kept his room as it has been the day he had left to join the Army. It didn't seem possible, over a year had passed since that day. As Cutler pulled on his clothes, he found that it felt distantly familiar to be putting on civilian clothes once again. Wearing his uniform had become second nature now, and although he had a spare one, both had been reduced a little shabby during the past year of wear and patching. The Florida troops, in fact, most of the Confederate soldiers, had taken pride in outfitting themselves the best they possibly could. True, many of the uniforms in the same companies often were cut differently and sometimes were of different shades of grey or butternut; some uniforms were even blue, but mothers, wives, sisters, and sweethearts had labored many an hour to provide the best they possibly could for their loved ones. Issued uniforms were the exception rather than the rule for the Southern armies, versus the regular issues of uniforms for the Union.

Sam Garnett was sitting out in the courtyard, between the main house and the kitchen. The Spanish-style house was built in the shape of a "U", the kitchen built separately in the center of the walled-in, coquina courtyard. Sam had kept most of the large trees and under them had placed iron tables and chairs. Except for rainy mornings, he always had his breakfast served under the trees; this was, of course, after his daily walk to visit the single, fenced-in tombstone, under the largest oak on his property. Emily, his wife, Cutler's mother, rested there, ever since the day of her son's birth.

At noon, he would eat at the large heavy wooden table under the portico. Supper was served in the main room. This room was dominated by a large stone fireplace with an ancient cypress mantel and stone firewood boxes. Sam's secret iron safe was under one of the firewood boxes. The ceiling beams were two feet wide and supported rooms upstairs. The furniture was also hand-fashioned from Florida live oak, cypress, and pine. The roof was covered with red tiles.

"Howdy, Pa, it sure is good to be home, and am I ever hungry!" the younger Garnett called out as he approached his father. He, too, had visited the spot under the large oak. Sam returned his son's grin and turned toward the kitchenhouse, "Yo, Mara, his highness is up an says he'll whip you if you don't bring him his breakfast." His voice was strong and clear.

A skinny colored woman in her early fifties calmly walked up the brick walkway from the kitchen. She was carrying, with both hands, a large tray, covered with a white cloth.

"Well, well, well...now I'se not gonna believe this hea royal son is gonna whoop this lady what used to wipe his bottom not too many years ago," she said in a singsong voice. Then sticking out her tongue at Cutler, she placed the tray on the table and began unloading its steaming contents on the table in front of him.

"Now, Mara, you know better than to believe everything that Pa says. You're family, and besides, ain't no better cook in the South...in the North, too, I reckon, but I've never been there, so I don't know." Eying the food, Cutler lost all interest in talking and proceeded to satisfy his appetite. Mara nodded to herself happily, patted him on the shoulder, and walked back to her kitchen, leaving father and son to their breakfast table under the tree.

Cutler spent the next several days helping repair the spring-house. The sulfur spring running through it had eroded much of the mud and sand, causing some of the coquina rocks to shift and the timbers to sag and crack. Two of the slaves worked with him, carrying stones, cutting lumber, and digging holes for the supporting of the walls and roof. Deep Waters would occasionally wander by silently, and watch.

It felt good to be home; it was almost like never having left. The war seemed far away. He certainly didn't miss being shot at, and shooting at Yankees wasn't done for fun. He was even starting to believe that some of the Yankees were human, too.

One evening a rider came in from Monticello with news. While having supper with the Garnetts he filled them in with some of the news of the war. Two companies of Federal troops from the 97th Pennsylvania had been scouring the countryside around Jacksonville looking for Confederate guerrillas. Captain Footman of Company F Florida, with forty of his men, had been scouting along the Fernandina railroad and had captured some of the Yankees of the 9th Maine Infantry. Men from the Saint Augustine Rifles and the St. Johns Grays had been sent to Virginia with the Second Florida Infantry Regiment. The Saint Augustine Blues had been sent from New Smyrna to Mobile with the rest of the Third Regiment. General Kirby Smith had recovered from his wounds taken at Manassas and was very disappointed that his home town, Saint Augustine, had been surrendered to the enemy. There just weren't enough men and materials to prevent the enemy from invading the land. General Robert E. Lee had notified Governor Milton that Brigadier General Joseph Finegan was to be the new Commander of the Department of Eastern and Middle Florida, according to Special Orders Number 80. Captain Smith and his men had ridden for 24-hours from Blue Springs to Saint Andrews Bay to try and recapture the steamer, Florida, but instead repulsed a landing by the Federals, killing most of them, with no loss to the Southerners.

Yes, the war was still in Cutler's beloved Florida, and the hard fact returned with sudden impact! Although he still had a few more days left of his furlough, his mind was no longer at home.

The next morning a letter arrived from Cora! Would he and his father come over and visit for a few days? She had received his letter that Jacobs had delivered. It was real nice hearing from him. Her daddy was well and back with the Company, and the store kept her very busy.

"Just my luck. Here I have to finish all this work just before goin back to soldierin, and I get an invite to go visitin someone that I wouldn't miss seein for the world."

Cutler was quiet at the breakfast table that morning. His father glanced at him a few times with a knowing smile, then said, "You know, I was thinking, we need to go to Ocala and pick up some supplies before you go back to the Army. Maybe you remember Sergeant Gordon's family invited me to go visitin, and being there are a few things we could use, maybe...if you don't mind, you could come along."

Cutler looked up quickly, but Sam was intently cutting the ham on his plate.

A few moments of silence, then the younger man admitted softly, "I received a letter this mornin from Cora Gordon. She invited us to go and visit for a spell. Pa, I'd sure like to go."

"Good," nodded Sam. "We'll leave as soon as I leave some instructions around and Mara has our lunch packed. I told her earlier we were going." Then he looked at his surprised son and grinned, saying, "The ole man ain't as dumb as he looks."

Mara's son, Jeffrey, drove the wagon while Sam and Cutler rode their horses about twenty yards ahead. The men spoke occasionally, but mostly they rode quietly, their eyes and ears concentrating on the forests and surrounding fields. The dust rose in little puffs from the horse's hooves, and the late spring heat began to rise as the day wore on. Occasionally, they would encounter a rider or farmer, and once a Confederate messenger rode swiftly passed them, waving his cap as he continued northward.

Whenever a civilian was encountered, all would stop and chat and exchange news. Jeffrey would overtake them and continue and they would then follow him, overtake the wagon, and slow back down to a walk. Cutler was glad to be seated on Rhona again. She had been his horse since she had been a young filly.

"Funny, before the war, there was a few of these folks I wouldn't ever had talked with. Now we're all in it together...notice everybody's armed?" murmured Sam.

"Yea, Pa, but there's a few I wouldn't leave my house unguarded for, or my back turned to. We got some of the folks that don't care what side wins, just as long as they can make a profit, and that don't matter how, either. That pair we saw by the waterin hole were eyin that big bay of yours, but I reckon they figured we had a mite more powder 'n lead than they'd care to mess with. I saw you shift your rifle across a tad."

Sam nodded, "Figured you'd noticed. They looked at your Apaloosa, too!"

The men didn't stop for lunch, eating while in the saddle. They watered the horses as they crossed a slow moving stream and got off for a few minutes and stretched their legs before moving on.

That evening they camped just east of Eustis, a small dusty town among a group of lakes. Sam caught three nice size bass in a lake while Cutler cut some palm hearts and Jeffrey watered and hobbled the horses and started the small cooking fire.

It wasn't long before savory fragrances drifted with the wood smoke through the shadows of the grey woods. Having eaten their fill, the men extinguished the fire, and wrapped in their light blankets, each with a small mosquito string net over his head, quickly fell asleep on the soft pine needle covered ground.

The next day, the ride continued uneventfully. The miles seemed to never end to the impatient Cutler. He continued to think of Cora as he remembered her the first and only time they had met on the pier at Palatka when he had been about to board the Hattie Brock. Cora's pale blue eyes had gazed directly through him, and he had melted like butter on hot corn bread. He tried to imagine how she would welcome him. Would she act cool and distant or like just a friend and that's all, or would she run to him. He could even fantasize what it would be like to hold her close...or even kiss her on the lips. Cutler had never felt like this. He felt like he had no control of his emotions and didn't know if he liked it or not. Sex wasn't the main thing that was bothering him. He had rolled in the hay before with several of the girls from nearby farms, even with the widow lady that lived at the northern neck of the lake where it joined the St. John. She had taught him a lot! Cora wasn't an object of lust to him. In fact, he just dwelled on the image of her face as he rode. He had found himself daydreaming about her several times in the past few months, but not as much as now as he rode closer to seeing her again.

It was dusk as the trio stopped in front of the Gordon store. A dim light could be seen inside the unpainted board building and two horses were tied in front of the low porch. Cutler tried to act unconcerned, but he couldn't help dismounting quickly and walking toward the porch before stopping and turning back and leading Rhona to the water trough upon hearing his father loudly clearing his throat.

"Son, I'll go on in. You and Jeffrey wait here," and the older man handed the reins of his horse to his disappointed son and stepped up to the porch and into the open doorway.

"Why, Mister Garnett, it really is good to see you again," Cutler heard Flora's excited voice from outside. "Cora, come out front. Mister Garnett is here, from Mellonsville." Cutler heard a door slam inside the building, some rapid footsteps, and then Cora's voice, "Welcome to the big city, Mister Garnett...did you come alone? I mean...that's a long way to travel by yourself, the war and all."

Cutler couldn't move. He just stood frozen, staring toward the doorway, still holding the loose reins of the drinking horses. Jeffrey had stepped down from the wagon and had gone around to the little trickle of water that fed into the hollowed out logs through the bamboo-like shoots from the natural spring in the ground. He had placed his upturned mouth to the clear water and it ran into his mouth and spilled over his chin and down the front of his dusty shirt. He stared at Cutler.

"Don't you two pretty ladies fret, I brought that heroic son along to entertain you two. He's outside now, too bashful to come inside. He's the white one," laughed Sam.

Flora and Cora were quickly in the doorway, and Flora placed her hands on her hips and looked down at the boy and said, "Cutler Garnett, what's the matter with you? Here I've been watchin my sister all this time, makin sure she doesn't run off lookin for you, and now that you're finally here, all you can do is stand there with your mouth open drawin flies. Come up here, boy, and give me a hug, and if it's not too much trouble, you can say hello to my sister...mind you, I'm watchin you two!"

Cutler went quickly up the steps and self consciously placed an arm around each girl and mumbled something. He could feel his neck and face getting very hot. "Good thing it's almost dark and nobody can see how red my face must be," he thought. Flora turned and walked toward the doorway, reluctantly, Cutler released Cora.

"Come on, Cora, let's close up and get on to the house and get these hungry men some supper," Flora called from inside.

The four walked along the wagon road the half mile to the Gordon house. Jeffrey followed with the wagon and horses tied to the rear. Sam and Flora talked about her father, while Cutler and Cora followed silently, occasionally exchanging quick glances, but mostly concentrating intently on walking, as if they would stumble. Once Cora's hand brushed his and Cutler's heart seemed to skip a couple of beats.

The Gordon house sat on a low knoll, surrounded by azalea bushes and orange trees. The two-story building was of whitewashed boards on a log foundation.

As they approached the house, Cora turned to Cutler and said softly, "Thank you for writing me the letter from New Smyrna. Ralph Jacobs brought it to me...it meant a lot to me," then she hurried into the house.

The men washed some of the dust from their hands and faces at the spring at the back of the house, bedded the horses in the open stalls, and Cutler and Jeffrey brought their bedrolls from the wagon to the tool shed, which was also used for overnighters that occasionally worked part time around the house and small fields. Thomas Gordon had some fields on which he grew a few vegetables, mostly for the family and a few friends. He even had a dozen orange trees, some pecan trees, and raised some chickens and hogs. Sam went inside with his bedding and bag. He would be sleeping in Thomas's room while in Ocala.

Cutler was self-conscious throughout most of the meal. The conversation was light, but he partook sparingly, feeling that Cora and he were really what was on everybody's mind. Even Jeffrey looked up at him strangely from his dinner where he was seated in the warming kitchen, when Cutler had gone into that room to help bring another platter of chicken to the dining room table.

The dishes done, the two girls joined Sam and Cutler on the front porch. Jeffrey had gone to the stables. The four had little to say, other than the weather had been pleasant and it seemed to be an early summer. Then, Sam started the conversation about Deep Waters, the Seminole who had become sort of a neighbor at the plantation. As the topic continued, Cutler joined in, telling stories of how his friend had taught him some of his skills in the forests. As Cutler spoke, he was stimulated about the life he loved, and forgot his self-consciousness and embarrassment. Cora watched his every move and absorbed every word.

"Well, you young folks can keep talkin, but, me for one, am

71

a tad tired and goin to bed now. That nice soft bed is callin. See you all in the morning," yawned Sam, and he went inside as the trio of "G'nights" trailed after him.

"When are you going back to the Army, Cutler?" asked Cora. She was leaning with her back against a porch post looking out into the darkness. She turned and looked at him as he answered, "I reckon the day after t'morrow. Pa's going on back with Jeffrey, and I'm headin to Amelia Island to join Lieutenant Dickison's company there." Flora turned excitedly, "Oh, we know J. J. Dickison. He was in Captain Martin's company, the Marion Light Artillery, from here in Ocala. Papa is still a sergeant with the company. Lieutenant Dickison keeps saying that they're going to make a change of part of the company and start some cavalry companies from the Third Regiment of Florida Volunteers. Anyway, Ralph said that Vito Forselli is with the group and maybe he, too, will get a chance to go there."

"It'll be good to be with my friends again, although I understand that some of them have gone with General Loring to Virginia. Can you imagine, two Generals in the Army from Saint Augustine? General Loring and General Kirby-Smith...ain't that somethin!" exclaimed Cutler.

Softly Cora said, "Do you think the war will last very long? I know it's very exciting, but I'm scared for our people. Everybody thinks it's a game."

"It's no game, but everybody says the Yankees are whipped good and it'll be over soon...Pa thinks different, and he might be right. All we got is farms, slaves, and spunk. That's not enough to beat someone that really wants to fight, and that crippled rat, Thad Stevens, keeps stirrin em up to steal our niggers. The only chance we got is to get the North tired quick, then they'll get disgusted and quit, but Pa don't think we can beat em if it strings out very long. But you know, they've had a lot of riots up there. People want the war to stop. Their police and soldiers have killed a lot of their own civilians. I don't know, some of the old timers think the way Pa thinks. They might be right and they might be wrong, we'll see...and we better not depend too much on England coming to our rescue so we can supply her with cotton. We sold a lot of cotton over there the last few years and even if they are dependent on it, I bet they have loaded up their warehouses when they smelled war," answered Cutler.

"C'mon, Cora, we better get to bed. We've got a big day tomorrow. All that grey cloth's got to get rolled and wrapped to catch that southbound wagon in the morning. G'night, Cutler. See you for breakfast." Flora, got to her feet from the chair she had brought out from the dining room, picked it up, and went in.

Cora hesitated, then turned to follow her sister. As she walked past Cutler, she touched his sleeve with her hand and turned her head, "I'm glad to see you again. G'night," and she was gone inside.

Before going to his own sleeping quarters in the tool shed, Cutler stood on the porch for several minutes savoring fond thoughts of the blonde girl.

17

Captain Dickison slowly rode down the sandy trail. The Captain's horse was sweaty and the trail dust, mixed into a gritty mud that ran down the animal's flanks and stained its hide into various shades of brown and grey. The Captain rode quietly, slightly bent over, but alert to the sounds of the thick woods and palmettos on either side of the wide trail. His scouts were well ahead; behind him trailed Company H, 2nd Florida Cavalry, seventy-five tired, thirsty and dirty officers and men. They had been at Yellow Bluff, north of Jacksonville, then had been sent to Camp Finegan. Now upon learning that the enemy had begun troubles in the Saint Johns area, they had been ordered to Palatka to protect that general vicinity.

Cutler was riding toward the rear of the column, dozing in the saddle, unmindful of the mosquitoes, buzzing around his face and hands. Occasionally, he would jerk his head upward and open his eyes, then swat a few of the mosquitoes as they settled. The sweat had thoroughly soaked his skin, and the mixture with the dust had made riding extremely uncomfortable. He and Forselli had been scouts all morning, and the night before. They had been up most of the night delivering messages and riding from one point to another among the scattered campsites at Camp Finegan.

Between thoughts of cool water, Cutler thought of Cora. The evening before leaving Ocala, she had kissed him lightly on the lips before running inside the house. They had been sitting on the steps of the porch, everyone else had gone inside, and they had been alone for quite some time. Some light conversation would start, but would die into embarrassed silence. Cora had finally said she had to go in, that it was late, and as he, too, had gotten to his feet, she had quickly turned and kissed him. He had been stunned, and then all of a sudden felt better than he had ever felt in his life. He thought all kinds of things that he had wanted to say to her now.

The next day, before mounting Rhona to leave, he had gotten enough courage to ask Cora to wait for him. They had held hands briefly, and she had said softly, "I will... please be careful. Come back to me," and with tears steaming, she had run up into the house. He had repeated her words to himself over and over the past months.

"Hey, sleepy, wake up. They just found a bunch of niggers runnin' away. We got to round 'em up."

Cutler woke, still in the uncomfortable saddle, and found himself kicking his horse to catch up with the rest of the column that had begun moving quickly up the trail.

The slaves stopped without offering resistance and were quickly circled by the soldiers. Among them were several Confederate deserters who were not treated as well, being cursed, shoved, and finally tied to trees.

Captain Dickinson and Lieutenant Brantly had taken two of the older Negro men to one side and all four were seated facing each other on four logs in deep discussion.

The remaining men, not guarding the prisoners or on picket, stretched out in the shade, most of them were quickly sound asleep.

Cutler slept about twenty minutes when First Lieutenant McCardell woke him, "C'mon, Garnett, you'n me and some boys are goin huntin Yankees," he said, as he squatted alongside the sleeping boy.

As Cutler got up and gathered his belongings, he noticed that the officer had six men waiting behind him holding their horses' reins; Cutler's horse was among them.

"The Captain says you're a good guide, and I agree, so we're turnin towards St. Augustine to see if we can catch us some of the blue-bellied troublemakers that have been stirrin up our niggers," continued the Lieutenant.

The little group mounted and turned back in the direction they had come earlier. They nodded as they rode past the rest of the troopers that were still awake.

The little patrol rode in silence until sundown, then the lieutenant signaled a halt. The men dismounted, grouped around the officer, and stood listening while stretching sore muscles.

"We've got to walk em from here on in. Keep it quiet and we'll set a trap by the crossroads into St. Augustine. Garnett, you go ahead and see if the road is clear. Some of those Yanks have gotta come by from the Fairbank place after goin around free'n slaves. We'll take em home with us."

The men walked their horses up to the crossroads, where Cutler was waiting. While two of the privates took the horses into the bushes to hold, one man backtracked, brushed over their tracks, and then hid in the underbrush. Lieutenant McCardell and the others hid along the trail near the crossroads.

There was a light breeze and the ghostly shadows played along the dirt road and among the trees from the bright three-quarter moon. The rustle of little animals and the calls of night birds were the only sounds heard. No sounds came from the hiding men or from the city, less than a mile away to the north.

The men waited almost two hours before approaching sounds came from the south. The murmur of voices, the creaking of leather, and the plod of horses' hooves moved closer toward the crossroads.

"Well, Sergeant, we'll be there shortly. I must admit, I'll be glad to turn this patrol to someone else tomorrow. Draining the country of contrabands and supplies isn't exactly my idea of war, although I'm sure it hurts the economy of the enemy and keeps some of their men out of the war," the officer in blue said.

"You're right, sir. Besides, my ass feels like it's been in this saddle a week. It won't be long the word will be out and we'll have all the blacks in the country runnin away toward St. Augustine. I guess that we'll have to feed them, too. Did you see the ones at the last plantation? Some cussed us out, some were scared and stared at us, some hid, and some clapped, cried, kissed our boots, and yelled, 'Jubilation.' I wouldn't be surprised that next we'll have some of them in uniform, too. Tomorrow I'll be glad to pull garrison duty," the second man in the column had answered his officer.

From behind a stand of pines and palmettos a loud voice was heard, followed by the heavy metallic clack of rifles, pistols, and muskets being cocked. "Friend, none of you have to worry about goin after no niggers tomorrow, but you do have a long ride tonight before you can rest your thievin asses. I suggest you drop your weapons and raise your hands."

Without hesitation, the Union soldiers followed instructions, looks of surprise on their faces as they vainly looked around in the darkness. The officer had a look of disgust.

The little group of hidden Confederates picked up the weapons and tied the wrists of the captured men behind their backs. They had captured a lieutenant, two sergeants, and two privates.

Lieutenant McCardell spoke with the captured officer for a few minutes, then the little column turned and moved briskly southward, Cutler riding point, the happy men in grey holding the bridles for their dejected prisoners.

The morning found the group on the eastern shore of the St. Johns river, across from Palatka. It wasn't long that a raft was sent over to ferry them to the little town.

Routine camp duty was boring to Cutler. Only the occasional scouting trips or raids helped break the monotony. News was always precious and couriers were the center of attention whenever they passed through with their dispatches. True, the officers received the report officially, but unofficially...

During September, Cutler became sick with dysentery and lost almost thirty pounds. By October he had not fully recovered and remained in camp as Captain Dickinson and most of his men crossed the San Sabastian river and rode to set a trap for the Federal troops that had been again visiting around the Fairbanks place and other plantations near Saint Augustine.

The Federals, instead, did not come out in the usual force or at the usual time. This time, six companies, about 350 men, crossed the San Sebastian river four miles below the point at which the Rebel forces had crossed, with the intention to capture their wagon train of supplies and cut off the Southerner's way of retreat.

A detachment held the Federals in check until the wagons could be drawn off, then Captain Dickison returned with his main force, charged, and captured the Union rear guard of one officer and twenty-six soldiers.

The heavy firing continued for some time as the Federals retreated toward Saint Augustive. Afraid of being drawn into an enveloping trap, the rebels broke off the engagement. Forty three of them had beaten six companies of regular Union troops, and with no losses to themselves!

The next night the jubilant little command returned to Palatka with their prisoners and the captured weapons. Forselli had been with the victorious group and gave all the details of the action to the jealous Cutler.

Captain Dickison and his men were building quite a reputation, according to the Union prisoners. Rumors had been that he had over a thousand men and heavy artillery. His nickname in the Federal camps was "Dixie."

Cutler was proud to be a member of this elite little group and hoped that he would soon be well enough to participate in the next battle.

Some bad news arrived. Saint Johns Bluff, a stronghold over-looking the river near Jacksonville, had been captured.

In September, the little fort on the bluff, really just some cannon and earthworks, had repulsed and crippled attacking Federal gunboats. On October first, six gunboats, two regiments of infantry, one battery of artillery, and several companies of cavalry, had returned. After being repulsed, they left for more reinforcements from Fernandina. This time when they again attacked they found the little fort abandoned.

The good news was that Jacksonville was again in Confederate hands, although the Federals retained Fernandina.

The Southerners had mounted a rifled 32 pounder on an armored flat-car and had shelled with uncanny accuracy into Jacksonville and the Federal gunboats. This was followed by an infantry attack. The Federal troops were forced to withdraw and abandon the city.

During that week, Dickison's forces were involved in several skirmishes around Jacksonville.

Upon their return to Palatka, they fought against the transport Mary Benton, carrying five hundred Negro troops of General Montgomery, Lieutenant-Colonel Billings commanding. Colonel Billings was wounded and over twenty-five of the negro soldiers were killed before the transport broke off the engagement and retreated northward.

18

Cutler had been receiving letters from Cora. In fact, one week he received two letters and was in a most jubilant mood. Every evening after supper he led the singing, mostly love songs, like Lorena, although Bonnie Blue Flag was sung at least once every evening and now the new song. Dixie, had become more and more popular.

With the coming of cooler weather, Cutler was thinking of the Christmas holidays, hoping that he would be among the men going home to their families. Of course, he wanted to go home and see his father, but mostly he thought of Cora.

On December 23rd, he was granted five days. Lieutenant Brantly handed him the signed paper and Cutler shook the officer's hand, spun on his heel, and ran to the tent he had been sharing with Forselli and two other privates, the Clifton brothers.

"I'm leavin, I'm leavin..." he shouted to the startled group. Then he quickly rolled his bedroll, his few possessions in between.

Cutler, whooped as he rode out of camp towards home. It took all his self-control to keep from galloping Rhona, but instead, he kept her at a slow trot southward.

It was December 23, 1863, the weather was pleasant and warm. Leaves had begun to turn from the rich greens of summer to the splashes of yellows, reds, and browns. A fresh light breeze came from the northeast, and with it, the clear salt air of the sea.

The smell of the sea reminded Cutler of his cousin, Orin. He was a seaman on the cruiser, Alabama, commanded by Captain Raphael Semmes. The new ship had already captured several enemy ships and looked as though she was going to become a threat to Northern shipping. Captain Semmes had previously commanded the Sumter, a tiny gunboat that had sunk or captured eighteen enemy ships. Now he was in command of the new speedy English built raider, and the one letter that Sam Garnett had received from Orin was full of optimism for the new venture. Orin lost two fingers on his left hand during one of the fights of the Sumter, he had gotten used to the loss by the time he had written the letter, and only mentioned it in passing.

Cutler remembered Orin as a chubby boy that would occasionally come and visit from his home at Cedar Key. He and his mother, Aunt Ernestine, the widowed younger sister of Cutler's mother, would come part way by train and then take a steamer south on the St. Johns to his father's plantation. Orin was a year older than Cutler, but had never been as active, preferring to "relax" by a stream with a fishing pole rather than do anything strenuous as his cousin.

They had gotten along well enough, but usually, after a visit of more than a week, the boys would normally spend little time together, each preferring to go his own way.

Cutler rode the small ferry across the St. Johns, then found his way to the Old Kings Road, a road left over from the English occupation of Florida from 1763 to 1783. The road led southward, past the abandoned plantations of John Bulow and Robert McHardy and James Ormond. The plantation of Bulow had been burned by the Seminoles in 1836 and was overgrown with vegetation. Much of the warehouse and factory and sugar mill was built of coquina stone, and still standing. Cutler dismounted, led his horse to the ruins of the springhouse, a little distance from the factory, in a low marshy area. He and Rhona drank their fill of the cool water. He then refilled his canteen, and led her to the creek a few dozen yards to the east. Peering out from among the palmettos, he looked carefully up and down the slow moving creek. Bulow Creek drained the swamps and saw grass, emptying into the Halifax River about a mile north of a large basin. A high spit of land on the southside of the basin had once been an Indian shell mound and village in the old days. Deep

Waters had taken him there on numerous occasions on hunting trips. The small deer had been plentiful and the tidewater stream feeding the basin was great for fishing. Of course, there were a fair number of alligators, but they seldom bothered anyone, contenting themselves to bask in the sun or slide down the banks into the stream. The water was brownish and depending on the tides, was either freshwater or salty.

Seeing no human activity near the creek, Cutler sat on a log and watched a long legged heron pick its way along the shallows of the opposite bank, occasionally pecking into the water with its long bill and retrieving a shimmering minnow. Eating some captured hardtack biscuits and chewing on some stringy smoked beef jerky, Cutler relaxed for fifteen minutes.

Finished with his light lunch, he rinsed his hands in the creek, wiped them dry on his pants and taking Rhona's reins, led her back to the old overgrown road.

Cutler rode passed the ruins of the McHardy plantation. Little could be seen of the once thriving community; the woods and swamps had reclaimed their own.

Reaching the larger stream that fed into the basin, he dismounted and tied his moccasins and weapons to the saddle. The silent duo then swam to the southern shore. Cutler saw a small boat in the distance and not knowing if it contained Federals, or possibly Northern sympathizers, he stayed in hiding among the fallen trees. When the boat disappeared around the spit of land, he dressed, mounted, and slowly walked Rhona to the main road again.

Cutler would have preferred returning home the short way, but before Lieutenant Brantly handed him his pass he had asked him to check out the area for Northern outposts on his way home, how could he refuse?

A chill went through Cutler's spine as he remembered the stories that Deep Waters had told him. how the ghosts of the long gone Indians roamed these thick woods of pine and oaks, smothered with grey hanging moss. How a rider would have the feeling of being watched and often at night many a traveler would see eerie blue lights in the woods following him. Some people stayed away from this area, swearing that the blue lights would chase them and if they were caught they would disappear from the face of the earth and return as wandering souls emitting nothing but blue light.

As the shadows deepened, Cutler turned Rhona westward at a fast walk, ever mindful of Federal patrols or bands of deserters from both sides. These small bands of outlaws were becoming bold, and had, on several occasions, ambushed lone travelers, killing them and taking their weapons, clothes and supplies. Mutilated, naked bodies, found on sparsely traveled trails were terrible evidence of this.

Having passed through several swampy areas, Cutler set up camp on a high spot in a grove of cedars. Rhona was hobbled loosely and watered, then he laid down on his bedroll and munched on some beef jerky in the darkness. He then covered his weapons at his side, closed his eyes, and while listening to the crickets, fell asleep.

Early next morning, Cutler and Rhona continued cross-country through forest, undergrowth, and swamps, finally coming to the Spring Garden road. With little urging, Rhona broke into a trot on the wide dirt and sandy road until the scattered houses of the little settlement were reached. They continued on to the spring and met with the small detachment of militia camped there. There were a dozen men at the little campsite in brand new uniforms and an assortment of weapons, ranging from muskets to flintlocks and shotguns.

The men were thirsting for news and Cutler talked to them for about fifteen minutes. The greatest shock to them was the death of General Stonewall Jackson at Chancellorsville on May 11th. There were tears in the eyes of the men who had never seen General Jackson.

After a long drink of cool water for both he and Rhona, Cutler returned on the southward road towards Enterprise. One of the militiamen rode to Fort Butler, near Volusia, with the news.

By late afternoon, Cutler trotted into Enterprise. On his right was The Brocks House, a large wooden resort hotel on the shore of Lake Monroe, built by Jacob Brock, the owner of the steamboats, Darlington and Hattie Brock. "Hey, Cutler, don't you say howdy to friends?" rasped a voice from the porch of the Mercantile Goods Company store. Reining, Cutler dismounted and walked up to the sun-tanned old farmer seated on the rocking chair in the sun.

"Howdy, Mr. Jed. Didn't see you right off. How's the misses?" said the young man as he reached over and shook hands with the old man.

"Feelin poorly, feelin poorly. But than again, she ain't happy less she's complainin. Where you been soldierin lately? Saw your pappy other day; said you might be mosyin this aways soon. Set a spell," answered the old, one legged man.

"Can't. Got to get on to home. Been with Cap'n Dickison on the east. Com-mon to the house and have some supper with us sometime. Bring the misses. how's the leg?"

"Aches on cool days, but the new wood foot shore makes walkin easier," answered J.J. Jed.

J. J. Jed. lost his left foot several years earlier to a hungry alligator while fishing. He had been sitting in his boat wiggling his bare feet in the water when a large gator had bitten him just above the ankle. The gator had tried to twist and pull him into the water, but had released his grip when J. J. shot it in the eye. The farmer bandaged his mangled limb and dragged himself home. That night his wife amputated the foot. One week later

J. J. was back working in his fields, a crutch under his arm.

Cutler remounted, waved, and continued southward through the dusty street, to Lake Harney. Several miles short of the lake, he turned on a path toward the west, reaching the St. John. He paid the riverman and walked Rhona onto the little ferry. The two men silently poled the craft across the slow moving stream. Cutler led his horse off the ramp, mounted, and trotted on the Mellonsville Road. Passing several neighbors on the road, Cutler greeted them without stopping, then taking the plantation turnoff, he rode up to the house among the barking dogs, and hallooed.

Mara came running out of the cookhouse and yelled, "Mr. Sam, yo boy is home," then she put her arms around Cutler.

"Howdy, Mara, sure missed you-all," said Cutler, as he embraced the slender black woman.

Mara let go only when Sam walked up and warmly shook his son's hand.

"Welcome home, son. It sure is good to have you back in one piece. Come on inside and have something to drink. Jeffrey will take care of Rhona."

Sam sat in his large deerskin-covered, stuffed chair. He watched his son seated across the room, his favorite old hunting dog at his feet. Cutler was sipping from a large glass of rum, water, and lemon juice. His uniform was dusty and worn. A large dark holster hung from his belt, his bone handle knife was in a leather sheath, tied to the same belt, on his left side. The moccasins he wore, reached almost to his knees, and these were covered with dust and sandspurs. The edges were frayed and a small knife and sheath was strapped with rawhide to the outside of the right one. He had placed his brimed hat on the floor. It, too, was dusty and sweat stained. His saber was thrust between his side and the armrest. There was rough stubble on his sunburned face and he wore a drooping mustache where before there had been none. His dark hair was mussed and long, reaching over the collar of his frayed grey tunic.

Sam was proud of his only son, but he was also worried and sad for him. He also knew that his worry and sadness must never show.

"Pa, we've really had some times. That Cap'n Dickison is some man!" exclaimed Cutler. "He really knows how to lead men and seems to always know what the enemy is plannin next. They're scared to death of him."

"Son," said Sam. "Maybe things look good to you, oh, I'm sure you're hungry and tired, but as you know, those things can be patched up in a day or two. But, let me explain a few things. When I finish you can tell me what you think." He paused, took a sip from his glass, and began.

"I'm sure you know all that's been going on in Virginia and the west. To start with, Antietam was a big defeat for us. Everybody says it was a draw. That if McClennan hadn't found Lee's orders of battle wrapped around those cigars, we would have taken Washington or New York by now. If, that's a big word. If we had won, the British, French and Russians would have recognized us as a nation, not just a bunch of rabble-rousing revolutionaries. In October, last year, they voted in London and we lost! That battle cost us that valuable recognition and a six months armistice. That armistice would have been between two countries, the United States and The Confederate States. That armistice would have ended the war. Europe would have made sure of that. They don't want the United States to be so big and strong. They want the Confederacy to succeed. That way, North America will be divided, and the real world powers would still be in the Old World. This, of course, at no risk to them! Britain wasn't happy about the War of 1812 and is still smarting over our winning the war with Mexico, beating most of the Indians, and mostly, getting Oregon. Don't forget, also, the North has high tariffs against British goods, the South is a free-trade area, no tariffs allowed, which if successful, could become a way for all countries, no tariffs!

"You know as well as I do, how much the South depends on cotton for exportation. Our currency is practically based on it, yet we burned almost two million pounds, just to try to keep Britain's demand for it real high. What stupidity! Not only did we hurt our image with our, almost allies, but we looked like financial fools. We should have listened to our Vice President! Stephens was right when he said we should export it, warehouse it, and use it for credit to buy supplies. Instead, now we have a problem getting it out of the country. Britain is buying the captured cotton from the Yankees, especially since they have the whole Mississippi under their control, and now India is starting to supply some of their cotton to the world, too."

Sam paused, then called Mara. "Get some water for our soldier. He's goin to take a bath shortly. He can't look and smell like that at the supper table."

After Mara left, Sam continued. "You know, the Court of St. James isn't dumb. They sell arms to both sides and they feel that if they risk recognizing the South they may have to go to war with the North. Sure, the North has her hands full with us, but she's got a lot of people that won't fight against us but will against the English. Also, the North pays cash for its war materials, we pay with credit. Lord Palmerton and Gladstone are also worried that another war might break out in Europe between the Polish people and the Russians. Then they'd have to get into that and be stuck with wars on two fronts. The Italians already have their own war goin on with the King and Garibaldi trying to unify the country against the outsiders and the Pope. Good thing too! Lincoln and Sanford offered Garibaldi command of all the Federal Armies, but he had to refuse because he was busy in his country. He's one hell of a leader. We'd a had some real problems."

Sam paused for a sip of his drink, then with a sigh, continued. "The Sumter, Alabama, Florida, and others of our cruisers, have made the waters of the world unsafe for the Federal merchant fleets. Hundreds of Yankee owned ships have been rotting in harbours, afraid to take to the open seas. Many of the bolder ones are now resting under those seas. The British ships have no competition on the world trade markets. Do you think they're goin to let that slide away? Oh, sure, they rattled their swords when that idiot Wilkes of the Jacinto captured the British ship, Trent, and took our ministers, John Slidel and James Mason, to prison in Boston. But they gave Lincoln and Seward plenty of time to back out of the predicament and return the two ministers. The North was lucky that the new Atlantic Cable to Europe must have broken and all communications slowed down again. This gave time for a lot of tempers to cool down.

Tell you the truth, we'd a been better off if the Yankees had kept those two idiots! Mason's a pig. He insults the upper classes in The Chambers. He even spits his chaw on the carpets there. This doesn't endear us to the British. Slidel just killed a Frenchman in a duel over an insult he made to the man's wife. Fine representatives those two have turned out to be! They hurt us badly in both England and France. So now where do we stand with the battlefields? This fellow Grant has the Mississippi, with Vicksburg fallen. Thomas' men took Missionary Ridge, and Chattanooga is lost to General Bragg. Bragg, being President Davis' brother-in-law, doesn't help us one bit. Joe Johnston hasn't a prayer against Sherman and Burnside. Antietam cost us a third of our army. Gettysburg cost us another third of our army. Although when Perry's Floridians and Wright's Georgians attacked Humphreys and broke through his lines, with more men, we could have won at Gettysburg! There are more and more desertions every day. Chancellorsville cost us Stonewall Jackson. We've lost our rams; the ram, Virginia, had to be burned. Our entire coastline is watched by blockaders. Our paper money isn't worth rollin tobacco in. And I'm sure you heard of Quantrill's raid on Lawrence, Kansas in August and in Arkansas in October. I'm ashamed his people are classified as Southerners. They're butchers and outlaws and certainly harm more than help our cause. The states west of the Mississippi might as well not exist to us anymore and our beloved state is constantly under threat of invasion. We now are the breadbasket for the armies. We can supply the food, but it can't get up there fast enough and safely enough. Did you know that two ships bombarded New Smyrna in July? Those sailors got even for the defeat of last March...

Sorry, son, I didn't want to come up with all this gloom. I just felt we should talk, just the two of us."

"I understand, Pa. I know a lot of things haven't been goin right. But you'll see. It's not over yet," answered Cutler. His tone of voice, however, held little hope.

Sam spoke softly, "Cousin Jonathan from Atlanta was killed at Missionary Ridge. His body was found with the body of a Yank from the 104th Illinois. They both had been wounded and must have helped each other before bleeding to death. They found them side by side under a tree." Jonathan had been a favorite of Sam Garnett.

"Oh, I'm real sorry, Pa," said Cutler. "I didn't know."

"I know, son...now, why don't you get cleaned up for dinner. We have company," answered Sam.

"Oh! Who's comin?" asked Cutler, as he picked up his hat and stood.

"Orin is here and his mother, Aunt Ernestine...and...The Gordons," answered Sam, with a sly grin.

The boy's eyes widened and he gulped. He could hardly believe what he had just heard.

"You mean, Cora...is here?"

"Not yet, but Cora, Flora and Sergeant Thomas Gordon are due to arrive this afternoon. They will stay with us for a few days. I hope you don't mind," answered Sam ingenuously. "Orin and Aunt Ernestine arrived this morning. Now go clean up. Mara has your good clothes laid out on your bed. We had hoped you would arrive. She probably has hot water ready for you by now. Now git!"

"Pa, you're the best!" Cutler walked to his father and took his hand in both of his, then turned, gathered his things, and left the room.

19

Impatiently, Cutler paced under the arches outside the large house. He walked to the stables twice and three times to the main gate. He stopped and sat on the rail fence and watched the cattle grazing in the large pasture. Rhona was brushed and fed some grain and he checked her bridle and saddle, replaced some of the leather traces and a broken buckle. Then hung these carefully on the wooden pegs in the tack room. The hot bath had relaxed him, but now as the shadows of twilight were approaching, he felt concern that Cora and her family had not yet arrived.

Orin, Aunt Ernestine and Sam were in the house, chatting. Aunt Ernestine was still the same slender, prim woman. A few gray hairs now showed in her hair. Orin had changed completely. He was thin and deeply sunburned. He had a confident air about him and talked constantly about Captain Semmes and the Alabama. He loved the life he led and the adventure had brought out a toughness of limb and quickness of eye that Cutler had never seen before. Orin seemed to have completely gotten used to the loss of the two fingers of his left hand. Now he was anxiously awaiting his new assignment as a mate on the C.S.S. Florida, under Captain J. N. Maffitt.

Cutler had seen both his relatives earlier and there had been a sincere and joyous reunion.

Cutler went back into the house. "I'm goin down the road, see if I can 'meet them," he announced.

Sam and Aunt Ernestine looked up. Orin stood up, "I'll go with you," he said.

The two young men walked to the stables and saddled two horses. Cutler selected two spirited bays, leaving Rhona in the pasture. Without a word being spoken, Orin and Cutler rode out the gate, each with a rifle across the pommel of his saddle.

For an hour the two horsemen kept their horses at a brisk trot. The thudding hooves beat a steady rhythm on the packed sand and shell road.

The forests were now dark. Little of the remaining twilight illuminated the road.

"What's that ahead?" asked Orin.

"Sh...don't know. Dismount. Here...hold my horse," whispered Cutler.

At a crouch, Cutler moved forward at the edge of the road, his rifle ready. Orin held the horses, as his cousin's dark form melted into the darkness.

Several minutes passed, then Cutler returned. "It's the Gordon wagon in the middle of the road. Both horses are dead, shot, still in the traces. There's blood on the wagon seat and a trail leading off to the east. I'm goin to follow it. Take my horse back and get Deep Waters back here, quick! I'll leave a trail." Cutler turned, and was gone into the woods.

Without hesitating, Orin mounted his horse and turned back toward Mellonville, leading Cutler's horse.

Cutler followed the trail of broken grass deeper into the woods. Despite the darkness, the scattered branches, and occasional footprint in the white sand, left a clear trail to his trained eyes.

He had gotten over his concern for Cora and her family. Now he was mad! Having traveled for over an hour, he cautiously approached a small clearing. He stopped at the edge of the dark woods in time to see several shadowy figures run into the woods at the opposite side. Without hesitation, Cutler ran after the fleeing figures.

Entering the thick woods again, Cutler heard the people ahead of him crashing and struggling through the underbrush. Suddenly a shot rang out. "Uhh...he winged me," a voice cried out less than twenty yards ahead. A scattering of shots followed, then another voice, much closer, called, "You all right, Scott?"

"I guess so, but the old bastard hit me in the arm. Come here. It stings and I'm bleedin like a hog."

Cutler grinned, as he crouched under a large live oak.

Sergeant Gordon was giving these rats, whoever they were, a run for their money. This meant that the girls were probably still all right. The old sergeant was fighting a delaying action while his family was fleeing through the swamps toward Volusia Landing.

Cutler waited, then he heard several low voices coming from where the wounded man had cried out. He painstakingly crawled in that direction.

Hiding, he listened and counted six crouching figures in the underbrush.

"Jamie, you said this was goin to be easy; one ole man and two girls to keep us warm. Instead, here we're in the middle of nowhere and two of us are carryin lead."

"Why don't you two rebs shut up. You, Scott, if you had shot the old man square, we'd be now passin those girls around. Bill and I were supposed to kill the horses and we did. Anyway, let's quit this arguin and go after them, then we can go back and get all their stuff out of the wagon and leave the area before word gets out that deserters are in the area. We'll have J. J. Dickison, his men, and half the farmers out after us."

Cutler could see the larger of the six men talking. He had on a dirty blue uniform. Jamie and Scott had grey jackets and the two other men that hadn't spoken were also in blue uniforms. Deserters! Bandits! From both armies, banded together to steal, kill, rape, and pillage the countryside.

Cutler watched these men and the hatred built up inside him, especially for the two southern men. He felt they were betraying their country, their neighbors, their families.

Deliberately, Cutler aimed his rifle and shot Jamie in the face. While the echo of the shot was still vibrating off the oak and pine trees, Cutler moved swiftly away from the startled group.

Circling the now alert deserters, Cutler stopped and reloaded his rifle. He laid down under some bushes and waited, trying to quiet his heavy panting.

Cutler waited patiently for the deserters to make a move. He figured that they now suspected that Thomas Gordon had made a quick sortie into their camp and then had retreated back in the direction his daughters had taken.

Cutler turned his eyes slightly to the right at the crackle of some branches. There was silence, then a movement in the tall grass revealed a figure creeping towards him.

Placing his rifle slowly on the ground, Cutler unsheathed his knife. The figure continued to move toward him. Cutler realized he had been spotted and sprung from his hiding place, his left arm forward, the knife in his right hand held tightly at his side. Instead of landing on the creeping man, Cutler rolled to his right out of reach of a stabbing knife. As he landed and rolled, he sliced upward with his right hand. Both men missed and now jumped to their feet. Cutler could barely see the face of the Union deserter, but he knew that this was one of the men that had been sitting quietly in the little group he had seen earlier.

Knives in their hands, the two circled each other, waiting for a move from the other. Cutler thrust forward and upward, but the deserter moved deftly out of the way and jabbed forward, just nicking Cutler's sleeve.

Realizing that the others could show up momentarily and this man was his match, Cutler turned as to run. The deserter, seeing his victim seem to run, jumped forward. Cutler dodged to the left, picked up his rifle by the barrel, and swung with all his might. The man screamed as the heavy weapon crushed his knee. The scream was cut short as a heavy blade almost severed his head.

With satisfaction Cutler looked down at the dead man. "You almost got me, but I'm not as easy as old men and women," he said softly. He quickly wiped the bloody knife on the blue jacket, then rifle in hand, disappeared into the underbrush.

Having moved about two hundred yards, still across the path of the attackers, Cutler stopped and waited.

He rested on a bed of pine needles at the edge of a partially burned out area of palmetto and blackened pines. Several dozen yards in front of him he heard scattered movements coming in his general direction. The deserters had formed a semi-circle and were moving forward cautiously as skirmishers. There were still four remaining.

"Time for new tactics," reasoned Cutler. Rising, he quietly retreated eastward several hundred yards, then stopped and waited at the edge of a cypress swamp.

It was twenty minutes before he saw the shadows flitting among the tall pines and palmettos. Once they had passed, he cupped his hands and gave the "rebel yell." A scattering of shots came from among the trees toward his general direction, but Cutler had already laid down on the ground and the lead went harmlessly among the trees and bushes. He then crawled in a northerly direction until he had gone about fifty yards. Lying on his back, he laughed as loud as he could, a long vicious laugh. Once again the bullets flew overhead, clipping leaves and twigs. Cutler crawled once again another fifty yards northward. Despite the mimicked laugh, Cutler had no smile on his face, only cold determination.

This time, he yelled, "Com'mon you dirty bastards. Here I am. Two down, four to go!"

The bullets flew harmlessly overhead, but this time Cutler had stayed up on one knee and watched the rifle flashes from the protection of a tree. He crawled in the direction of the flash on his far left until he had gone about fifty yards, then he turned slightly to the left and continued slowly another twenty yards. Cutler slowly stood in the shadow of a large pine and looked to his right.

Five minutes of watching, his patience was rewarded by a slight movement less than twenty yards in front of him. He barely heard the faint rustle of palmettos.

Cutler brought up his rifle, aimed at the dark patch among the palmettos. Quickly he cocked the rifle, fired, and dropped down low and ran forward at a crouch. He found Scott dead, a large hole through his neck. Cutler picked up the man's pistol, moved a few yards, reloaded his rifle, and yelled, "Three down, three to go!"

He then moved quickly in an easterly direction for several hundred yards. Cutler was cautious. He knew that the deserters were jumpy and had little stomach for fighting, but also he certainly didn't want to be shot at by Sergeant Gordon, by mistake.

After some searching, Cutler found the trail made by Gordon and his daughters. Cautiously, he followed it.

The three remaining deserters had finally gotten together and, in a clump of underbrush, they conferred in whispered tones. "I'm for gettin out of here. I'd a stayed in the army if'n I wanted to fight. There's a devil out there and I don't think it's that ole man," said one of the men.

The others nodded. The men stood up and cautiously began moving in a crouch, back in the direction they had come. When they finally arrived at the large clearing, they waited and listened for any foreign presence. Finding none, they hurried their steps to cross the open space.

As the men reached the center of the clearing, two shots rang out. Two deserters fell to the ground, dead. The third man, the largest, started running in a panic, but before traveling more than twenty yards, a figure sprang from the ground in front of him and struck him in the forehead with a tomahawk...The last deserter fell to the ground without a sound, his head cloven to the chin.

Deep Waters and Jeffrey continued on the Gordon's trail, the Indian stopping occasionally to hoot like an owl. Twenty minutes later, the bird call was answered, and from behind some fallen trees, emerged a grinning Cutler.

"Am I glad to see you all. The Gordons are still up ahead. I haven't come up to them yet. I didn't want to get shot at by the Sergeant. Let's go find them. Where's Orin?"

"With the horses by the road. Massa Sam be with him, too," Jeffrey answered. "Yo all right, Massa Cutler?"

Cutler nodded and patted the young black man on the shoulder. "Thanks for comin. I won't forget."

Without a word, Deep Waters took the lead, and in single

file the trio continued eastward into the dense woods.

They traveled more than a mile. Deep Waters stopped, then pointing toward a dense clump of undergrowth. "They in there," he muttered.

Cutler called out for Sergeant Gordon and identified himself. The underbrush parted and a sweaty Tom Gordon emerged, followed by Cora and Flora. Flora held a pistol loosely in her hand.

"Is it really you? We're sure glad to see you!" exclaimed the Sergeant.

Cora ran and put her arms around Cutler, her face buried in his chest. She was sobbing! Flora walked up and quietly gripped his arm, tears of gratitude streamed down her cheeks.

Tom Gordon was standing, leaning on his rifle. A tight bloody bandage was tied around his left thigh. Part of his shirt was gone, to make up the bandage. His face was scratched and smoke blackened, but he had a faint smile on his lips. "We didn't know who was out there givin those rats hell, but we figured we'd just stay back and not get in the way and wait."

The girls were similarly scratched and dirty, their long hair mussed and disheveled, black circles under their eyes from the mixture of mud, sweat, and tears. Their long new dresses, especially made for the holidays, had many long tears and some of the fringes on the sleeves were hanging in strings.

Cora finally let go of Cutler, but as they traveled back toward the road, she held his hand tightly in hers.

Deep Waters and Jeffrey took the weapons and haversacks from the dead deserters as they passed the bodies and continued silently in the lead.

Finally arriving at the road, the little party found Sam and Orin waiting, rifles ready, their horses hitched to the wagon. With few words, the grateful Gordons stepped up into their wagon. Sam took the reins, Tom sat alongside, the girls sat on the blankets in the rear.

Cutler, Jeffrey, Orin, and Deep Waters, mounted the other horses that had been brought and hobbled alongside the road.

20

Mara and her young daughter, Cindy, helped the girls change and clean up, cleaned and dressed Tom Gordon's leg wound, and placed the food on the table. The men took care of the horses and brought in the Gordon's baggage, cleaned up, and changed, and were now sitting in the big room, sipping French cognac that had been brought in through the blockade.

"Well, gentlemen, I believe the ladies are ready and dinner is on the table," announced Sam. Motioning toward the dining table, "Shall we?"

The men finished their drinks and went to the dinner table. The large fireplace burned brightly, the mantle decorated with mistletoe and poinsettas, and the many candles illuminated the house cheerily. The heavy wood table was also lit up with candles. In the center were several huge platters piled high with venison, turkey, rabbit, ham, beans, corn, koontie bread, sweet potatoes, squash, wild onions, bowls of pecans, and several bottles of imported wines. The men stood waiting and conversing, but stopped as Aunt Ernestine, Cora, and Flora, walked in.

The girls looked very pretty and had changed into dresses they had brought in their baggage. Except for the scratches on their arms and a few on their faces, the events of the past few hours were not noticeable.

Sam sat at one end of the table, Deep Waters at the other. On one side was Cutler, flanked by Cora and Flora. Opposite them were Aunt Ernestine, with Orin and Tom Gordon at her side.

Sam stood, "I believe that today, the day before Christmas Day, we all have a special thanks to be grateful for. There's not much more to say. Let's all bow our heads in silence."

After a few moments of silence, Sam called, "Mara, Jeffrey, Cindy, come in here." The three walked quietly into the room and stood by the door.

Sam continued, "Today, I have an announcement to make." Reaching into his coat pocket, he produced a bundle of papers.

"These documents have been properly written, signed, witnessed, and recorded. As of today, you three faithful slaves, and our two field men and their families, are no longer...slaves. I have legally set you free." In the stunned silence, Sam cleared his throat and continued. "I hope that all of you will continue here as servants and workers. I will pay the field hands ten dollars per month, Jeffrey and Cindy eleven dollars, and you, Mara, fourteen dollars a month. Your lodging will be included. What you say to that?"

There was more silence, then everybody started talking at once. Mara ran up to Cutler and kissed him on the cheek, Then with tears streaming, went to Sam and kissed his hand. Sam stood up, "Now, no more of that," embracing her, he said. "Now, you all can't stand there a blubberin if you want to earn your pay. Get back to earning."

Once Sam was seated again, Cutler stood. "Mara, I'm happy for you. You've been a second mother to me. That doesn't change. I'm happy for your family, too, but please serve the wine. I've got an important toast to make."

Cutler stood patiently as Mara and Cindy poured the wine, still sniffing tears of happiness. Cutler continued, "A toast to a grateful holiday, to good friends, to the greatest father in the world, and...to my future bride! This evening Cora said she would marry with me."

Above the chorus of congratulations, Sam's voice was heard, "Son, you outdid me." Everybody went to the blushing Cora and hugged her and then shook hands with the beaming Cutler.

With no words, but sparkling eyes, Deep Waters removed the shiny green stone he had had hanging from his neck from a beaded chain for years. He solemnly walked up to Cora and faced her. Then with the chain in a loop with his one hand he lowered it around her neck. Taking Cutler's left hand and Cora's left hand, he held them in his for a few moments. During this little ritual, not a sound was heard.

Deep Waters returned to his seat and began to eat.

21

On January 7, 1864, Jacksonville was once more reoccupied by the Federal forces. Dickison and his men remained in the area and along the East Coast, discouraging the northern troops from further raiding into the heartland of the state.

Cutler became friendly with Sergeant Charlie Dickison, the Captain's son. The two became mess-mates and spent much of their free time together roaming the woods. Charlie was a chess player and taught the game to Cutler. Many quiet evenings in camp were spent playing the game and, on rare occasions, Cutler would win over his teacher.

The men were kept busy on patrols and light skirmishes until February. Then Captain Dickison received orders to travel to Fort Meade in southwest Florida to work with Colonel Brevard against the enemy in the Fort Myers area. Baggage packed and equipment readied, the company moved southward.

Having traveled a few miles, Cutler was sent for by Lieutenant Brantly and instructed to ride to Cedar Key with some dispatches. Once these were delivered, he was to rejoin the company in south Florida. With many hand waves, Cutler turned Rhona at the next crossroads and trotted westward toward Cedar Key.

Florida had few railroads at the time. The Florida Railroad that started at Fernandina traveled southwest through Baldwin, Starke, Waldo, Gainesville into Cedar Key. The Florida Atlantic Railroad went from Jacksonville to Baldwin, Olustee, Lake City, Madison, Tallahassee, and Quincy ending near Chattahoochee. The Mobile and Pensacola in the western portion of the state was only restricted to the immediate area. In many cases, the rail travel was so slow that it would take up to two and a half days to travel the width of the state. Some rails were made of wood and the trains rarely traveled at night.

Cutler traveled the distance in two days using roads, rail beds, and trails learned during earlier hunting days with Deep Waters.

Although alert, the young man daydreamed of Cora and the impending wedding. They had not yet set a day, but had agreed that they would marry in the spring. He could hardly wait!

During his travel, Cutler encountered a dispatch rider riding in a hurry. The man informed him that the Yankees, 1,400 strong, under General Seymour, had moved within three miles of Lake City, fought against 600 entrenched Confederates, and then withdrew to Sanderson. They were regrouping, expecting reinforcements, and then planning to take Tallahassee, the Capital.

The rider moved on and Cutler picked up his pace with this additional information toward Cedar Key.

Cutler delivered his dispatches, picked up several bags of fresh salt from one of the remaining salt works that Federal raiders had not destroyed, and the following morning, with thirty other soldiers, rode along the railroad bed northeastward. That night they camped in a pine forest and were shortly joined by ten more soldiers; among them was Ralph Jacobs. The two friends had a great reunion and later spoke for several hours, in low tones, about the Gordon sisters, while the rest of the men slept.

The following morning, before dawn, the little group of men continued on their way.

By midday, another group of twenty men were encountered near Gainesville and informed them that the Confederates were grouping at Ocean Pond, near Olustee, just east of Lake City. The men turned toward that direction.

Cutler knew that by now word had been sent to Colonel Brevard and Captain Dickison to return to meet the new threat. It would have been pointless to rush down to meet them and then turn around and rush back.

Riding all day and much of the night, with few periods for rest, Cutler and his companions arrived at the Confederate encampment early on the morning of February 15th. There, they found a busy army of several thousand men under General Joseph Finegan. The men's horses, being quite tired from the journey, were ordered tied in the rear by the old house being used as a hospital. The group was ordered to report to Lieutenant Thomas J. Hill of the Sixth Florida Battalion on station at the extreme right flank of the Southern troops.

The battalion was near the East/West railroad and to their right were the cannon of Guerard's Battery. The cavalry, commanded by Colonel Caraway Smith, was on station to their rear.

The Confederate line extended with its left flank to Ocean Pond, a sheet of water two by four miles, extending to the right to another pond about 250 yards in width. It then continued another 400 yards to the railroad and then another 200 yards beyond. Major Clarke, of the engineers, arrived and fortifications were built along the entire line. The 6th Georgia was at the extreme left of the Confederate line, reaching Ocean Pond, followed by the 32nd Georgia, 1st Georgia, 23rd Georgia, 64th Georgia, 28th Georgia, 19th Georgia, and 6th Florida. In reserve were the 27th Georgia and 1st Florida.

On the morning of the 20th, the Federal troops advanced in two columns, pushing rapidly towards the waiting Confederates.

Confederate cavalry was sent forward and shortly the sound of musketry was heard several miles to the east as cavalry and skirmishers of both sides made contact. Shortly afterwards, parts of Colonel A. H. Colquitt's Brigade was sent in support of the cavalry. Cutler and Ralph Jacobs were part of that brigade.

As the two friends moved out from behind their fortifications, they turned to each other and with grim expressions shook hands, then turning, advanced with the line towards the increasing rattle of musketry. Shortly afterwards, Colonel George P. Harrison, the other brigade commander, also ordered his men forward.

The musket fire became general, interrupted with explosions from the cannon of the two opposing armies. The soldiers in blue could be seen about two hundred yards to their front, the flashes from their muskets penetrated the thickening acrid smoke of battle.

Cutler heard the swishing of shrapnel and zip of minie balls. The air seemed full of missles. Pine needles, branches, and bark filled the air, torn from the trees by the flying lead. After several organized volleys, Cutler fired as rapidly as he could, stopping only when loading. During these moments, he would select a tree to stand behind. He was conscious of men falling around him. He looked for Ralph, but he was nowhere to be seen.

At one time during the battle, the Confederates expecting a Federal cavalry charge formed into a square, the defense against cavalry. A normal battle line could easily be penetrated by massed cavalry who, after overrunning the men on foot, could turn and attack again from behind. The square formation eliminated this situation.

The Northern cavalry turned out not to be a threat and after clashing with the Southern cavalry, returned to their own ranks.

A Southern cavalry officer grabbed the blue banner from his standard bearer and waving it, galloped across the lines rallying the sagging offense. With the Stars and Bars and battalion flags streaming, the lines in grey charged with a crescendo of rebel yells.

The Northerners wavered momentarily but then reinforcements arrived and the fight came to a standstill, casualties mounting. Facing the 6th Florida on the Northern left, was the 8th U.S. Colored troops commanded by white officers. The untrained black men fought as well as their white comrades, except for a few who threw down their weapons and ran in panic.

Most of the Southerners stopped advancing and were carefully picking their targets while standing behind trees or kneeling. Cutler ran out of ammunition, turned and retreated his steps several yards before finding a wounded companion who volunteered his powder and ball. The man was bleeding heavily from the knee. Cutler bandaged it tightly for him, using a torn section of the man's shirt. He then cut a sturdy pole and helped the man to his feet. The wounded Confederate nodded, then hobbled toward the rear, using his rifle in one hand and the pole in the other as two canes.

Cutler returned to his former position, kneeled and continued firing and loading. He noticed the Confederate fire had greatly diminished. Looking around him he saw a great many of his comrades kneeling or standing behind pine trees, but not firing their guns. They had run out of ammunition!

Cutler crawled over to two men kneeling a few yards to his right and divided up his powder and shot with them. "We better use this carefully. Save some in case the Yanks charge us," he shouted. The two men nodded and loaded their rifles. The Federals, noticing the diminishing musketry, began advancing again.

The weather was crisp by Florida standards and the warm sun penetrated through the tall pines and smoke, warming Cutler's shoulders. This same sun shined into the eyes of the Federals hindering, in many cases, their aim.

Colonel Colquitt had his staff and couriers dismount and employed them as ammunition bearers, bringing much needed powder and shot from the ammunition railroad cars half mile in their rear.

To Cutler's left, the 64th Georgia, the 32nd Georgia, and the 6th Georgia were completely out of ammunition. The 1st Florida battalion charged from the entrenchments and joined the 64th with ammunition. The sudden combined firepower caused the Federals to hesitate and then begin a general retreat. The retreat became faster as the victorious Southerners advanced more rapidly with less fire coming towards them and many stopping long enough to take ammunition and new weapons from the fallen Federals.

Cutler, flushed and excited, joined in the chorus of Rebel Yells as he ran toward the receeding blue line. He passed many dead and wounded and was in the spirit of the chase when he felt a solid whack to his body and was knocked off his feet.

Lying momentarily stunned, Cutler regained his senses and tried to get to his feet. A sharp pain shot through his chest and right shoulder. It was then that he realized he had been shot!

After a few moments of panic, Cutler decided to lie still. He knew that soldiers would be shortly roaming among the bodies looking for wounded to take back to the old house by the railroad being used as a hospital. As the battle continued to move eastward, he was conscious of the moans and occasional screams of the wounded strewn throughout the battlefield. The sound of musketry had continually diminished. The Southerners had won a decisive victory, the battle being hard-fought from 2 P.M. to around 6 P.M.

As dusk settled, torches and lanterns searched throughout the woods, stretcher bearers hurried with their painful loads back to the hospital, companions searched among the bodies for their friends, and in many cases turned away from still forms with tears in their eyes. A screaming horse was put out of its misery with a merciful shot. Its hind legs had been blown away by a cannonball. Its rider had been decapitated.

Meanwhile, surgeons went to work on their bloody tables, as piles of amputated limbs grew outside of the old wooden building.

Quiet settled throughout the darkened battlefield. Small animals scurried among the cool bodies of men in blue and grey. Union losses were 1,861, the Confederates lost 946. Many families would mourn February 20, 1864.

Cutler regained consciousness as dusk turned to dawn. He was lying on some straw, his chest and right shoulder tightly bandaged. He was covered with an oil cloth and several blankets. Ralph Jacobs was seated, leaning against a nearby pine tree, his hat over his eyes, an old torn horse blanket covering him.

Looking around, Cutler saw that he was surrounded by sleeping forms. Nearby, in front of a captured tent, several men were making coffee and frying bacon. On several ammunition boxes were piled all types of canned goods and cases of food. On the ground were piles of filled Yankee haversacks. A line of horses were tethered in the background, happily munching on captured oats. Among them, Cutler spotted Rhona. Several colored soldiers in blue were brushing and watering the horses. A young Confederate soldier leaned lazily on his rifle and watched them while crunching on hardtack. His pockets bulged with the hard crackers.

Cutler struggled to a different position and Ralph was quickly by his side. "Well partner, how you feelin?"

The gruff friendly voice was like music to the wounded man's ears.

"I reckon all right. How's the wound?", Cutler's voice cracked.

"You picked up a ball through the shoulder. You're lucky. It came clean out the back. I told the doctor you'd probably did it on purpose so you could go fishin. But really I think you did it so you could go a courtin. You thirsty?"

"Yup, powerful. What happened to your head?" A bloody bandage shown from beneath Ralph's hat.

"Well, we barely got goin', when the next thing I knew I was on the ground. Had a terrible headache and blood all over the place. Thought I was dead. Well, it seems that some Yank cannon tried to hit me, missed, an' hit a tree. A big branch flew down and bonked me on the skull. When I woke up it was all over. Missed the fun, so I went lookin' fer you. You were sleepin' peaceful like. Didn't know if I should wake you. I'll get us some coffee."

Ralph walked back from the fire with two steaming cups of coffee. Handing one to Cutler, "Watch it. It's a mite hot. You hungry?"

"A tad, but as soon as I finish this cup, I'd sure like another.

Sure am thirsty."

Ralph went back to the fire, refilled the cups and brought back two plates. On these were fried hardtack, bacon, a roasted ear of corn, and a handful of dried raisins. "These are compliments of Mister Lincoln. Eat up."

Dragging over a short log, Ralph propped Cutler so he could eat, then he sat cross-legged on the ground by his friend and had his breakfast.

The Confederate camp was stirring. Men were wandering around, gathering belongings and beginning breakfast. Some patrols were still out, while others were arriving. Prisoners were watched and fed and normal camp routine began to take place, as much as expected by over five thousand individuals of different units brought together under an emergency situation to form an army.

Cutler fell asleep after breakfast and awoke several hours later. Looking up, he saw Ralph, Forselli and Charlie talking.

"Hey, what's goin on?" he called.

The three turned to him. "You lazy fellow. Why you sleepin so late? What's the matter. A little piece of Yankee lead keepin you down?", remarked Charlie, a wide grin on his face. Both he and Forselli looked very tired and saddle worn.

Dickison and his men had force marched from South Florida to the battle sight but had arrived twelve hours after it had ended. They did, however, capture forty Union stragglers on their way.

"Hey, does Lieutenant Hill know I'm here?" asked Cutler. In a low tone, Ralph answered, "Lieutenant Hill is dead. Too bad. he seemed to be a good officer.

"Oh,...I'm sorry," murmured Cutler.

Later that afternon Captain Dickinson visited Cutler and told him that he envied him for having been in the fight. He did also tell him in his usual humorous way, however, that he did not envy his wound, although he would now have some time to recuperate and would probably be sent home for awhile as soon as he could travel. There was a private from the First Florida that was traveling home with light wounds and that on his way would stop at Mellonville and tell Cutler's father.

The Federals retreated in disorder to Sanderson, leaving over four hundred wounded and two hundred prisoners. They then

retreated to Barber's Plantation and Baldwin and finally Jacksonville. The Confederates, not being in sufficient force, did not
pursue. The Union held Jacksonville with entrenched troops of
approximately 15,000 plus four gunboats.

Cutler and many of the wounded were taken to Baldwin and
several of the less serious were placed in private homes. Here the
best and most affectionate care was given them by grateful
citizens.

On February 28th, Sam Garnett, Jeffrey and Deep Waters
found him and carefully loaded him in a straw and blanket lined
wagon and took him home to Mellonville.

The joyous and tearful welcome by Mara and Cindy embarrassed
the young sergeant.

The following day, while pampered on the large couch in the
main room. Cutler wrote to Cora. Jeffrey rode with the letter
that afternoon.

Four days later Jeffrey returned followed by Cora, a rifle across
her saddle. Cutler had just walked from having talked with
Rhona, who was grazing in the pasture. Cora galloped up to
him, jumped out of the saddle, dropped the rifle and flew to
him and embraced him tightly. Tears streaming, she buried her
head in his chest.

Cutler held her tightly with his left arm, the right one still
in a sling.

They stood holding each other in the pasture for quite a while.
Then hand in hand, they slowly walked back to the house. Cora's
horse left to graze, the rifle in her left hand.

"I was so worried when I heard about the battle. I just knew
you were there, and then when Jeffrey arrived with your letter,
I told Flora I was leaving that moment. I ran to the house, packed
a few things to eat, some clothes, and Jeffrey and I left. I was
going to ride all night, but he insisted on stopping for the night.
He's real nice and thoughtful. Oh, how I missed you."

"I missed you, too, a lot. I thought about you all the time,"
answered Cutler.

That evening at the dinner table, Cutler told everyone of the
battle. Mara, Jeffrey and Cindy listened, standing by the kitchen
door.

"Paw, I'll be well and ready to report back in a couple of

weeks. Cora agreed to get married before I leave. We can send for Flora and Aunt Ernestine. What do you think?"

Solemnly Sam said, "You know you don't need my approval, but thank you. Yes, I'd like to have Cora as a daughter as soon as soon possible."

Cora got up from the table and hugged Sam.

The next few days the women spent in hectic preparation. Sam and Cutler were told in forceful words, to stay out of their way!

News arrived that Captain Dickison and Company H, with one hundred and forty-five men, joined Lieutenant Colonel Harris of the Fourth Georgia Cavalry, with one hundred and twenty-five men, at Sweetwater Branch, about twelve miles distance from Palatka. The Union had made a landing with a force of five thousand men. The Confederates kept the larger force contained behind strongly fortified entrenchments with constant skirmishes with their pickets. Once the Federals sent a battalion to attack them, but to little avail. Another time, two regiments were sent forward, one white and one colored, but finally withdrew at nightfall with heavy losses.

The wedding was held at the Garnett house on the morning of March 6, 1864. Flora, Aunt Ernestine, Deep Waters, and the servants watched as Sam gave the bride away. Preacher Harver from Enterprize, the slim, elderly minister, performed the ceremony.

After a scrumptuous meal and many toasts, the newlyweds left with the decorated wagon for Volusia Landing. Taking the ferry across the Saint John's, south of Lake Monroe, they rode to Enterprise, took the Spring Garden Road and arrived at Volusia late that evening. Their hotel overlooked the river.

After a light dinner downstairs in the plain, sparsely furnished dining room, they walked along the moonlit bank and listened to the night birds, then bashfully returned to their room. Bashfulness melted into passion.

22

Two men rested quietly staring into the small fire, each wrapped in his own thoughts, oblivious to the normal sounds of the surrounding forest. A blackened coffee pot sat by the fire, two empty tin cups alongside it. The singed ends of green palm frond sticks were smoldering where they had been placed over an oak log. Some stringy remains of two rabbits still sizzled as they dried and popped.

Both men were barely twenty years old, but their faces betrayed weariness and hardships and even if the dust of the trail and the five day stubble had been removed, they still could have passed to be in their thirties.

They were both seated on a bed of pine needles, wore frayed deerskin moccasins that reached almost to the knee, and were dressed in faded and well-worn grey uniforms. On their heads were sweat stained, droopy, wide brimmed hats. To ward off the March chill, each had a blanket over his shoulders; one was blue and the other grey.

Occasionally, one of the horses that was ground hobbled nearby would look up and perk its ears up momentarily before returning to munching clumps of grass. Both horses still had on saddles with loosened chinches.

Cutler was thinking of Cora. It didn't seem possible that they had been married two weeks already. There had been one week of blissful days and nights at Volusia. Then they had returned to the Garnett home and after many sorrowful goodbyes, he had ridden away. He and Ralph Jacobs had met on the road. Ralph had been shadowing a Union patrol of ten men that recently had crossed to the west side of the Saint John River, and Cutler joined him. They had now been trailing the Federals for six days and that patrol was camped peacefully once again by the banks of the Saint Johns. The two Confederates decided to backtrack deeper into the forest, rest, and have a hot meal.

Cutler had been a little shocked upon returning to his home to find that Aunt Ernestine had moved in with his father. He had never seen his father with a woman, and although his mother had died giving him birth and he had always liked his aunt, things had seemed out of place and strange. He hadn't felt that his father owed him an explanation, but yet he woud have felt more comfortable if they had talked about it first. He did realize that Aunt Ernestine's house at Cedar Key had been burned by the Yankees in one of their raids, but he wondered how his cousin Orin would react when he found out that his mother was.....

"How do you like bein married?" asked Ralph. He had murmured almost as if talking to himself.

"Huh? Oh...good, real good. But bein away from her isn't so good. How about you and Flora. When you'all gettin married? It's about time, you know."

"I don't know...I don't have anything to offer her, you know," answered Ralph dejectedly.

"What do you mean? I thought you were goin get that property alongside the Gordon property and farm it and build a sawmill by that creek?" answered Cutler.

"Aw, I ain't got any money. When the war started I was a carpenter in Gainvesville, and practically starvin. I ain't got any kin. Folks died of fever and my older brother went out west in '49 and we never heard from him again."

"Ralph, damn it! Flora's not after you for your money, you fool. How long do you need to wait? Do you want to lose her?"

"Well, my pappy's not rich like yours. It's easy for you to talk! Oh, shit, I didn't mean it," apologized Ralph after his short outburst. "I've just been mixed up and don't know what to do. I want her, sure as shootin, but also I don't want to be selfish about it. I've seen what the wives of some of these starvin farmers look like. I couldn't bear Flora livin like that, and I wouldn't take money from her father."

Both men were silent for awhile, then Cutler spoke again. "You know, I'm plannin to do a lot of work at the plantation. I'll be addin to the place, to the barns. We're goin to build a wharf on the lake, some flat boats to get up into some of the narrow streams, a lot of fencin and stock pens. Now, if I had a lumber mill nearby, say by that spring that runs pretty quickly down to the Saint Johns, and a reliable man to build and run that mill...I might consider selling him some property for the mill, and use some kind of reasonable trade for the lumber and carpentry he provides me. Now, I'm not sayin that you're the man for the job, you bein single and not a stable married man and all, but maybe I can find someone...Think about it." Then with a chuckle, he continued, "or maybe you may know of someone that you could recommend."

Ralph looked up with a grin, "You know, you're really somethin, and not too bad for a Gentile."

Cutler grinned back, "You're a pretty fine fellow, too, for a Jew." Then the two friends laughed quietly and began gathering their equipment. The fire was put out, and in single file, they led their mounts to a grove of cedars and pines a mile to the northeast of their camp. Still only a mile from the Federal camp, they tied their horses, gathered pine needles for beds, and wrapped in their blankets were soon asleep.

As the early morning grey was melting into daylight, the two men crept close to the awakening Federal camp. The men in blue were leisurely preparing their breakfast and a few had gone to the slow moving river and thrown in some fishing lines. Cutler and Ralph could smell the coffee boiling and the bacon frying, shortly mingled with the aroma of freshly caught bass sizzling over hot coals. The two Confederates chewed on stringy beef jerky in silence.

Cutler watched the enemy's horses picketed twenty yards from the camp, contentedly chewing on grain that had been taken from Florida farms. Remembering his and Ralph's horses as they had had to make do on sparse clumps of grass the previous evening, bitterness towards the Northern intruders led to a plan of revenge.

Motioning to Ralph to return on their tracks, the two quietly crawled away from the camp.

In whispered, abbreviated sentences, Cutler outlined his plan to capture the enemy horses. There were fifteen including the pack animals.

Carefully they poured black powder into six large magnolia leaves, wrapped them tightly with grass and packed with river mud, then laid then in a row on a fallen log. More gun powder was poured in a narrow line connecting the six mud balls and a small hole poked into opposite ends of each to the line of black powder. Ralph nodded in satisfaction and Cutler left in the direction of the picketed horses.

Fifteen minutes later, Ralph struck a match and lit the far end of the trail of black powder, then quickly walked in the direction his friend had taken.

Cutler was lying on the ground behind a large cypress less than than twenty feet from the horses when the first explosion startled the enemy camp. The men were in confusion grabbing their weapons and tripping over equipment as they ran towards the northern perimeter of their camp, from where the noise had come. When the second explosion was heard, the men in blue were behind logs and trees, weapons pointed in the direction of the expected attack.

With a few quick strides, Cutler reached the horses, untied the halters, jumped onto the back of a large black, and began striking the other animals with the stock of his rifle. The frightened animals galloped into the woods as the startled Federals turned around and saw the wild-eyed Rebel driving their horses southwards.

Another explosion sounded and the Federals hesitated for a few seconds. Then six of them ran after the escaping horses while the remainder returned to face the direction of the explosions.

Keeping the horses from scattering in all directions was a difficult task for Cutler, as he guided his mount by its mane and his knees, crashing into palmetto, thorny vines, and through low-hanging tree limbs. A rifle shot near his side told him that Ralph was in position covering for him.

Herding the horses into a clearing several hundred yards from the camp, Cutler stopped. Two of the horses had escaped somewhere into the woods, but the remainder of the herd was milling about in the clearing. He slid off his mount and gathered the trailing halters of his little group. He tied the big black to a tree for Ralph to find, then mounting one of the bay mares, he led the remainder of the horses through the woods towards where he and Ralph had left their own animals.

As Cutler reached the grove of cedars and pines, Ralph galloped up behind him. "Let's get on our own horses. I'll take half of this string and let's get out of here." He exclaimed breathlessly. "I doubt if they try to follow us. They've got a wounded man to take care of and it looks like they'll have some searching before they find the other two horses," he continued, as he counted the captured herd. "We did good."

Mounted on their own horses, the two Floridians trotted northward, each leading a string of U. S. branded horses. Revenge is sweet, thought Cutler, as he led the way towards the Palatka road.

23

Ralph and Cutler arrived at the Waldo camp with the captured horses in the middle of a violent thunderstorm. Charlie Dickison was among the dripping crowd to congratulate them. The horses secured, the Clifton brothers, Cutler's former tent-mates, broke out a jug of their "finest," to celebrate the occasion, and to "dry your inards." As they said, "This here stuff will melt horseshoes."

As he nodded through watering eyes, Cutler agreed with them. His breath and speech was gone, but the second sip, or maybe it was the third, cleared his throat. The next morning, he couldn't remember which.

During the month of March, the Confederates fought and beat a larger Union force at Three Mile run, General Beauregard visited the state on an inspection tour, the Union gunboat, Columbine, captured the steamer, Sumter, on Lake George, and numerous small skirmishes took place throughout the state, keeping the scattered eight thousand Confederate troops occupied.

Cattle were constantly being herded through towns and transported by rail or driven to the Southern armies in Virginia and Tennessee. The Florida drovers used twenty-four foot bull whips to keep the cattle moving, snapping these with loud cracks over the heads of the stubborn animals. Whenever a herd of cattle was driven through a town, the people would call out, "Here come the crackers," referring to the riders and their whips. Hence the name "Florida Crackers," came into being.

Many outraged discussions were held over the news that Federal Colonel Dahlgren had raided toward Richmond. He had been killed by the Confederate cavalry and many of his men captured.

On his body were found papers outlining plans to burn Richmond and capture and kill President Davis and his cabinet. The Southern papers condemned this "low down Yankee" way of waging war. Most of the Northern journals either denied the existence of the documents or ignored the entire affair. Copies of the documents were sent to Union General Meade but knowledge of the entire affair was denied, although a brief investigation was started.

The Confederate submersible, Hunley, went out and attacked Federal ships at night and sunk the warship, Housatonic but the Hunley and her crew never reappeared.

Federal gunboats had been navigating the St. John's with relative ease. To prevent this, a number of underwater explosives, or torpedoes, were placed in the channel, fifteen miles above Jacksonville. The Union transport, Maple Leaf, struck one of the torpedoes and sunk, leaving her superstructure well out of the water. The following day, Dickison went with some men to burn her upper works. On board was found enough garrison equipment for three regiments. She had been a large, double stack sidewheeler. A few weeks later, another transport, The Hunter, exploded another torpedo and sunk near the wreck of the Maple Leaf. This second steamer had been carrying quarter-master supplies.

Heavy skirmishing took place near Palatka with the five thousand Federals in the vicinity. Cutler participated in several of the raids and returned from each without a scratch.

On April 15th, another steamer, the Harriet A. Weed, was torpedoed twelve miles below Jacksonville.

News arrived that the Hattie Brock had been captured by the Federals south of Lake George and towed north. Miss Hattie Brock had tearfully watched as her namesake went past The Brock House on Lake Monroe.

On April 30th, Captain Dickison received information that the enemy had a regiment stationed at Fort Butler, near Volusia. On May 11th, he received orders to "strike the enemy whenever you have an opportunity of doing so to advantage." That night, Captain Dickison took two men and scouted the enemy outpost opposite the town of Welaka.

The following evening, the Captain and thirty-five of his men, including Cutler Garnett, Ralph Jacobs, and Vito Forselli, rode out of camp. Captain Gray, of the Second Florida Cavalry, and twenty-five of his men, joined the small command.

Reaching the Saint John's river, they crossed in small boats, the horses swimming alongside. At daybreak, the tired troop of cavalrymen arrived at Welaka, completely surprising the Union garrison there, that entire command surrendering without a shot being fired.

The river was recrossed and a short but well-deserved rest was granted. They had captured a Captain, a Lieutenant, and sixty-two men.

That afternoon, they were on the move again. This time only a total of twenty-five men participated. Forselli and Cutler stayed behind to help escort the prisoners to camp.

That evening, Captain Dickison returned with thirty-two additional prisoners, two farm wagons, and twelve recovered slaves. The following evening, Sergeant Charlie Dickinson returned from a long and roundabout march through swamps while avoiding Federal cavalry. Not one gun had been fired during the entire raid. Celebration and rejoicing were in order until later in the evening when the sorrowful news of Jeb Stuart's death at Yellow Tavern arrived by messenger.

The next few days were spent in rest for men and animals; restful but busy days of repairing and cleaning equipment and uniforms. Some of the evenings were spent singing songs by the fires under the towering pines. Two men had recently arrived from Hood's Texas Brigade and they added "The Yellow Rose of Texas" to the collection of campfire songs.

The men had plenty to eat—sow belly, corn, goober peas, swamp cabbage, alligator, deer, possum, jerked beef and gopher stew, plus captured Federal rations of hand tack, coffee, compressed vegetables, desiccated potatoes, dried split peas, Yankee beans and many different tins of delicacies.

Two days later, Captain Dickinson held an inspection and review which inspired the officers and men. They were all proud of their little company.

News arrived of the battles of Spotsylvania and the Wilderness and the heavy losses suffered at these battles. There had been no victory or defeat. Forselli was grief stricken. His younger brother had been killed at the Bloody Angle! Preferring to be alone with his sorrow, he rode quietly out of camp as the others stood helplessly watching. Two days later, he quietly returned to camp.

The Southern forces in Florida were sparcely positioned throughout the state and still more men were being called and sent to the armies in Virginia and Tennessee. Colonel Scott's battalion was now at Camp Milton, Lieutenant-Colonel McCormick's second Florida Cavalry was near Cedar Creek, Gamble's artillery near Baldwin, Captain Dickison's Company H, and Captain Gray's Company B, on outposts between Green Cove Springs and Palatka. The Sixth Battalion Infantry, with some of the First, Second, and Fourth, were at Waldo. These units were commanded by Colonels Hopkins, Brevard and Martin.

On May 22, 1864, a courier galloped into Dickison's camp near Palatka. He excitedly reported that the river was full of gunboats coming up the river. The previous day, Lieutenant Bates had reported to Dickinson with twenty-five men and two cannon, a 12 pound howitzer and a Napoleon. Captain Dickison now ordered this artillery to the hill overlooking Palatka and the river. Captain Gray and Captain Dickison joined Bates with most of their men.

Two gunboats and four transports were seen coming up the river. The Floridians dismounted and concealed themselves behind the old earthworks in the town.

As they watched, the transports moved to the opposite shore of the river and landed two regiments of troops. These formed and marched away into the forest. The gunboat, Columbine, passed near the hidden Confederates, but not close enough to be fired upon. She continued up river.

Captain Dickinson hurriedly mounted fifty of his men and taking the artillery, tried to intercept the gunboat several miles upstream at Brown's Landing, but arrived too late. Disappointed, the little troop started back towards Palatka. They were soon met by a courier sent by Captain Gray. The other gunboat, The Ottawa, and a transport were coming their way.

The men returned to Brown's Landing, dismounted, and scattered among the cypress trees in the swamp along the river. The artillery was unlimbered and pushed to the landing. By dusk, the ambush was ready.

The two boats anchored less than two hundred yards from the

hidden Confederates. Unaware that their enemy was hidden nearby, the Federal ships were lighted for the night and presented perfect targets.

Charlie, Cutler, Ralph, and Vito, were among the excited soldiers that delivered the first well-aimed volley. The two cannon thundered, their echoes crashing through the trees.

Twenty-eight rounds of artillery fire tore into the two helpless boats while confusion reigned.

Finally, the transport hoisted her anchor and without firing a shot, moved off. The Ottawa finally fired a broadside which, despite the noise, passed harmlessly through the trees. Gradually, she began to find the proper elevation, firing at the flashes of the Rebel cannon. The battle, now being mismatched in favor of the Federals, Dickison moved his cannon and men away into the darkness.

Upon asking for a casualty report, he was relieved to hear that no one had been hurt.

That night, camping on high ground with no fires, the men ate cold rations, then wrapped in blankets, lay on beds of pine needles.

Cutler was restless and walked back to the river. He found several sentinels watching the gunboat. She was still at anchor. Sounds of repairs drifted across the water.

"Wall, I favor we hurt them a tad," said one of them. "Too bad we can't take her. Too many cannon, and they're ready now."

"I wonder if a surprise boarding party could get at her." answered Cutler, thoughtfully.

"The Cap'n's got other plans. I think he's thinkin of the other gunboat that went up river. Maybe he's going to surprise her, but if we attack this 'un, we might be the ones gettin surprised. This 'un can't move and come to the rescue of t'other 'un if'n we go after that 'un," reasoned the sentinel.

"Yea, you're right. Anyway, the Captain knows what he's doin."

The men stood silently watching the dark gunboat. Then Cutler yawned and turned, "Reckon I'm goin back. Night."

"Night."

The next morning, Captain Dickison with sixteen sharpshooters, Cutler and Vito included, and Lieutenant Bates' battery and men, broke camp. The little command rode to Horse Landing, six miles from where the Ottawa was still at anchor. The cannon were positioned on the wharf and the sharpshooters hidden behind cypress trees a short distance to the left.

Some of the men dozed while others waited patiently. Around three o'clock in the afternoon everyone was alerted. The Columbine was seen steaming back down the river.

Captain Dickison cautioned his men not to fire until he gave the order.

The boat was barely sixty yards up from the landing when the hidden cannon fired, immediately followed by a volley by the sharpshooters.

The surprise was complete! Before the Federals could react, a second volley erupted from the shore. This time the cannon fire disabled the Columbine and she drifted onto a sandbar less than two hundred yards from shore.

The men on the vessel regained their composure and began returning their fire. She was armed with two large cannon and over one hundred and fifty men with rifles and pistols.

Cutler found himself firing and loading as quickly as possible, his gun barrel becoming hot to the touch. At his side, Vito Forselli was loading and firing, shouting loud rebel yells after each shot. His canteen, hanging from his shoulder, had been hit, water pouring from the two holes soaking his side, but the slender man never noticed.

It seemed as though the battle went on for hours, but only after forty-five minutes, the Columbine hoisted a white flag.

The silence was welcome, although the heat of battle, with its deafening noises, smell of burned powder, and uncomfortable zip and thunk of bullets striking all around, was exciting, the aftermath was always a strange relief. Cutler remained outwardly calm, but inside, his entire system was in turmoil.

Lieutenant Bates and a few men went on board to receive the surrender. He found death and destruction. Of the original complement of one hundred forty-eight Federals, only sixty-six were still alive, and twenty-five of these were wounded.

The Commanding Officer of the gunboat was the only officer left standing. The others were dead or wounded.

The prisoners, dead, and weapons were removed and then the

114

boat was burned. It was impossible to save her because of the other gunboats nearby on the river.

The dead were buried, except for the First Officer, who was wrapped in one of the captured flags at the request of the Union commander. The body was taken to Captain Dickison's headquarters for burial. Surprisingly, the Southerners suffered no casualties.

Dickison and his jubilant command returned to their headquarters near Palatka.

24

Skirmishing continued throughout May and June, with raids by both sides. On July 1, 1864, Cutler and Ralph received permission to visit their families and friends for ten days.

The two friends rode quietly in the dusty heat, alongside the railroad. The sun was extremely hot. Little relief from the bright fireball could be appreciated even in the limited shade from trees along the rail line.

Only one train, going in the opposite direction, passed them, and that one, with three flat cars half-loaded with lumber and a few barrels. The engineer and a solitary guard waved half-heartedly to them as the little engine labored through clouds of oily smoke and cinders.

Cutler and Ralph reined in front of the Goods store in Gainesville. There were few people moving in the wide streets in the stifling early afternoon. A few horses stood dejectedly at the hitching rail in front of the store, their muzzles dripping after drinking the warm water in the trough.

Inside the stuffy little store, while sipping cold cider, they heard of the terrible battle of Cold Harbour. Some of the old-timers heard that Grant had ordered charge after charge against the Confederate earthworks. It was said that over seven thousand Federals had fallen in thirty minutes. In some places, the dead had been piled three deep. The victory had been complete for the South, but it seemed that Grant, unlike previous Federal

115

Commanders, was a stubborn and determined man and had not retreated before Richmond.

The bad news was that the CSS Alabama had been sunk off the French coast on June 19th.

After the short rest and exchange of gossip, Cutler and Ralph continued on to Micanopy, a small sleepy town near the Chatal Hammock, a dense tangle of swamp, sawgrass, and underbrush. The two riders stayed on the narrow road, avoiding the forbidding rotting vegetation surrounding them.

"Well, you haven't said a word about the sawmill deal." questioned Cutler.

In fact, Cutler had waited to hear from Ralph, feeling sure that his friend had certainly considered the offer he had made. Now that they were on their way to Ocala, and Ralph would be seeing Flora, some type of planning for their future would certainly be discussed between the two of them. Flora would most naturally be wondering whether she was to be included in Ralph Jacobs' plans for the future. The fact that her younger sister was now married and living away from home, her father away in the army, and she living by herself with plenty of time to think and no one to talk to, probably made her feel that she could easily end up becoming an old maid.

"You know damn well I've thought about it," turned Ralph. "But, you hadn't mentioned it again, so I thought maybe you'd changed your mind, or maybe it had been only talk."

"I meant what I said. I was waitin to hear something from you. I thought maybe you weren't really interested, or thought Flora wouldn't leave her pa alone in Ocala with the store after the war. You know she'd go anywhere just to be with you! You know that, don't you?"

"Yea, I guess so. Well, I'm interested, if you really mean it...really interested. Course, I'll have to talk to Flora about it, you know."

"That's what I figured. After all, you're not the boss...yet. But I guess, with that little filly, she'd be the boss and let you think that you were."

Ralph grinned and nodded, "You're probably right, but I bet that Cora's got you pretty well twisted around her little finger."

"Got to admit it, she does get her way....I don't mind. You

know, you and I've got to be neighbors. How'll we figure out those two sisters if we don't compare notes?"

"Right you are, my Gentile friend."

Cutler slyly answered, "You're goin to have to spend Christmases with us. How does that sound?"

"Kiss my ass," laughed Ralph.

"Seriously, do you think there could be a religion problem? You know that the Gordons come from old Baptist stock."

"We'll work it out," answered Ralph quietly.

The separate late afternoon shadows were merging into one, as the fading sun lowered itself beyond the trees, when the two tired and dusty riders looped the reins of their footsore mounts to the scarred hitching rail in front of the Gordon store.

A pale yellow light from a lantern shown through the window panes and open front door. Cutler had barely taken two steps from his horse as Ralph bounded past him, went through the open door and exclaimed, "Flora!"

They were holding each other tightly when Cutler strode into the room, leaned against the long wooden counter and said, "Howdy, am I interruptin something?"

Reluctantly, the two parted. Then Flora rushed to him and gave him a big hug. "I'm glad to see you, too, you old married man, you. Have you heard from Cora?"

"Yup, bout two weeks ago. I'm on my way now."

"Oh no, you don't. You're staying here with us tonight. You can continue in the morning. Besides, it's dark and you don't want to get there in the morning, unless you're well rested...do you?" she smiled wickedly.

Ralph spoke, "Right, stay tonight. You'll be able to leave early in the morning. It's still a twelve hour ride and your horse is a tad tired, even if you're not."

"Guess you're right. I'm tired, dirty and hungry...not necessarily in that order," Cutler reluctently agreed.

After blowing out the lantern, taking the money box, and locking the door, Flora joined the men as they finished watering their horses.

Ralph and Flora walked hand in hand down the sandy road as Cutler followed, leading the horses. As he watched the two figures in front of him, he longed more than ever for Cora. Common sense told him to wait until morning but...he wanted to see her, hold her, as soon possible. It had been over three months since they had been together. It seemed like a lifetime!

During the entire meal, Cutler could not help but notice the affectionate glances that passed between the two lovers. The conversation was mostly light and some about the war. After dinner, while the three were comfortably seated on the front porch, Raph approached the subject of marriage. Cutler was surprised that he was present when Ralph blurted, "Flora, Cutler has offered me a chance to run a sawmill on his property after the war. Do you think you could leave your Pa and the store to live there?"

With a look of surprise, Flora turned to Ralph, "Why Ralph...are you proposing to me? I was hoping you would, eventually, but somehow I pictured it differently. Just you and me, maybe you on your knee...or something like that. No offense, Cutler. You are like family, but...some things are...well, you know...private and personal."

"Aw, I'm sorry," said Ralph. "I guess I didn't think. It's just, I've nothing to offer you, and now...Cutler's offered something I can start with, and a chance...with you."

"Ralph, I know what you don't have, but I just wanted you. That's all I need."

Cutler stood up, "Folks, I think I'll check the horses. Make sure they're...you know," he said quietly, knowing full well that he had brushed, fed, and watered them himself in the stable a few hours earlier.

Nothing was said as he walked down the steps toward the path around the side of the building.

"Aw shit," he thought. "That fool. He could've waited until I had gone to bed. Maybe he felt safer with me there, to help him convince Flora to move, but he should discuss it with her first, just the two of them. Oh well, I guess she'll pout for awhile, make him feel guilty and eat crow, and then she'll come around."

It was completely dark, the only light coming from a hazy moon. He sensed the animals rather than actually see them other than dim outlines.

The horses looked up as he entered the three-sided stable and tool shed. The loft was well stocked with hay. This was where he and Jeffrey had slept the first time he had visited Cora. It seemed too long ago.

Cutler went to Rhona and scratched her ears and rubbed her black muzzle. She nipped at him playfully and then reached down for another mouthful of hay.

He went back outside and sat on the wooden bench beside the wooden building. With his legs stretched out in front of him, his moccasins in the powdery dust, he leaned back against one of the heavy wooden roof supports. He looked up and watched the quarter moon as it moved slowly through the blackness of the tree branches and Spanish moss. There was a circle of mist around it. "Probably rain tonight or in the mornin," thought Cutler.

An hour passed, then he heard the whisper of footsteps on the sandy path by the house.

"What ya doin here by yourself? My best man's supposed to be up at the house helpin us plan the weddin." Ralph's dark form loomed out of the darkness at Cutler's side.

"I reckon you'all made up and you got on your knee," said Cutler. "You asshole."

"Yup," answered Ralph, as he sat down on the bench. "All fit 'n proper. Like I shoulda in the first place. I think she kinda likes the idea of the sawmill, and livin near her sister, too, but she didn't say so...yet. I reckon she'll talk to her Pa. It bothers her some leavin him here alone with the store and a big empty house."

"He can sell the house and the store and come, too. My Pa would enjoy his company in the evenings. Someone to argue with," answered Cutler. He ignored the fact that his father now had Aunt Ernestine.

"Really? You think he could come, too?" asked Ralph excitedly. "That would be just right. I like ole Tom Gordon. He's a tough ole codger, that one, but he's fair. He'd probably work his ass off, too."

"Sure, why not. If you think you can get along with your father-in-law, it'd be fine with me. After all, Cora's gettin along with my Pa...I think."

"You're a good friend, Cutler," spoke Ralph, in a rare display of emotion. "In fact, tell you what I'm gonna do. Next time I have a fat blue-belly in my sights, I'll let you have first shot. That's the least I can do for a guy that's seen the elephant with me so many times." Then he laughed and punched Cutler, not too gently, on the arm.

In the dim predawn grayness, Cutler saddled Rhona and led her out of the stable. He had quietly slipped out of the parlor, Where he had slept on blankets on the floor, the settee being too short for his long legs. Ralph was still asleep in Tom Gordon's room, although some time during the night, Cutler heard stockinged feet shuffle upstairs, through the hallway towards Flora's room. When Cutler opened the front door to leave, Flora had suddenly appeared with two packages. "Here, one's your lunch and the other's a gift for Cora. Have a nice trip. I guess I'll see you when you return on your way back for Ralph," she whispered. She was dressed in a long grey housecoat, her nightgown just barely showing at the hem. She kissed him lightly on the cheek and went back inside, closing the door quietly.

As Rhona trotted down the road, the light mist turned to a warm drizzle, and although he wore his rubber slicker, the water found its way passed Cutler's collar and tricked down his back.

Late that afternoon, a thrill of excitement ran through Cutler as he saw the outline of his home through the screen of grey-green moss dripping from the trees. The warm rain was still falling as he wearily led Rhona passed the kitchen house. A thin column of smoke was fighting its way through the rain. The aroma of freshly baked cornbread assailed his nostrils as he dutifully unsaddled and brushed Rhona with dry hay from an empty stall.

Having dried his gear and put it in its proper place, he walked toward the house, his rifle in hand and saddlebags and saber over his shoulder. None of the dogs were out in the wet weather, preferring the dryness beneath the slave cabins beyond the corral.

No one had seen him as he quietly opened the door and stepped into the large main room. No fire was burning in the large hearth, but several candles brightened the empty room. Cutler put his equipment on the floor, shut the door quietly, and walked over the bearskin rugs into the dining room. The table was set for dinner and sounds of preparations were heard in the warming room, adjacent to the dining room.

Although there were no place settings at the opposite end of the table, Cutler quietly pulled out his customary chair, sat down, and waited patiently.

As Sam, Ernestine, and Cora came down the stairs, Sam called, "Yo, Mara, I hope supper is ready, cause we're coming down now."

Mara burst out of the warming room with two bottles of wine, "Don't you fret Mista Sam. We is ready..." She then spied Cutler sitting calmly at the table and screamed. Cutler jumped and caught the bottles as they fell from her outstretched hands. He placed them on the table as Sam ran into the room, followed closely by Ernestine and Cora.

"You son of a gun," was all Sam could say as he embraced his son briefly. Cora practically pulled him aside and was shortly in Cutler's arms, squeezing him with all her strength. Aunt Ernestine quietly put her hand on Cutler's shoulder and said, "Welcome home, son."

Sam turned to wipe a "so-called cinder" from his eye, but boldly he said to the still gaping Mara, "Well, aren't you going to welcome our boy home, too?"

Cora slowly stepped away as Mara, eyes streaming, hugged Cutler and sobbed. Jeffrey and Cindy were standing by the door, broad smiles on their faces.

"Now, let's all sit down for supper. We can all look at him and talk to him as we eat," said Sam as he seated Ernestine at his left and sat down. He had regained his composure.

Cutler pulled out Cora's chair, also to his left, but sliding it closer to his, then sat down.

As Cutler and Cora held hands, Mara poured wine and Cindy placed table settings for Cutler, while beaming broadly. Jeffrey began placing platters of food on the table.

"Well, Jeffrey, how're the fish biting?" asked Cutler.

"Tolerable, Mista Cutler, right tolerable. Caught a cat yesterday. Mista Sam says it weigh onto ten pounds, he says. Right good, too. We ate it last night. Mista Sam, he got a big stallion; white one, too. He say he savin him for Rhona, he says. Wild one, that one."

"Well, that's good. Maybe we'll have a new colt next year," answered Cutler.

Cutler talked about the war and the offer he had made to Ralph. His father approved and mentioned selling lumber to plantations and boatyards.

Throughout the meal, Cora had little to say, but gazed adoringly at Cutler, touching his hand, and several times rubbing his leg with her foot.

Ernestine said she had heard from Orin. He was still with the cruiser, Florida. Captain Maffitt was no longer in command of the raider, being of poor health. Lieutenant Morris was now in command. In Orin's last letter, he has said that they had captured or burned twenty-six ships and visited many ports around the world.

Cutler and Ernestine were friendly with each other, although both felt uncomfortable. Cutler knew that just the two of them would have to talk, eventually.

Later, as all were seated in the big room, sipping their respective drinks, Cutler mentioned meeting the owner of the Kingsley plantation.

"Now that's a story," said Sam. "Back in '11, President Madison wanted West and East Florida as part of the states. He tried to make it sound that West Florida was part of the Louisiana Purchase and had all kinds of sneaky things goin on there. Here, in the East, he sent a man named George Mathews to get so-called patriots, most of them Georgians, took St. Mary and Fernandina, then gave them as presents to the U.S. Government. They then moved down the St. Johns' and did the same everywhere they went. They had some American troops as backing and even some of Campbell's warships. They got almost to Saint Augustine and there was a short fight at the Moosa Old Fort, you know, where runaway slaves had formed their own colony, protected by the Spaniards. These so-called patriots, formed the Republic of East Florida and John McIntosh was one of the ring leaders. When Madison and Monroe decided that their sneaky dealings were going to get them into trouble, they pulled out and left everybody high and dry. The U.S. troops and warships left and the patriots retreated. The Seminoles and their slaves got into it, too, torturing some of their captives near Picolata. It was a mess. In the meantime, the war with the British was going on and things were going badly. Kingsley got the McIntosh plantation, proclaiming he had been forced to go along with patriots. Everything was hush-hush, but the news was in all the papers. I wasn't born, yet, but I remember Pa telling me about it and how he had refused to join the group. Spain had always been pretty decent with the settlers, he felt. Anyway, Florida was bought legal-like in 1819, when Spain knew that the territory would eventually be taken, one way or the other. The Seminole Wars continued on and off, but they really started because of those first patriots. The Indians weren't bothering anybody. I could be classified a traitor for his, but the white man has always caused troubles and the red yellow and blacks have had to suffer."

"But, Pa, what about now? We're not fighting any other race. In fact, this war sure isn't about slavery, although the Yankees are now making it an issue, and that rotten book, Uncle Tom's Cabin, has stirred up a lot of garbage. You know, as well as I do, that that book is trash. True, there are a few slaves that are badly treated, but who would want to mistreat his own property? That's stupid! Slaves with whip marks lose their value. In fact, now there's been talk of arming them. The Yankees have. In fact, there were a lot of them at Olustee. Some of them ran but a lot of them fought just as good as their white comrades."

"Son, did you hear about the battle of Fort Pillow? I'm sure you have. General Forrest took that Yankee fort, but did you read about the casualties? Most of them were the colored soldiers. That's right, and it's said that they were shot after they had surrendered. Our men slaughtered them. Now, I know war 'is killing, but that's not right. No, sir." Sam was visibly upset.

"I know, Pa. In fact, we talked a lot about it in camp. Captain Dickison said that if that was what really happened, it makes him ashamed that those kind of people are fighting on the same side with us. I really don't think that General Forrest had anything to do with it, though."

Cutler knew that, although his father and many of the slave owners in the area would not betray the Confederacy, the policies of some of the officers and men of the South were against their principles. Several of the smaller ranches and plantations had freed their slaves and retained them as workers, as his father had.

"Enough about problems and war," interrupted Cora. "How long will you be staying, dear?"

"I have a total of ten days, so allowing for travel, I'll be here five more days before I have to leave and meet Ralph. Oh, by the way, I have something here for you, from Flora."

Cutler opened his saddlebags and handed Cora a small package wrapped in brown paper.

Cora tore the paper and opened the small box. Inside were baby clothes. She looked up at Cutler and smiled. "No, I'm not expecting a baby, so you can take that surprised look off your face. I haven't seen you since March, you dummy. Don't you think that I'm still...rather thin. This is for the future."

25

Thoughtfully, Cutler gazed down at his mother's grave. He never failed to visit this spot whenever he returned home from his army duties. The leaves of the umbrella-like liveoaks in the grove, screened most of the summer sun. Along the path from the house, in the patches of sunlight, grew dozens of Crepe Myrtle bushes, their delicate pink flowers thriving in the hot sun. Sam Garnett kept these bushes well trimmed, contributing to their healthy blossoming throughout the summer.

Cutler's daydreaming was interrupted when he heard footsteps and the rustling of skirts coming down the path.

"I saw you take the path and realized this was the perfect opportunity for us to talk," said Aunt Ernestine, as she joined him in the shade.

"Yes ma'am, I know we both care for the same person, but we have a need to understand each other," he replied softly.

"Cutler, I'm a widow, your father is a widower, and has been, since the day you were borne by that wonderful person lying there. I loved your mother very much. For that reason she married your father. Neither ever knew, but I cared for your father, too! No, don't be alarmed. I cared for your father secretly all the while he was courtin Emily, and I never let on. When they were married, it broke my heart, but the tears they all saw at the wedding were thought to be for joy. I was married shortly afterwards to a sea captain. He was much older than I, and shortly after Orin was born, his ship was lost at sea during a voyage to the Japans. Orin was all I had left, and you were all that Sam had left."

Ernestine's voice was strong, but her eyes were misty as her gaze looked past Cutler, back into the years. "Son, I'm barely forty years old. To you, that may be old, but I feel that I'm still young, and when Sam offered me a place to stay, now that my house was gone, it stirred old memories and feelings. I came here with no intentions, other than to help a dear and wonderful man that was offering me a roof. It's just that...well, things happen, and that lovable wife of yours, understood and never batted an eyelash. I hope that you'll understand and accept me, too."

Cutler cleared his throat, "Aunt Ernestine, I didn't know about the past, but I do understand and am happy if you and Pa are happy, it's just that...I was taken by surprise and although I didn't expect to have been asked permission, I was disappointed that Pa never said anything to me, and completely avoided discussing the subject, with me. He and I have always talked about everything, and most of the times we would come to an agreement, or at least some type of compromise."

"I know, and we know he should have. He said so to me. But now he feels that since he didn't say anything in the first place, he was just going to let things go, maybe hoping for another opportunity, or...hoping you and I would take care of it, for him, as we are."

"Well, we certainly are, but...how about Orin? What will happen when he get's back? He may be embarrassed or resentful."

"I wrote to him...I told him that I was moving to Mellonville, just casual like. Later I wrote again, and told him a little more. I haven't heard from him. Maybe he hasn't received any of my letters. I don't know where the Florida is, where she's been, nothing."

"Aunt Ernestine, why don't you and Pa just get married?" asked Cutler, pointedly.

"Oh! Why...we've discussed it but, that was all. Do you think so? Well, We thought that you would be against that very strongly."

"I'm not against it. I'm sure Ma would prefer it that way, too. And before a lot of gossip starts around Mellonville and around the farms, I think it would be a good idea. Of course, you have to get Pa to propose."

Cutler turned and took one of Ernestine's hands, and continued, "I'd be right proud to have you marry Pa, although it'd be hard to call you 'Ma'...I never called anybody that before."

Ernestine's voice broke as she said, "Thank you, son. I love you for that." She turned and hurried back up the path, her handkerchief wiping her eyes.

Cutler walked up the path and then turned toward the field where Cora was helping Mara gather various vegetables for dinner. Leaving Mara to finish, the two returned to the house, Cutler carrying the basket of produce.

"Well, Aunt Ernestine and I talked and discussed the situation and we both feel better. I gave my approval, and I think that she and Pa will probably get married."

"I figured that was what happened. I saw her returning to the house and then you coming up afterwards. I'm happy. We don't need hard feelings. Believe me, your father is great, but when you're away, I sometimes feel like a temporary guest," answered Cora.

"I'm sure. I guess it'll take time. You know, this place is mine, too, and what's mine is yours."

Cora squeezed his hand.

That evening, under the arches, before dinner, Sam came up to his son, put his hand on his shoulder and quietly said, "Thanks, son. You showed more brains than I did, and more understanding than I gave you credit for."

Cutler grinned, "I was raised right, Pa. Will you invite me to your wedding?"

Getting in the spirit set by Cutler, Sam answered, "Maybe, seeing you couldn't make it to the first one." And he smiled.

26

Cutler was quietly brushing the big bay he had been riding. Rhona was now at home, hopefully benefitting of the services of the white stallion Sam had bought.

As the young sergeant cared for the horse, brushing the dust and ticks from the animal's coat, putting salve on leg and saddle sores, and trimming its hooves, he sadly thought of the events of the past month.

He and Ralph Jacobs had returned to camp and had joined the company in constant skirmishes the rest of the month. Fights had been along Cedar Creek, Trout Creek, Baldwin, Higginbotham, and on the King's road near Callahan. Two scouts of the Second Florida cavalry had been captured by Northern sympathizers and then had been murdered.

As he worked, Cutler chewed on a mixture of wild onions, corn, dried meat, and garlic cloves. The strong mixture had been pounded into a crumbly dry paste. Blue Waters had taught him that this nourishing food could be easily preserved and it helped repel bugs and mosquitoes. Of course, the aroma was far from pleasing when you sweat a lot.

On August 2, Sergeant Charlie Dickison had been killed. This tragic event deeply affected all the men of the little command, and they all felt so helpless for the sorrow of their commander over the loss of his only son.

A few weeks before Charlie's death near Palatka, Cutler remembered well that evening during one of their chess games, Charlie had looked into the nearby glowing embers and said, "Cutler, this chess set has been in our family for generations. I want you to have it."

Cutler had looked up from the board, "What?" He glanced at Ralph, who had been watching the game. "I'm not that good, yet. You can't give up the game, just because I beat you one game this week."

"No, that's not what I mean," replied Charlie, quietly. He was still staring into the red coals "Don't think I'm joking. I've never been more serious in my life. I don't know exactly when, but it won't be long, and I'll be dead. I want you to have the chess set, and whenever you play on it again, I want to be remembered."

"Aw, come on. You're too mean to die. I expect to visit with you when you're ninety years old."

"Really, I'm not joking. The set will be yours, and there's a letter in my pocket to my father. Make sure he gets it. Deal?"

127

"Come on, Charlie," answered Cutler, but he was getting worried with his friend's words.

"Deal?"

"Deal!"

Later, that same evening, Cutler motioned with his hand, to Ralph as he walked towards the shadows to check his horse. Ralph glanced at the still brooding Charlie, got up from the log, and followed.

What do you think?" asked Cutler.

"Dunno."

"Well, I'm worried. I've never seen him like this."

"Do you think there's anything to it?"

"Who knows. Blue Waters used to tell me that sometimes when Indians went into battle they used to sing their death songs, and sure enough, they'd get killed."

"Well that may be, but I also heard that they all used to paint on death masks and a bunch of them sing and then not get killed and act like they were all reborn all over again, and next fight, do it all over again."

"Charlie's no Indian!"

"Well, we'll see."

"That's what I'm afraid of," answered Cutler.

Now, Cutler remembered that conversation, while he cared for the horse. He also remembered the looks he and Ralph had exchanged the day of Charlie's death.

The Federals had landed a large force of men at Palatka in July. Upon hearing of this, Captain Dickison, hurriedly sent a small detachment of fifteen men on reconnaissance. They were met by a battalion of Northern cavalry and were forced to retreat in a hurry. Three of the men were captured. Meanwhile the militia from Orange Park, and Company H joined Captain Dickison, and the next morning he advanced on the enemy.

The Confederates encountered a large force of cavalry and defeated them six miles from Palatka. Meanwhile, in Palatka, the main Federal force of over three thousand men waited in defense.

Cutler was near Captain Dickison and about thirty other men, as they were engaged in close fighting with pistols and sabers. Then the opposing commanding officer ordered his men to cease firing. Believing that the enemy was surrendering, the Southerners also ceased firing and rushed forward to stop any of the Northerners from escaping.

On the opposite side of the enemy column, Sergeant Charlie Dickison, Sergeant Crews, Forselli, and two others, closed in on the Federals. All of a sudden the Federals started firing again and Charlie was shot. As he fell from the saddle, Sergeant Crews caught him and lowered him to the ground. Captain Dickison rushed up and dismounted. Most of the Federals, at this time, surrendered, with just a few escaping.

Charlie breathed a few more breaths and with a sigh, died in his father's arms. Cutler rode up, just as the tearful Captain began the long ride carrying his son's remains.

The enemy had lost fourteen killed and twenty-eight captured, and many wounded. The 2nd Florida Cavalry has lost Charlie!

The silent column wound through the forest. The fearful prisoners were also silent in their terror, expecting reprisals at any moment, for their part in this shooting during an apparent surrender.

Later Sergeant Crews took the body to Orange Springs and the people of that town buried Charlie Dickison among their own. Captain Dickison returned to his duties.

The following day, the Federals evacuated Palatka. The fierce attack by such a small force had convinced them of the possibility of more Southerners in the immediate area.

Meanwhile, July 11 was a day of panic throughout the North. General Early and his small army threatened Washington City and contemplated attacking, but then observed reinforcements moving into the capital from Grant's army and during the night decided to leave. He was criticized by some in the South who felt he could have taken the city.

On July 17, General Johnson was relieved by President Davis, and General John B. Hood was appointed to take his place.

Hood attacked McPherson and Sherman in several actions in an attempt to break out of Atlanta and almost succeeded several times, but was repulsed with heavy losses each time.

On July 30, the terrible mine exploded under the Confederate trenches at Petersburg. The attacking Federals planned to race through the breach and split the defenders. Instead they found themselves in a maze of trenches. The Confederates collected themselves and trained their artillery into the hole. The Federals did their best in hiding. Meanwhile the all black, IX Corps, also attacked but to no avail and finally the surviving Union troops rushed back to their lines leaving almost four thousand casualties. On the same day, Confederate cavalry burned Chambersburg, Pennsylvania, after not receiving the ransom demanded from the city. The real reason for burning the town was in reprisal for Union General Hunter's raids in the Shenandoah Valley.

On August 5, Admiral David Farragut's fleet defeated the Confederates and captured Mobile Bay.

On August 5, the CSS Tallahassee arrived in Wilmington, North Carolina. During the past three weeks she had captured thirty-one Union ships, most of them off the coasts of New York, New Jersey, and New England.

The war continues, with minor and major engagements, the South winning some and losing some. But always losing!

27

One Sunday evening, Ralph and Cutler were quietly writing letters, seated on logs in the firelight's glow. There were few insects in the cedar grove, and fewer yet over in Cutler's and Ralph's tent, thanks to bay leaves, cucumber peelings, and garlic cloves, scattered round, per Mara's and Blue Waters' instructions. Cutler also cooked with bay leaves and garlic, and ate cucumbers, so nothing was ever wasted.

To rid their clothes of greybacks (lice), the men would place them on a hill of angry ants.

Whenever issued soap, store-bought soap, or captured soap, were not available, he made it, using fat and ashes or lye when it could be found. Sometimes he had to use the root of the Yucca plant, or bear grass. Thanks to his father, Blue Waters, and Mara, Cutler was able to make an othewise miserable existence, tolerable.

"Oh, oh, here comes trouble," said Ralph, as he looked up. Cutler looked up. "He's at it again. Well, let's take care of him again."

Vito Forselli staggered towards his two friends. He gripped a bottle in one hand, wore no shirt, his skin being all sticky with sweat and covered with sand, pine needles, and several scratches. He was barefooted, his feet covered with dirt and ashes. One big toe was bleeding heavily, having been stubbed more than once.

"There they are. I've been lookin' a lover fer my two buddies. In fac...I've had to sacrifice an drink moss of thish here bottle m'self cause you all weren't around to share it wish me." Forselli spoke thickly, his breath was foul, and his eyes were half-shut.

Cutler and Ralph shrugged, and resignedly put away their unfinished letters. Then they patiently turned their attention to Forselli who now was sitting cross-legged on the ground in front of the log, grinning foolishly.

"C'mmon, fellers, lesh have one...or two."

As Ralph and Cutler each took a sip, he watched each patronizingly, but slightly out of focus. "Thash my frens, my drinkin buddies, my Famous Fightin Florida Fools. How's zat for poetry? Purty good? I'll bet we'll be shootin' Yanks purty soon, betcha. Ole Dixie ain't goin' to let us ress much, no siree bob, h'aint. An I'm goin' to kill me a passle of them there Yanks, purty soon, yup. But right now I got a secret, yessirree...(hic) bob."

"OK, what's your secret?" asked Cutler. He and Ralph were being as patient as possible with their friend. Ever since Forselli had heard that his brother Joe had been killed in the Bloody Angle at Spotsylvania in May, he had become slovenly in appearance and had been drinking heavily. Ralph and Cutler had tried to cover for him on numerous occasions, but Forselli was smart enough to sober up when he knew that he was being noticed by the officers. During times of crisis or battle, he had always been seemingly sober and prepared to fight. In fact, his agressiveness could almost be termed suicidal.

"Well now, if'n I tell you, it won't be no secret," and he winked and tapped a dirty finger at his temple, knowingly.

"You're right," answered Ralph, "but what fun's a secret unless you tell your two best friends? Then it's our secret, and we won't tell nobody."

"Wellll...maybe, you shore you ain't funnin me?"

"I'm sure!"

"Well,...alright...but first..." and he took another healthy swig from his bottle, and then belched loudly, and showed a satisfied smile on his face.

"The good ole Cap'n agreed to transfer me."

"He what!?", said Cutler. Loud enough for several men in the vicinity to turn their heads in his direction.

"Shhh...I thought thish was goin to be our little shecret?" whispered Forselli, a finger over his lips.

"Sorry, what's the matter? Don't you like us here any more. You sure can't complain about the action, or the being mistreated, or the food. What is it?" asked Ralph.

"I want to go to Virginia and get shom of them Yankees that killed my Joe, and the Cap'n has approved me goin to Bobby Lee's Army of Northern Virginia up there by Richmond," sobbed Forselli.

Then he put his head down and shut his eyes as tears rolled down his dirty, sunken cheeks, and dripped from the scraggly whiskers on his chin onto the ground.

Cutler nodded to Ralph, and the two picked up Forselli, "Com'mon, Vito, lets walk some, it'll do us all some good," and the three left the glow of the fire and walked to a nearby lake.

Campfires dotted the area surrounding the lake, their yellow sparkles intermingled with the pale reflections of the stars, on the still surface of the shallow lake.

"What do you say, let's cool off in the water. I need a bath and my clothes do too," said Cutler. "Sides, no one can hear your secret if we're away from the shore.

"Fine", mumbled Foreselli.

Ralph and Cutler removed their moccasins, and then waded into the refreshing waters with Forselli. The sandy bottom made walking easy, with few stones and shells.

"You know, there's a bunch of caves around this area, some are underwater and connect one lake to another. I know for a fact that this feller drowned in one lake and a few days later he surface in another," said Cutler.

The three young men were now almost chest deep in water, and Ralph and Cutler ducked under water and then came up sputtering, "Try it Vito, it'll help clear your head and wash your face too."

Good naturedly, Forselli imitated his friends.

"Look, fellers, I know what you're doing, an I appreciate it, but I'm shtill drunk, dirty, feelin' sorry fer myself, and don't give a damn bout nothing no how; sides I'm goin, to avenge my brother, and that's final."

Ralph turned Forselli by the shoulders, and said sternly, "Look, asshole. We're your friends, and if you want to leave for Virginia, we understand. It's no more dangerous there than it is here, and we can understand your feelings, but gettin' drunk all the time, turning into a slob, and generally not givin a damn, that's shit! You understand?"

"Mind your own damn business!"

"You *are* our business," answered Cutler.

"He's right," added Ralph. "We've stuck together, helped each other, fought together, ate together, and generally been each other's keepers. We know that we can't take your brother's place, but we've been good friends the past few years and...like it or not, we've been like brothers, and you know it."

Forselli bowed his head, "You're right," he said quietly, and nodded his head.

"Now your talkin," said Ralph. "Now let's get your nasty ass washed up and then go get somethin to eat." Later that evening, after Forselli had been escorted back to his tent and was snoring loudly, Ralph asked whether he thought the problem had been solved.

"Temporarily, and I don't think it'll get any better once he's gotten his share of Yankees up in Virginia, either!"

28

Early on the morning of August 16, a combined Union force of five thousand infantry, four hundred cavalry, and several batteries of artillery, left Jacksonville and Green Cove Springs. Their missions were to destroy Captain Dickison's forces, and other Confederate troops in the state, disrupt communications, and raid the various plantations and small towns.

The Federals advanced on the Confederates at Baldwin, drove them across the little Suwanee river, then flanked the Confederates at Lake City, turned to Fort Butler, and circled the railroad town of Starke.

The railroad tracks were torn and all telegraph wires were cut. Not until sundown did the news reach Captain Dickison and his force at Waldo.

There was little confusion as the battle-tried veterans of Company H, joined with men from the Fifth Battalion, and a section of artillery, prepared themselves to move out. Joining them were about ninety new recruits. Captain Rou and his detachment of twenty men that had just arrived with the news, completed the entire force, a total of one hundred and eighty men.

"Holy shit, I guess the ball is about to begin," exclaimed Ralph. "Mr. Boulware just came in. The raiders burned his plantation and now over five thousand are camped there. I just heard the cap'n say that their cavalry, the 75th Ohio is movin on to Gainesville. Betcha that's where we're goin."

"Wouldn't surprise me a bit," agreed Cutler. "Have you seen Forselli?"

"Yup, he's already up ahead. He seemed to be in purty good shape."

"Hope so."

The Confederate cavalry moved briskly in the bright moonlight, in the wake of the Federals, these not yet aware of being followed. The Northerners stopped at plantations and farmhouses on their line of march, sacking these of all foodstuffs, negroes, and livestock. They took over one hundred and twenty-five slaves and four large wagons loaded with furniture, clothing, and valuables from the Lewis plantation. Mrs. Lewis had hidden the wagons, but her slaves, being threatened by the Federals, told them where the wagons had been hidden. William Lewis and his son, were both members of Company H. Captain Dickison offered to allow them to stay at the plantation, but they preferred to continue with the company.

At daylight, Captain W. Owens, and his small detachment of fifteen men of the State Militia joined the little command.

These were all men, who because of age, or illnesses, could not be in the regular service, but whenever a state of emergency existed, they would report to fight where needed.

The silent column continued rapidly, Captain Dickison and the surgeon, Dr. Williams, in advance.

The enemy rear guard was spotted and the column halted, allowing the Federals to continue unmolested and unaware.

"We must almost be in Gainesville. I know the railroad depot is pretty close," whispered Cutler.

"Well, we better be ready, cause all hell's goin to bust loose purty soon," answered Ralph.

"Well, all we have to do is follow Lt. McCardell, and you know damn well we'll be in the middle of it, that's for sure."

McCardell's men were ordered to dismount and move off to the left. Ralph and Cutler handed their reins to the horse holders, and filed quietly behind the Lieutenant.

Suddenly, the crash of one of the Confederate cannon, shattered the stillness of the morning. Startled birds fluttered away as the second shot echoed through the trees and dusty streets. The attack had begun!

Ralph and Cutler advanced side by side toward the railroad depot, with other dismounted cavalrymen in a long skirmish line. Lieutenant McCardell walked ahead of them, his saber in his right hand and pistol in his left. The rest of the men had left their sabers and scabbards on their saddles, taking rifles and pistols only.

As another cannon shot whistled high above their heads, the Confederates started their run towards the enemy. Captain Dickison remained mounted and led the center of the line with Lieutenant Dozier and his men. On the right flank was Lieutenant McEaddy and his men, one platoon remaining mounted.

The Federals began firing, but the Confederates held their fire until their officers halted them, gave the command to aim and fire. The devastating volley killed and wounded many of the defenders. A Union cannon, in the vicinity of the wooden Beville Hotel, fired several rounds towards the Confederate's cannon, but with no effect. Gradually the defending cannon was silenced, many of the artillerymen and most of the horses, having been killed in the cross fire of the attackers who had now taken the

135

railroad depot and now both attacking wings were starting to envelope the Federals in a pincers movement.

A courier reported to Lieutenant McCardell that the Captain wanted all the men mounted at this time, and charge the enemy for he expected them to break and retreat.

Just as the horse holders were brought up, Cutler saw a group of the enemy rush behind one of the homes bordering the main street. "Common Ralph, let's hurry after those," he shouted, pointing toward the scurrying Federals. "It looks like they may try to get in that house, and I saw a bunch of women by the door and windows just a minute ago."

Ralph nodded, and ran alongside his friend, neither waiting for their horses.

As they rushed down the dusty street, several minie balls hit around their feet and buzzed uncomfortably close to them.

"They've got Spencers. Hurry," panted Cutler. Both men hit the dirt before the porch just as a dozen more bullets passed where they had been.

The two rolled and crawled under the porch, and then stopped for a few seconds to listen and catch their breath.

Cutler signaled that he would go around one side of the building and Ralph, the other. Ralph agreed and crawled to his right. In the meantime, Cutler turned and moved cautiously in the opposite direction. Just at that time, the charging Southerners, now mounted, swept through the streets, shouting "Remember Charlie," led by Captain Dickison. There were civilians cheering them on, unafraid of the flying bullets.

Cutler crawled to the corner of the house, under the porch. The dust was dry and choking, and his eyes felt like they were full of scratchy gravel. He stopped, and resisted the temptation to rub his eyes, knowing this would make them worse. He peeked around the corner. Seeing nothing, he shuffled out from under the porch into a stooping position. Still seeing no one he moved along the whitewashed building. The small-arms fire was scattered and fading in the distance when Cutler stopped under an open window and heard a muffled voice coming from within. Not wanting to be seen, he refrained from looking into the building.

"Les, you stay with the old lady. Tony, you hold on to the

brat. I'll stay close to the sweet thing. Now, hold the pistols on them and follow them real close out the back way."

Cutler heard and moved quickly to the rear of the building. There he saw Ralph about to burst into the back door.

"No, wait...they've got three hostages. They're goin to try to escape...can't let them get away," Cutler quickly cautioned. "You get behind that stack of boxes and shoot as soon as I distract them."

Ralph nodded and moved quickly behind a stack of wooden crates a few yards from the back door. Cutler ran quickly in the opposite direction to a low white picket fence bordering the back yard of the house. He quickly jumped the fence and laid down in the low grass just as the back door slowly opened.

A young face wearing a blue forage cap, showed out the door. Two eyes searched the area for intruders. Satisfied that no one was to be seen, the head disappeared inside and shortly a grey haired lady appeared outside. She was short and plump, her skirts were dark blue, and she held her head proudly. Her chin was thrust firmly forward and led the way. She was followed by the young soldier in blue holding a pistol pointed at the old lady's back.

Another figure emerged through the doorway. This one was a little girl dressed in white of about eight years old. Her eyes were wide with fear as she stumbled forward as the next soldier appeared with his left hand gripped tightly to her long dark hair. The man was thick-set and bearded and looked about slowly, his pistol in his right hand pointed upward, ready to shoot in any direction. Next appeared a dark-haired girl of around eighteen. She was wearing a pale yellow dress and white apron which was tied in the back and was held by the next soldier. Cutler thought she was very pretty and could tell by the red of her face and flash of dark eyes, that she was very angry and would probably fight all three men if she wouldn't jeopardize the lives of the others.

Cutler stood quickly, pointed his pistol at the beared soldier, and squeezed the trigger.

The top of the man's head disappeared in a spray of blood, hair, and fluids. His trigger finger jerked, and a shot went up into the air. The little girl screamed as the man fell forward and knocked her down. Cutler turned his pistol toward the last man and fired, his shot hitting the man in the left shoulder. The force of the lead shot forced him to release his prisoner and knocked him to the ground.

As Cutler's shot hit the bearded soldier, the first man in line instinctively turned left toward the sound of the shot and shifted his aim from the old lady, to Cutler. As he did this, Ralph shot him between the shoulder blades. The man landed flat on his face in the dust, arms outspread.

Ralph scrambled over to the man that had been shot in the shoulder and kicked the pistol out of his hand. Pointing his own gun between the wounded soldier's eyes, he screemed, "You low-life bastard, you don't deserve to live!" His trigger finger tightened for a moment, but then with a sigh, Ralph lowered the pistol.

For few moments no one moved. Then the old lady turned and helped the sobbing child to her feet and hugged her tightly, caressing her dark hair. The young woman stared at the shattered head of the dead soldier practically at her feet, then turned and hurried to the wooden boxes and was sick.

As Ralph checked the dying soldier and the one wounded in the shoulder, Cutler went into the house. Satisfied that no one else was inside, he picked up a towel that was on a table, returned outside, and handed it to the young woman.

"You fellers all right?" asked Forselli as he rode into the garden accompanied by several other soldiers. His face glistened with perspiration and had streaks of burned powder and dirt from the heavy fighting. His uniform was soaked from a bucket of water he had just poured over himself. There was a growing blood stain seeping through the cloth of his right leg.

"Wow, was that a good fight!" "We really whupped 'em good. They had four hundred men here, and from what we can tell, only their Colonel and ten men escaped. The rest are like the three rascals you got here, dead, wounded, or prisoner. Their dead are scattered all over the town and in the woods and on the road to Newnansville. We'll take the prisoners, then join us by the square. I've got to get this scratch looked after afore all that good shine leaks out."

Forselli and his men loaded the dead man and the dying man, and with the captured weapons left, the wounded Federal, walking meekly in their midst.

That evening, as the victorious Confederates occupied the grateful town of Gainesville, many stories of heroic and sometimes comical events were circulated about the campfires. The citizens of the town happily supplied an abundance of food for supper and tended to the wounded. Dickinson's men had suffered light casualties, five dead and three wounded. One of the stories was of Sergeant Poer and three men who had been out on patrol the day before, and were just arriving at the start of the battle. On the road they ran into a Union officer and thirty men running to beat the band. The four, leveled their rifles and called for the retreating Federal Cavalrymen to surrender, which the Federals complied with immediately, naturally supposing that many more Confederates were coming up behind these. On their way back to town, the Federal Commanding Officer, Colonel Harris and his men, came galloping up the road and seeing the prisoners and four captors, instead of attempting to rescue them, turned in the opposite direction, and with the remnant of his men, made his escape.

"Hey Poer, I heard that the Cap'n is sendin youall to Washington City to capture the whole Union army," joked one of the men seated around the campfire.

"Well, I reckon, Jim, but he says that we got them so skeered that all four of us won't have to go, so I'll send just Richard and Caleb."

The men around the fire laughed, Cutler only smiled. He was troubled. He was thinking of the events of the morning and of Lydia Taylor, the young woman he had helped rescue.

The strong perfume of night-blooming jasmine filled the air.

The following evening First Sergeant William Cox, Assistant Adjutant, read this congratulatory order to the assembled troops:

"Officers and Soldiers: Again we have met the enemy and signally routed him. The victory at this place is equal, if not superior, to any in the history of the war. We met an enemy of superior numbers, with all the improved equipments which Yankee ingenuity could devise; but, trusting in the aid of Divine Providence and the justice of our cause, we have put him to shameful flight and confusion.

"Their purpose was evidently invasion and a permanent occupation, as evidenced by the papers of the Colonel in command

139

captured in the victory.

"For awhile your country has been saved from desolation and ruin. Only those of us who followed in his track of destruction and pillage can properly appreciate its importance. In their march, families were robbed with highhanded impudence, and homes made desolate. By your bravery and courage, this property was restored to them.

"But above all this, the victory which you have gained, by your coolness and gallantry, has saved your bleeding country from the polluting tread of the invader.

"But, my brother officers and soldiers, let me, in parting with you, warn you not to become indifferent by your success; let me urge you always to be ready, keep your arms in your hands, preserve your organizatrions, and be ready upon the first sound of the tocsin alarm to rally to your country's cause. With such indomitable courage, coolness and bravery as you have exhibited, you may be killed, but never conquered.

"If your State should again be invaded, which I pray God to avert, I hope to be with you, and in my humble way, to contribute in saving our homes, property and beloved country.

"J.J. Dickison, commanding forces."

Captain Dickison then stepped out and said, "Gentlemen, I salute you!"

The captain came to attention and saluted his troops. The men whooped and cheered as the onlooking townspeople clapped.

Lydia Taylor clapped loudly as she watched Cutler from across the square.

Dickison's forces remained four days in Gainesville before returning to Waldo headquarters. More letters of congratulations were read to the men from high-ranking Confederate officials during dress parade on August 28th.

"Well now, I'm glad that's over," sighed Ralph, as he unsaddled his horse. "These here fancy parades and inspections just don't do a thing for me. I sweat too much...and gettin all fixed up purty-like, that's only good when there's women around to watch and admire you. Don't you think so?"

Cutler nodded and continued brushing his horse, "Yea, all well and good," he thought. "But, if you don't know which woman you're thinking of and you get all confused and guilty, then all you want to do is crawl into a hole and be left alone and hope it resolves itself."

Ralph watched his friend, shook his head and said no more.

Meanwhile, General U.S. Grant declared that the exchange of prisoners would no longer be allowed. He wrote to General Butler as follows:

"It is hard on our men in Southern prisons not to exchange them, but it is humanity to those left in the ranks left to fight our battles. At this particular time, to release all rebel prisoners North would insure Sherman's defeat and would compromise our safety here."

The bitterness in the South increased. The desperation to the sufferers in both Northern and Southern prisons became more acute.

Reading of the raid on Gainesville and surrounding communities in the *Lake City Columbian*, Sam Garnett slowly began accumulating his valuables, trading Confederate dollars, no matter what the loss, for gold or silver, and hiding these at night, in the iron safe by the fireplace.

Forselli was in the Confederate hospital at Camp Log, near Madison, chaffing over this delay in his transfer. The other Confederate hospitals in Lake City, Quincy, Tallahassee, Madison, and Marianna with a total of almost six hundred beds, stayed almost full most of the time.

29

The Southerners did their best in keeping up with the events of the war. They valued any bit of information received, either by telegraph, newspaper, courier, or rumor. Rumors were, of course, constantly flying, some being completely false, but many having a shred of truth, somewhat distorted through fabrication or misinterpretation when relayed from messenger to messenger.

The average soldier, if there is such a thing as an average human being, did not fight blindly for "The Cause," he didn't agree with all the policies of The Confederacy, and he certainly did not believe in the infallibility of his political leaders. These men came from every conceivable ethnic background, and had many variations of religious beliefs. To say that President Jeff Davis was revered, would be a complete falsehood. In fact, he was considered by many in the ranks, as a despot, with a blind, and corrupt central government. The initial idea for withdrawing from the Union, had been for States' rights and freedom. Many had considered this war as the second Revolution. Along with Jefferson, Hamilton, Franklin, Madison, and a multitude of other patriots, George Washington had led the first Revolution. These founders of a new way of life, new beliefs, and representative government, had also been called traitors and rebels. The Confederate soldier certainly didn't mind being called a rebel or a traitor. He was now, in his own mind, being classified with the signers of The Declaration of Independence, the founders of The Constitution, and The Bill of Rights. What more of a compliment could one ask for?

The fact that Jeff Davis and his cabinet, were mere mistake-prone, greedy little men was ignored. Well maybe, as the Floridians thought, Secretary of the Navy, Mallory, wasn't too bad. After all, he was from Florida and had supplied the raiders Alabama, Florida, Tallahassee, Sumter, Georgia and others. And let's face it, the North sure had some terrible generals, compared to the South's.

After the war, these problems would be solved and removed, and after all, who needs a centralized government? States' rights! That's the issue and, by God, once the war is over, our own people, from our own state, will straighten up the whole shebang and we'll all be friends again and everything will be back as it was. To protect our homes and way of life, that's part of it…most of it.

And besides that, whose statue is it that is most admired in Richmond? Why, the one in the main Square, George Washington.

So what if a Confederate note isn't worth a… Continental!

Marianna is a quiet town of two thousand people in West Florida. The nearest railway is fifty miles to the east at Quincy. St. Andrews Bay, is fifty miles to the west, and Federal gunboats have been blockading there.

Most of the people of the area are planters from Georgia and North Carolina, but had been against secession until the outbreak of the war. Then they decided instead to go along with the Confederacy. In fact, many of the men joined the Southern Armies. Pensacola, is occupied by the Federals and is the largest naval station in the south. The state capital, Tallahassee, is to the East through wooded rolling country and still firmly in Rebel hands.

Occasionally, the alarm is sounded that the "Yankees are coming," and the inhabitants become concerned and some measures for defense and protection of property are thought of, but not much more than that. Usually by the time that the patrols have been activated and notified, the alarm is found to be false.

Colonel Mortgomery, a former United States Army officer, is in command of the scattered forces in the vicinity. These are small cavalry detachments in various towns and on patrol throughout the area.

In the town of Marianna, other than at the post hospital, there are a few Confederate soldiers, mostly at home on sick leave, and a scattering of old men and young boys armed with antique weapons and shotguns. This loose-knit organization has called itself "The Cradle and Grave Militia Company."

Two roads lead into Marianna, both from the West, Campbellton and St. Andrews Bay roads. The roads intersect in the center of town, forming the main street. Another road circles the town from the rear. At the center of town stands the Episcopal church and opposite it, a wooden, two story boardinghouse. A small cemetery is adjacent to the church.

On the morning of September 25, 1864, the alarm sounded that Union forces had been seen by scouts, and this force was advancing toward Marianna. To confirm this report, Colonel Montgomery went himself to see. He found the Federals to be moving toward the town, their probable intended destination to be Tallahassee.

Montgomery sent couriers out to his scattered forces. The town's people met and voted to fight the invaders and then voted Captain Norwood as their Captain. He and his men reported to the Colonel. Hurriedly, a barrier of defense was decided. This barrier was a single line of hastily piled logs, barrels, and wagons, formed from the boardinghouse to the church.

Early that afternoon, the small band of defenders, saw the advancing Federal skirmish line. The defenders fired, a few men in blue fell, and then the skirmishers retreated.

All too soon, the jubilant Rebels found the main body of attackers advancing. Battle flags flying, the troops neared in lines of battle.

The Federals consisted of three companies of Florida Union troops, the Second Maine Cavalry, and two full companies of Louisiana Negro troops. The Union commander, General Ashboth, had over six hundred, well equipped men at his disposal.

The main body of attackers moved forward while a part of the command was detached to flank the village. The defenders maintained constant fire on the attackers, but were shortly hemmed in from all sides. The Northerners set fire to the surrounding buildings and pressed the attack from the rear.

The Militia, realizing that further resistance would be useless, laid down their arms in surrender. The excited Negro troops, ignored the attempt at surrender, and gave no quarter. Some of the now defenseless men and the wounded, were cut to pieces and thrown into the flames of the burning church. Twenty-one year old Little John Myrick, picked up his musket and was swinging it by the barrel, when he was finally bayonetted to the ground. The remaining defenders did their best to escape, by scattering into the woods, as some of their comrades burned to death. Colonel Montgomery and his staff made a fast retreat, but he was unhorsed and captured.

The Federal officers stopped the slaughter and the remaining Southerners were captured alive. Fifty of the defenders were able to cross the Chipola River and destroy the bridge. Later that evening they were reenforced by the detachments of patrols sent for early in the day.

The Northerners lost eleven dead and twenty-five wounded in the hour long fight. The remainder of the afternoon was spent plundering and terrifying the remaining inhabitants.

At midnight, the Federals evacuated the town and returned to Pensacola with their prisoners and loot. General Ashboth was forced to return by carriage, having been wounded during the battle.

The Confederate forces were finally strengthened enough the following day for a desperate pursuit, but the raiders, having had many hours head start, were not caught.

The Federals, in their rush to leave before regular Confederate forces could arrive, abandoned their wounded. In town, there was talk of "stringin' em up," or better yet, "frying them in their own fat," but this was stopped immediately, the wounded taken to a large, wooden, columned house with the round front veranda. The wounded black troops, had been crying and pleading for mercy.

The dead, along with the charred remains, were buried in the little cemetary alongside the family plots of the Aldermans, Calloways, Miltons, Merritts, Davis', Daffins, Pittmans, Benedicts, Cahouns, and other local families. The body of Stephen Kinley, killed at Sharpsburg, Maryland, was now joined by his friends and relatives. General Barnes, C.S.A., was later laid to rest in this elite company.

The mounds would be still fresh, when less tham four months later, the Governor of Florida, John Milton, would be brought here, death by suicide.

Later, memorials would be placed of the many that died in prison at Elmira, New York.

The little town of Marianna, Florida, paid highly in blood for that hour in September, 1864, and over the years there would be many different versions of that one hour in September.

The citizens of the state were horrified at the indiscriminate slaughter, and the men of Dickison's command hoped to be sent to the west to avenge the massacre.

Cutler cursed the black race with every word he could think of. Then he thought of Mara, and Jeffrey, and Cindy, and people that had worked at the plantation. He was confused at his contradictory emotions and prejudices. He realized then, that he couldn't blame a race for the sins of some.

Cutler and Ralph shook hands with Vito Forselli early the next morning. The September feeling was in the air, the summer heat was gradually decreasing in the humid days. Sleeping at night had become easier, and the nets kept the increased mosquitoes from disturbing the nights with their sharp stings and annoying whine.

There was more standing water in the woods and swamps, and unless well oiled, metal seemed to rust within hours, especially the gun barrels, from the highly corrosive black powder. Leather....well, that turned powdery green, and smelled musty, just like the clothes the men wore. Fungus itch was giving some of the men fits, and scratching....well, you could scratch until you bled, and then it still itched.

"We'll miss you, ole man. Wish you the best of luck, and if you have the chance, write a letter," said Cutler, as he shook Forselli's hand in a tight grip. He wondered if he would ever see his friend again.

"Now, you'all know I'm not much of a writer, but I promise to send word on how I'm doin. You'all take care."

Forselli jumped on his horse, brushed his eyes before turning around then waved, as he kicked his horse.

"Say howdy to Marse Robert," shouted Ralph to the waving figure as it galloped up the road to join the twenty other riders going to Virginia. The Army of Northern Virginia was needing more men again and the Eleventh Florida Regiment had been bled heavily.

"I reckon a little somethin died in that Eyetalian when his brother was killed," said Ralph.

"They're emotional people," answered Cutler. He had a lump in his throat.

Fort Sumpter was bombarded most of the month by the Federal squadron. Colonel John H. Morgan, the famed guerrilla fighter, and over one hundred of his men were trapped and killed in Greeneville, Tennessee. Early in September, General George B. McClellan had accepted the Democratic nomination for president. Cavalry General Wade Hampton and his men rustled over three thousand head of cattle at Coggins Point, and delivered these to a very hungry Confederate army at Petersburg. On Lake Erie, a daring Confederate plan to capture ships and free Confederate prisoners being held at Johnson's Island, failed. After months of fighting, General Early's little army was defeated by Sheridan near Winchester.

But the biggest news was the evacuation and burning of Atlanta. General Hood, and what was left of his army remained in the area to harass Sherman while General Forrest and his cavalry continued to hit at positions in the Federal rear.

During the Jewish New Year, Cutler and Ralph discussed the increased bigotry in some areas, against Jews in the North and the South. Ralph encountered no problems within Dickison's command, but several newspapers printed anti-Semitic articles. In the North, General Grant expelled all Jews from his department, back in December 1862. Closer to home, several problems brewed in several cities in Georgia, upsetting the Jewish population of the state, and especially the many Jewish soldiers in the armies. Thomasville, Georgia, was the center of the scandal, having expelled all Jews from the community, and allowing the families only ten days to leave. This brought about a boycott to that city, by many citizens of the South.

Drovers from the little village of Orlando passed through Waldo with a herd destined for Virginia. The little village was prospering since it's start nearly twenty years earlier. There now was a sawmill, a grist mill, a cotton gin, and now the merchant, John Worthington, had been named postmaster. There were almost two hundred people living in the vicinity.

Fort Lauderdale, on the East coast, had become a haven for fugitives, deserters, and desperados. The fort had been built during the Seminole wars by Major William Lauderdale. His second in command had been Lieutenant Robert Anderson, the same man that surrendered Fort Sumpter to General Beauregard in 1861. Now, abandoned Fort Lauderdale was being used by men with no loyalties.

30

Cutler received two letters, one from Cora, and one from Gainesville...Lydia had written...again. She had answered his short note and was also informing him that she would be visiting Starke next week and would stop in Waldo on her way. "On her way, my foot. What's in Starke? Just the railroad, and that's not much of an excuse, but I am surprised she hasn't come sooner.

We're only fifteen miles from Gainesville," thought Cutler.

His real problem was that he didn't want to see her and he did want to see her. He didn't know which.

She had to know he was married. After all, he wore the gold band. He rubbed the ring thoughtfully. He had to admit that he hadn't out and out told her he was married. Well, she hadn't asked, either.

"You've got more letters than my dog's got fleas," said Ralph, as he walked up to the log where Cutler was seated. "Cora must be really lonesome..." then he faltered as he saw the frown on his friend's face and the two distinctly different handwritings on the envelopes on the log, "aahh...they're not all from Cora, are they? Well, if you ever want to talk about it, let me know."

Ralph hesitated a moment, then receiving no response, he shrugged his shoulders and walked on. He didn't need to be hit with brick. He knew what was going on. Besides, he had problems of his own. The religious difference had him concerned about his relationship with Flora. He had put it off long enough and it was past time to either do it or not. This last letter from her had shown a very real impatience as to when the wedding would take place. He thought, "Yea, but how about where? Church or Synagogue?

The following week Lydia arrived. The carriage was driven by an elegantly dressed black coachman, and she was accompanied by her sister, Mrs. Dawkins, and husband, Judge Dawkins, a friend of Captain Dickison.

Cutler met the carriage as it arrived into camp. His eyes were only for Lydia as he greeted the Judge and his wife. The visitors were escorted to the Captain's tent and Cutler retreated as the young officers congregated around the attractive young woman.

"What do I care," thought Cutler, as he sat on his favorite log, "she's nothing to me...I'm a real beaut, and Cora's home thinkin I'm here defending the country. Instead, I'm slobberin over a woman that I haven't said ten words to. I must be crazy."

"Now what'r you mumblin about," asked Ralph?

Cutler looked up and saw his friend standing by him, watching him intently. He realized that he had been talking to himself.

"Oh, hell. You know. I don't know what to do. I'm married to one...and I care for her, I really do! But now I'm mooning over another one, too," Cutler answered, disgusted with himself.

"Yea, I know. Now why don't you and I go take a long walk, avoid everybody else, and talk about it."

Cutler nodded, and followed Ralph.

The two stopped at the tent and picked up a bottle Ralph had bought from the Clifton brothers, strictly for medicinal purposes, of course, then they continued on a path in the woods.

They returned late that night. The bottle gone. The problems of the world solved. The bonds of friendship renewed, and very drunk. The carriage had departed much earlier.

"Com'mon thare feller, get yore ass up otta that rack." Cutler painfully opened one bloodshot eye. The other one resisted and resented the intrusion on its rest. To further aggravate his abused body, a hand was violently shaking him by the shoulder.

"I never seed you sleep that soundly. You were powerful drunk last night," the voice continued. Cutler finally discerned it to be the drawling voice of one of the Clifton brothers. He never could tell one from the other.

"You better get a move on. First thin the Cap'n says to me this mornin, 'Get at air Sergeant Garnett here to ma tent, rat now!' So here I be."

Cutler jumped from his comfortable bed, which was really a pile of pine needles held in place by logs. His head throbbed, his eyes ached against the early morning sun, and the rest of him just wished it belonged to somebody else.

Buckling on his pistol and buttoning his jacket, he walked rapidly to his Commanding Officer's tent. He hesitated, then knocked on the table just outside the tent flaps.

"Come in," a voice called from inside.

Cutler entered and saluted, "Sergeant Garnett reporting as ordered, Sir." He remained rigidly at attention upon receiving a brisk return of his salute.

Captain Dickison was precisely dressed in his long grey coat, red sash, and pale grey gauntlets. He was seated at his desk, several papers under his left hand. His right hand was on a large black bound book.

Captain Dickison stared at Cutler for a long moment. There was a no usual twinkle in his eyes, nor smile on his face. He didn't tell the young soldier to stand at ease, and now Cutler knew there was something drastically wrong.

"Sergeant Garnett, do you know why I have ordered you here this morning?"

"No, sir."

"Well, I'm going to tell you, and I cerainly do not plan to mince my words, so I suggest you listen attentively."

"I normally do not interfere with the personal affairs of my men, but in this case I am honor-bound to do so. You have been a good soldier, and I commend you for that, but, it has been brought to my attention that, you, a married man, have been trifling with the affections of Miss Lydia Taylor. Now, sir, I will tolerate none of this in this command. I thought you a gentleman, and know you are from an honorable and upstanding family. I pray that this is only a misunderstanding and will be cleared up in a satisfactory manner. I promised Judge Dawkins that I would attend to it personally. Have I been mistaken or misinformed? If so, please state so, and I will apologize to you, and the matter will be forgotten."

A very uncomfortable Cutler listened to his Captain, the man that, other than his own father, he admired and respected more than any other in the world. He perspired under the uniform from nervousness, guilt, and alcohol. It was difficult looking into Captain Dickison's dark eyes.

"You are correct, sir," Cutler began. "I am a happily married man, and I love my wife very much. I must admit, I found Miss Taylor to be a very attractive, and fascinating young lady. I assure you, sir, that I have done nothing...ungentlemanly, and although there has been an attraction between the two of us, and we have corresponded, nothing has actually been done or said, other than perfectly legitimate. I must admit, I did not tell Miss Taylor that I was married. I avoided her last night when she was in camp."

"Thank you, Sergeant Garnett. It was what I expected, but I feel that your little escapade could have gone further, if allowed to run its course, and then it would have been regrettable to all concerned. Last night, you may have thought that getting drunk and avoiding the young lady was the solution to avoid an embarrassing situation, but it may have been the coward's way out. The young lady was much distressed and finally when you could not be found, she and the Judge confided in me. I do suggest that you contact Miss Taylor, and explain your marital status. You may, if you wish, go to town and do this. I do not recommend that you send the apology by mail."

"Yes, sir. Thank you, sir. I would like to clean up and take care of the problem today...Sir, may I take a friend, as...escort?"

"Yes, Sergeant. you may have Jacobs accompany you. Feel free to talk with me if there are any more problems."

"Yes, sir. Thank you, sir. There will be no more problems. I promise you that."

"I'm sure. And, Sergeant Garnett, be assured that this conversation will not leave the confines of this tent."

"Thank you, sir. I appreciate that."

"Dismissed."

It was late morning when Cutler and Ralph rode into Gainesville. They had dressed in their best uniforms, and although these were tattered and mended in places, they were clean.

The two riders discussed Cutler's embarrassing situation at length and Cutler rehearsed, in his mind, what he had to do. "I sure wish this was over with," he muttered. "I'd rather eat shit with a spoon than have to do this."

"Well there, oh great lover, you may just have to do that, too," kidded Ralph. "Just stick to what you said, and don't let those dark eyes get to you, and you'll get away free. We both know that you've got a weakness for the ladies, so, don't get yourself in a fix any deeper than you have. I'll be nearby, so you can use me for an excuse if you feel uncomfortable, and need to escape."

The two dismounted and tied their horses to the rail in front of the porch they had so recently dived under. Bullet scars still showed on the posts and building.

Cutler knocked on the front door, which was immediately opened by Lydia Taylor. She had a big smile on her face and her dark eyes flashed. Cutler stood dumbfounded, his hat in his hand.

"Miss Taylor, I have come here to talk to you and explain a misunderstanding......May I come in?"

"Why, certainly. Please do." Then she looked at Ralph questioningly.

"Howdy ma'am. I'll just wait out here."

"Lydia nodded to Ralph, then moved to one side and held the door wide for Cutler.

They walked into the parlor. No one else seemed to be in the house. Lydia motioned for Cutler to sit down, but he chose a chair rather than the settee near her, where she had motioned.

Lydia frowned. "I was concerned," she said. "I looked for you last night at camp, but now I'm glad you're here."

"Miss Taylor..." started Cutler.

"Oh, please...call me Lydia."

"Yes,. ma'am. There's something very important I must talk to you about. It isn't pleasant, and you may hate me when I finish."

"Oh, Cutler, I can't hate you. You and I...well, we seem to have an understanding. I can tell. And, after all, you saved my life. Remember?"

"I remember, but...well, the understanding that we have, is...wrong." Cutler fidgeted with his hat, turning it slowly in his lap. He had started the conversation and knew there was no backing out of it this time. He could tell that she was still very glad to see him, and had misunderstood his visit as, calling on her...or more appropriately termed, courting. Courting! He knew he had better straighten this out quick!

"Well, you see...I'm married."

"Oh, I know that, silly."

Now Cutler felt he was in a corner.

"I said I'm married...to a girl."

"Of course, to a girl. I know that, too. But I also know that you and I have been attracted to each other and I'm here, now, and your wife is not. And...who knows what could happen?"

"No...nothing is going to happen. I don't believe what you said, but although I would like for us to be friends, you must know that I love my wife, very much. I am guilty in being attracted to you. I don't know what I was thinking."

Lydia Taylor tightened her mouth, and said, "Well...my my, aren't we saintly. All of a sudden you change your stripes. I saw the way you watched me, the second meaning in your letter, but now all of a sudden a touch of conscience."

"Miss Taylor, Lydia, I'm sorry. I...I admit I was wrong in my interest in you, but nothing happened, and although we both were attracted to each other, I know it's my fault that I didn't tell you that I was married. I'm very surprised that you knew it all along and it made no difference to you. That surprises me...a lot."

"Oh, you make me sick. Just leave....Go away, just leave me alone," she shouted.

Lydia stood, stamped her foot, and left the room.

Cutler hesitated, then walked to the front door, opened it, turned and mumbled, "I'm sorry," to no one, and walked out on the porch.

Ralph had been leaning against a post and walked up to Cutler when he saw his friend come outside.

"Well?"

Cutler shook his head, went to his horse, quickly mounted and trotted back in the direction to camp.

Ralph mounted and hurried to catch him. "Now what," he said to himself.

Once the two had traveled out of sight of Gainesville, Cutler slowed to a walk, and with Ralph alongside, he recounted the conversation in the parlor.

"Good riddance," was all Ralph said.

As they rode further, Cutler said, "You know, she was really mad. What if she tells Cora?"

Ralph answered dryly, "When in doubt...lie."

31

Sam Garnett sat under the huge live oak, admiring the fading rays of sunlight as they slowly lost their strength to the advancing dusk. The hum of insects grew more intense, although a few mosquitoes didn't seem to bother him. Appetizing aromas drifted from the kitchen building where Mara and Cindy were preparing dinner. It would be only a few more minutes before he would be called to the supper table. Ernestine and Cora were doing whatever women do. The table had been set. He sure was happy that Ernestine was here. She was...comfortable, and he really cared a lot for her. He found himself looking forward to the day they would be married, although the role of husband and wife was being lived now...to its fullest. And Cora, what a wonder! Cutler sure hit it right with that one. She sure acts a lot older than her real age.

Sam cracked another pecan and picked at it carefully, eating the tasty meat inside. He knew that if caught eating pecans before dinner, Mara would scold him, and Ernestine and Cora would look and smile, saying nothing.

There was rustling in the underbrush. Sam knew it was an armadillo without turning and looking. The dogs, however, charged the bushes, prefering to check first hand on the identity of the noisemaker. The armadillo, a recent inhabitant of Texas, dodged from side to side, ran unbelievably fast around a tree, then scurried into his hole and safety. The dogs barked and pawed the ground around the hole where the armored animal had disappeared.

Sam chuckled and whistled for the dogs.

"Well, now..." Sam thought, "I hate to admit it, but... the South is sinking. I hope I'm wrong, but it doesn't look good, and here in Florida things are better than most places. I hope I'm doing the right thing, although it doesn't seem very patriotic."

Sam had sold most of the cattle herd, most of it to the government, and he had taken the chits and gradually traded them at reduced value for gold, silver, diamonds, U.S. greenbacks, whatever he could get. His cotton was stored in a hidded barn in the woods, known only to himself and Blue Waters. The hard cash, was hidden in the iron strongbox by the fireplace.

The resin and turpentine from his harvest of Naval Stores yielded by the forests of longleaf and slashpine trees, was buried in barrels, deep in the woods. The corn from his fields had been taken to the mill and the meal not needed for the livelyhood of the plantation, was bartered for implements of agriculture and tools for woodwork. These tools were buried under the stalls of the horses. The perishable foods had been continued being used and stored in the springhouse. Most of the meats were smoked, dried, or salted, and then stored in barrels. Many of these barrels were hidden in the area of Blue Waters' shack, an area unlikely to be searched. The balance, were stored in various places, "Not all your eggs in one basket," reasoned Sam. Just in case the raiders come, or worst yet, deserters or outlaws."

Sam also knew that there were some of his neighbors with divided loyalties, and yet others that were jealous of his prosperity and would have turned him into some sort of traitor for freeing his slaves and hoarding goods in case of disaster. Some of the other planters that had freed their slaves, had been subjected to abuse by some of the so-called patriots. Of course, these flagwavers were not among the soldiers defending the Confederacy. By one method or another, most of these had somehow avoided conscription. Sam did have to admit, that there had been some question as to how he had avoided it himself. He had been able to convince the authorities that he was more valuable to the Confederacy supplying cattle and food for the army, rather than just another rifle. Besides, his only son was known to be doing his share towards the defense of the state.

Sam realized that, no matter how the war turned out, things could never be again as they had once been. The era of the plantations, very rich, slaves, and very poor, would evolve from its agricultural society to more industrialization, it had to! In fact, if there had been more industry in the first place, possibly, the war would never have had happened.

Sir Walter Scott with his book, Ivanhoe, and chivalry, and all that life of fantasy, had helped many of the dreamers in the South look at the world with a false image of euphoria and security.

"Oh, well, gettin about supper time. Guess I'll go clean up and join the ladies," Sam muttered, got up from his seat and walked toward the house. He stretched his arms and moved his shoulders around. His muscles were still firm and strong.

"Damn, some of these people think a man in his forties is fallin apart and not worth his salt." He grinned, "Ernestine sure knows better!"

On October 4, 1864, after a successful cruise, the C.S.S. Florida, with a total of thirty-seven captured enemy ships to her credit, sailed into Bahia, Brazil. Orin watched the anchor splash into the blue-green waters of the harbour. They had been at sea almost continuously since February, when they left France after almost six months there for refitting, and recruiting. Orin had certainly enjoyed his stay in France. In fact, he had almost gotten married while there...at least once or twice!

The black smoke curled skyward from the two large, black, smokestacks, the stillness of the day allowing it to disappear high in the sky.

Now that the ship was in a neutral port, minimal vigilance would be maintained, and Orin hoped to be allowed ashore at least once during this stay at a liberty port. Little attention was paid to the United States Steamship, Wachusett, moored out into the harbour.

The noisy little port was nestled in surrounding hills, lush with tropical vegetation. Many small boats were docked at the stone wharves by the lower city, the upper city, instead, having many colorful colonial style houses, all with the traditional red tile roof.

The bay or Bahai in Portuguese, had been discovered in 1501 by an expedition headed by Amerigo Vespucci whose name the American continents were named.

The large Catholic church, Sao Francisco de Assisi, was on one of the hill crests, its interior heavily adorned with gold, evidence of the wealth of some of planters owning their fasendas, or plantations.

Orin looked forward to tasting some, of the African exotic dishes, plus some fresh pineapples, bananas, and coconut milk.

A large slave population and many dark skinned Indios, seemed to dominate the European inhabitants that actually controlled the harbour city.

Lieutenant Charles Morris, the present commander of the Florida, had the loads drawn from the guns, and gave his crew liberty on shore as each watch was relieved.

Orin was among the first group of fortunate seamen and officers allowed to take one of the ship's boats, into the port. Proper diplomatic procedures had been made with the port authorities, and the Confederates were welcomed with sincerity. The country of Brazil also allowed the institution of slavery, and felt more than just neutrality for the new southern nation.

Orin was well in the grips of inebriation when the slender Indian girl helped him up the narrow stairway to her room and brought him to her bed. He was sound asleep by the time she undressed, in the dark and joined him. Maria was not surprised. She had seen many drunken sailors for her seventeen years.

Orin barely made it to the little boat to his ship the next morning in time for his watch, but as soon as he was permitted, he left the ship again to visit the young Indian girl. This time he arrived sober.

Orin spent two days of bliss. Whenever on land, his shipboard duties seemed to be mere interruptions from where his real desires lay. Maria, was, besides her other attributes, a good cook and good housekeeper. In her limited, accented English, she informed Orin to bring her all his laundry and sewing, which she busily washed and repaired during his duties on board.

The next night, Orin had the watch. It was a dark night, no moon and few stars to brighten the skies. He leaned on the railing and gazed toward shore. A few pale flickering lights shown, most of the town being asleep. Orin searched in the direction of Maria's room, trying to discern the dark shapes of walls and roofs, and penetrate the darkness with his mind.

He could smell the odors of the town, the rotting garbage, the open sewers, intermingled with fragrances of spices and fruits. a dog barked twice, from a distant building, then stopped abruptly with a squeal.

A steam engine chugged in the bay, and now the swish of water could be heard against a hull as it sliced through the water. It was unusual for vessels to be moving in the darkness because of such a danger of collision with the many anchored craft.

Suddenly a shout came from the stern. "There's a ship on a collision course. Show a light!"

There was running on deck, then another voice called out, "Veer away, damn you! Can't you see us?"

Orin turned and saw a ship bearing down on their starboard quarter, the pointed dark bow getting bigger by the second at the same time, Lieutenant Porter ran on deck and shouted, "Beat to quarters, prepare to be rammed. It's the Yankee ship, and she's headin straight for us. Prepare to repel boarders!"

The crashing impact threw Orin off his feet, then the Wachusett fired two shots from her battery and poured a volley from small arms onto the decks of the Florida.

Several bullets passed where Orin had been standing. Other

men were not so fortunate, and fell to the deck with wounds.

A voice from the attacking ship called for surrender, but the irate Southerners on deck replied with pistols and muskets. Orin fired his musket at a figure on the rat-lines of the enemy ship, and had the satisfaction of seeing the figure tumble into the dark waters between the two ships. Orin grabbed another weapon, fired again, and then saw a hoard of borders jump onto his ship. He swung the musket and another sailor in blue dropped in his tracks, then realizing that this was a futile fight, Orin jumped overboard.

As Orin swam toward shore he realized that others also had jumped overboard, and were swimming in the dark waters, shoreward. Rifle and pistol fire could be heard from behind him on the ship, then he noticed the zip of bullets hitting the water around him and his companions. To his horror he realized the Union sailors were shooting at the swimmers!

Orin dived, took off his shoes and trousers, and then continued in the same general direction underwater as long as he could. When finally he gasped for air he looked about and saw that only a few swimmers could be seen. He again dived and continued underwater until again, he was forced to surface. This time he saw no one in the water and the shooting had ceased, so he quietly resumed swimming toward shore, using the dog paddle and listening for foreign sounds.

Meanwhile, Lieutenant Porter had no choice but to surrender the defenseless ship and shortly, the Wachusett towed her out toward sea. A small sloop-of-war, the only Brazilian vessel present, fired a few shots at the Union ship, but these were ignored. The fort also fired a few rounds, but because of the darkness, discontinued for fear of hitting some of the other ships in the bay.

Orin was helped on the wharf by some Portuguese seamen. In a few minutes a large crowd gathered around him. Among them was Commander Morris and several of the sailors that had been in town. Upon being questioned by the officer. Orin answered the best he knew. Meanwhile, the bodies of nine of his comrades were fished out of the water. Orin and five others had survived the swim to shore. The balance of the officers and sailors that had been on board had been taken prisoners.

One of the dead sailors had been one of the fire gang, a negro slave that had come aboard to be with his master's son, one of the officers. The young officer knelt beside the body and sobbed, "Poor ole Jim, I see the Yankees finally freed you."

Maria made her way through the crowd and stood by Orin's side during the questioning. Later she took him to her room.

32

Cutler's letters to Cora usually described normal everyday camp life, occasional antics of his companions, and unusual things he himself would do. He described in detail, the skirmishes or attacks that Dickison's command would participate, explaining his point of view of the battles and the movements of the troops and any actions by his friends or himself. He seldom mentioned any gruesome details, mellowing out the horrors of war.

Explaining the battle of Gainesville, in his last letter, Cutler narrated his and Ralph's participation in the saving of Lydia Taylor. "That way," he reasoned, "in case Lydia writes that she's involved with me, Cora will understand that it's only appreciation for saving her life, and anything else could be imagination or infatuation. I hope!"

Cutler soaked a hard-tack biscuit in his coffee, before munching the hard cracker. Although his teeth were good and strong, he had heard of men breaking teeth in an effort to eat the crackers. The coffee and biscuits were taken from supplies the Federals had abandoned at Gainesville.

Cutler was awakened from his daydreaming by Ralph, "Hurry, we're movin out."

The camp awoke from the relaxed routine of the evening, to the hurried preparations of saddling horses and grabbing bedrolls, food, weapons, and ammunition, In less than ten minutes a detachment of Company C, a detachment of Company H, and a 12-pounds howitzer were ready to move out. Captain Dickison was in overall command with Captain Chambers in command of Company C, and Lieutenant McCardell commanding Company H. Sergeant Crews commanded the artillery. In all, ninety men were ready to ride.

Cutler and Ralph rode side by side, following Lieutenant McCardell, ready to relieve the other scouts who were riding far in advance and on the flanks of the column. Captain Dickison did not believe in being surprised.

A dispatch received from Lieutenant Haynes of the Fifth Battalion, cavalry, on outpost near Green Cove Springs, informed Dickison that he had met the Federals in considerable force and had driven them back three miles. They would, undoubtably, return, and be ready for a fight. Captain Dickison thought this would be an opportune time to, not only stop and drive the enemy back, but to whip him good.

After riding all night and not finding the Union troops near Green Cove Springs, the tired Confederates continued on to Finegan's Ford. Ralph was on scout at the time, and returned with information that a cavalry force had crossed at the ford and then continued up to Middleburg, along Black Creek. The tracks were confused and intermingled, but the signs were certain to be the well-shod hooves of Federal Cavalry-a lot of them! They had obviously gone on a raid and most probably would return on the same road. Ralph was soaked with water and sweat as he reported. He, his horse, and equipment were mud splattered but, although tired, he had a triumphant glow in his eyes.

"The Cap'n is really gonna trap 'em this time," he whispered, once back alongside Cutler. "I feel it in my bones."

Dickison, not wanting to risk missing the return of the Federals, placed a detachment on each of the two roads, just in case the Federals returned by a different route. His two detachments were close enough for one to reinforce the other, if need be.

The men dismounted, and lay on the ground, their bridles in hand. The scouts, hid further up each road. The sun had risen above the horizon, the rays reached far up into the sky, but not yet penetrating the Florida wilderness.

"Here they come. Mount up," came the hushed order. The Federals were on the road heading toward McCardell's command. Leaving a handful of men to watch the other road, Dickinson's men mounted and waited for the enemy. They sat across the road two ranks deep, overlapping into the field and trees on either side. Not a word was spoken as the figures in grey waited as if on the parade field. Not a movement or sound came from the men. Occasionally, a horse would move, but a strong and impatient hand would bring it back into line.

The Federals, driving a large herd of captured cattle, and being thus occupied, did not spot the waiting Confederates immediately. Suddenly seeing Dickison's command, the Federals halted in their tracks.

Their Captain, quickly gave orders for his men to form in two columns of fours. He calmly inspected the ranks, the cattle having been sent to the rear. Satisfied that his men were ready, he wheeled his horse to face his enemy. He carried his saber straight up by his right shoulder. "Draw sabers," he commanded. As one, the men in blue flashed their polished blades, the sun's rays, now reaching above the trees, reflected as crystals the front ranks.

"At a trot, forward."

The still waiting Confederates had not yet moved.

"Charge!"

The galloping horses pounded closer.

Ralph and Cutler exchanged glances, then to their relief they heard Captain Dickison's clear voice. "Draw rifles!"

Most of the men were now armed with Spencer short carbines, captured from the Federals in earlier fights. These weapons, were now drawn from the scabbards. The men were also armed with sabers and pistols, many wearing more than one. In fact, Captain Dickison, did not have a rifle, but did have his saber and always carried four pistols.

Ralph turned his head, and spat on the ground.

"Ready...aim." More than fifty rifles were brought up to fifty shoulders, fifty hammers cocked.

"Fire!"

Most of the front rank of the charging men in blue disappeared. Screaming horses, and falling men confused the tightly packed attacking columns. Their Captain, miraculously, was unharmed. He quickly reformed his command, wheeled again, and charged, sabers extended, this time, the men yelling as they attacked.

"Ready...aim...fire!"

The attackers were again stopped by the deadly volley. Then the center of the Confederate line moved aside, exposing the cannon of Sergeant Crews.

The roar from the cannon startled some of the Confederates' horses. The shrapnel was devastating to the men in blue and their horses.

Dickinson's men continued firing, the cannon roared once more, then Captain Dickison called, "Cease firing!"

The Captain trotted out in front of his men, "Draw pistols." He turned, drew his pistol, "Charge!"

The two ranks of Southerners attackers the confused Northerners, firing their pistols and yelling the Rebel Yell as they galloped.

The fight lasted less than an hour. The Federals had twenty-one casualties, and lost sixty-five prisoners. Only three made their escape, among them, their captain who was badly wounded. The Southerners had no losses.

"They sure were brave, but I guess they haven't learned yet that bullets reach further than sabers," remarked Cutler.

The next battle took place several days later near the Fairbanks place, above the San Sebastian river. Neither Ralph nor Cutler were involved in this fight, having been selected, instead, to help return the cattle to the ranches where they had been taken.

The battle at the Fairbanks plantation was also a success, despite Saint Augustine being less than two miles distant, and occupied by Federal Forces.

Captain Dickison and his men returned the following day with thirty-five prisoners, weapons and horses. Again, none of his men suffered any casualties.

Throughout the month of October, the Confederate forces on both the East and West Coasts of Florida were kept busy, constantly skirmishing with detachments of Federals and their raiding parties. The Confederates consistently held their own, defeating the Union troops on these frequent expeditions. The Florida civilians suffered.

Sam Garnett packed his many books and valuables into heavy wooden boxes, and with the help of Ernestine and Cora, pried the heavy floorboards in the house every night. They dug a small cellar under the stairs leading to the first floor. The dirt was scattered in the gardens and the boards replaced every night after the work was done. Within the month, a room ten feet by ten feet and six feet high, was completed. The sides were lined with vertical pine logs and the board ceiling braced with heavy cypress timbers. Boards and brush were placed on the floor to help guard against humidity. Sam also packed several weapons wrapped in oiled rags plus ammunition. Once all the valuables were hidden in the room, a trap door was put over the hole in the ground, covered with dirt, then the heavy flooring was nailed back in place as originally built.

On November 27, 1864, Sam and Ernestine were married in the main room of the big house in Mellonville. Cutler, home on leave, and Cora, were present as witnesses. Blue Waters, Mara, Cindy, and Jeffrey, also watched. Afterwards, the servants, still sniveling, served a huge dinner on the everyday dinnerware. The "good stuff," remained hidden. Blue Waters even showed a hint of a smile as he stood silently watching the ceremony. He did, however, say briefly to Ernestine, "He my brother. Now you my sister."

None of the nearby planters or townspeople were invited. As with Cutler's wedding, the Garnett's preferred "real" people, rather than onlookers, backslappers, and people that were "just plain curious," and later would gossip all over the county about who said what and who wore what. The next time on errands, Ernestine would ride the wagon with Sam, and he would simply introduce her as his wife.

Neither Ralph nor Tom Gordon had been able to leave camp, but both sent their greetings. Flora, also, had been unable to leave the small harvest of crops she had. She had been forced to hire a man to pick for her while she attended to the store.

Preacher Harver conducted a very short service (at Sam's insistence) that sunny afternoon. Cutler watched his father. His face was glowing with happiness. This was the first time he had ever seen him so happy, really radiating!

Cutler had seen him enjoy himself, of course, occasionally joke with his usual dry humor, and always glad to see his son return from the war. Cutler remembered, when he was still a young boy, how he and his father would take long walks together, often for hours, on paths or in the woods. Sam would point out different features of the terrain and woods, but more important, he would include examples, stories about thoughts, feelings, and truths. These truths would always follow a story about something that had happened to him or to someone he had known. Cutler never knew whether these people or incidents were real or fictional, but the stories were always interesting, and left an impact, or moral to the story. Each night afterwards, Cutler would lie awake and think over his father's words.

Cutler remembered once that he had wanted a special favor. He couldn't remember now what it was, but he had been very insistent about this favor. Thinking about it now, Cutler said to himself, "I was really rotten. Pa should have given me a good whippin."

Instead, Sam had explained that life was like a scale; on one side was privilege, on the other was responsibiity. Too much of one or the other would upset the balance of the scale. If Cutler wanted and felt he deserved a privilege, then he should be willing to accept an extra responsibility. On the other hand, if Sam felt that he was old enough to be given more responsibilities, then these should be, in some way compensated by additional privileges.

Cutler remembered once being very tired during one of their long walks. He sat on a log and said, "Pa, I can't walk no more." His father coaxed him patiently to the next log and on to the next until they arrived home. Later, Sam explained to his young son that if he *really* couldn't have made it, Sam would have carried him, but he knew that his son wasn't a quitter. After that, Cutler's pride would not have let him quit even with two broken legs.

Shortly afterward, Cutler was given a little filly. He named her, Rhona. The pleasure that he enjoyed from the little Appaloosa more than compensated feeding her, cleaning her stall, brushing her, and generally being responsible for her. One cold night, Cutler wasn't able to sleep. instead, he dressed quietly and tiptoed to the stable with the heavy quilt from his bed. He found Rhona curled up by her mother.

Sam heard the front door close, and when he entered the barn he found the mare, Rhona, and Cutler, all curled up on the straw. All three were covered by the quilt.

The mare looked up at his entrance, Rhona opened one eye, but Cutler was startled. All Sam said was, "Sleep well son. Keep warm. See you in the mornin," and he walked back to the house.

"That's my boy," he thought. "He's got a good heart, like his ma." With a lonesome, sad smile, Sam returned to his room.

Now, it was Sam's and Ernestine's day, and Cutler tightened his arm around Cora. She looked up and smiled at him, a broad smile on her wet face. "I wish Flora and Pa could have been here," she whispered.

"Ralph, too," answered Cutler.

Ernestine was thrilled with the bottle of expensive French perfume that Cutler and Cora gave her. The bottle had come by way of blockade runner.

Sam smiled knowingly as he unwrapped his gift. The small gold-covered figure of a blindfolded lady holding in her outstretched hand a pair of scales touched his heart.

Sam looked at his son and smiled. With the pleasure and privilege of marriage, he realized that he had also acquired a responsibility.

The statue was eventually re-wrapped and hidden in the iron box by the fireplace.

33

The news from the main battlefields was not good for the men of Dickinson's command.

Except for minor battles and skirmishes won by Southern Forces, the overwhelming supplies of men and materials commanded by the population and manufacturing centers of the north were continually apply more pressure on the dwindling Confederacy.

The North is amazed at the resistance against her. Many of the Union soldiers secretly admire the ragged scarecrows in grey they encounter on the battlefields. "Johnny Reb" doesn't know that he's beaten, and "Billy Yank," although winning, is paying a high price in blood and dollars.

On October 19th, a small group of Confederate raiders, led by Lieutenant Bennet Young, crosses the Canadian border and descends upon the small Vermont town of St. Albans. The men rob three banks of over $200,000 but are thwarted in their plans to burn the town. Eleven of the raiders escape back to Canada. They are later arrested but then released. The same day, General Early's little army attacks General George Crook's army. The Federal's left flank, completely surprised, falls back in disarray. General Sheridan, on his way back from Washington City, strives to turn the thousands of stragglers retreating down the Valley Pike. By the time he arrives at the front, his divisions are regrouped to the west of Middletown. Meanwhile, the Confederate charge slows to a stop as soldiers fall out of line to loot the Union camps for food, clothing, and shoes, many of them being barefoot. The Union counterattack defeats General Early once and for good, putting an end to the Confederates' last major threat in the Shenandoah Valley.

In Missouri, the Federal force of twenty thousand men defeats eight thousand Confederates in the Battle of Westport.

General Hood's army wanders through Alabama and finally engages against General Schofield at Franklin, Tennessee. Although the Union Army retires, the casualties for the Army of Tennessee are staggering, brought about by the head-on assaults and hand to hand fighting.

On November 16th, General William T. Sherman and his army leave Atlanta on its march to the sea. The army is composed of four columns and a total of sixty-two thousand men, with twenty days rations. After that…live off the land!

Opposing them are General Wheeler's ten thousand cavalry and three thousand militia. The defense and harrassment is valiant but pointless.

Brazil is outraged with the Federal government over the capture of the CSS Florida in their harbour at Bahia. They demand her return with all Confederate prisoners. Meanwhile, the captured vessel is "accidentally" struck by an army transport while in Hampton Roads. Then to avoid anymore accidents, she is moored above Newport News, but on November 28th she sinks. It is apparent that the water-cocks have been opened and she has been sent to the bottom intentionally. Meanwile, the Condeferate prisoners are badly treated in prisons at Point Lookout, Washington and Fort Warren.

The CSS Olustee, having run the Federal blockade outside

Wilmington, North Carolina, is preying on Northern shipping.

Southern sympathizers in New York set fire to ten hotels, two theaters, and the Barnum Museum. Little damage is done, and one man, R. C. Kennedy, is caught and executed.

But what really upsets the South, more than anything else? On November 8, 1864, Abraham Lincoln is re-elected!

"We're in deep shit now," said Ralph. "He doesn't want this war to end with a truce. We've gotta be beat and punished or the war's gonna continue. Lincoln gettin re-elected proves that enough people are behind him to get the job done. All they gotta do is keep squeezin us, just like oranges. Purty soon all the juice will be gone."

Cutler nodded. He and Sergeant Crews were playing chess with the set Charlie had left to him. Both men sat straddling the log, the set balanced on a flattened area between them.

"Ha, I got you in a world of hurt now," exclaimed J. C. Crews. he moved his Knight, "Check!"

Cutler looked at his opponent and smiled, "You really think you got me, huh?"

"Well I do...don't I?" A questioning tone betrayed J.C.'s doubt. "Oh com'mon, I know I got you now, sure as campfire smoke follows a man around a fire."

"You sure," teased Cutler?

"I'm sure, dammit!"

"Well...then," and Cutler moved his Bishop from across the board. He had purposely ignored that corner to lure J.C. who was still a new player and very excitable. "Poof...and now, no more Knight. Thank you very much."

"Shit fire!"

"Your move, J.C., and watch the whole board. That's how Charlie used to get me all the time." Then realizing what he said, Cutler said, "Aw, I'm sorry."

Crews had caught Charlie in his arms when he was shot and fell off his horse.

"That's all right, t'weren't your fault. We all miss him," answered Crews in a subdued voice.

Migrating birds by the thousands flew overhead—the sky was dark with them. In the distance a few shotguns fired, and duck was roasting over a few campfires later than evening.

The leaves that remained on the trees lost their lushness of summer, many trees now being completely bare, standing stark in the warm Florida sun. Several weeks had passed since the last cold snap, and now, the frost forgotten, the weather was pleasantly warm again. With the setting sun, the fires would draw the men closer, and the coats would be thrown over their shoulders.

"Funny, how a few years ago we all thought that this was going to be a glorious, exciting venture," said Cutler, thoughtfully.

Ralph nodded as he stared into the fire, "Yea. I heard some of the younger ones sayin, nothin could be more glorious than dyin on the battlefield facin the enemy, with blood on the breast, and having saved our country's flag. What horseshit."

"Well, were you one thinking that way?"

"I guess so, but it sure seems a long way off, and I was more interested in returnin to Flora as a hero, crisp new uniform, and a splendid charger. Oi Vey, I even thought of comin back a Colonel or even a General."

"Well, when the war started, I didn't have Cora, or anybody else, but I imagined comin back to the plantation in grand style, and havin all the pretty gals makin eyes at me whenever I went somewheres. As for dying on the battlefield, that's crap. Those glorious dead are now just piles of rotting meat and bones, maybe covered with maggots. At least I think so. As for their souls, they're not in the grave anyway. Did you ever notice how bodies look on a battlefield?"

"Well, I never made a study of it, but they look like piles of disfigured, broken trash, all piled up and swollen."

"I couldn't have said it better myself, and those are the bodies that are lucky. How about the ones that were blown to pieces by shrapnel, or bled to death when a leg or arm is blown off, or the ones that couldn't move away from the burning woods. My God, what're we talkin like this for?"

"Dunno, but I'm willin to change the subject if you are."

"Damn straight."

"I got a letter from Flora today."

"Yea, I know it. Saw you readin something, and sittin there feelin sorry for yourself."

"Kiss my ass."

"Ha, your mustache is in the way."

"Seriously, I've gotta tell you about what's goin on...You know that I've been worried about the religion deal."

"Right." Cutler didn't want to say more for fear of offending his friend and saying the wrong thing.

"Well, Flora is gonna meet me in Savannah in December. I don't know yet when. She's got some distant cousins there, and it seems that these relatives have a store and are partners with a Jewish family. Well, to make a long story short, this family talked to their Rabbi about me and we're gonna, be there and discuss the whole deal, and if it works out...that's a big if...we'll be married right then and there."

"Hey, that's great. Will Tom be able to attend?"

"He's gonna try. I doubt if Cora can go. What do you think?"

"I doubt it, but it's up to her. You know that I won't be able to come, don't you. I just got back last month from my Pa's wedding."

"Yea, I realize that. Sorry, I'd like to have you there. My main man, but I can't see any other way to do it."

"No problem. You know I'll be thinkin of you both. Good luck, ole man." Cutler patted Ralph on the back.

"Thanks," but Ralph did not have much of a smile on his face. "Too many 'if's'," he thought. "Plus, this damn war. Savannah isn't the safest place in the world."

Word came that General Finley's Florida Brigade, under General Bate had suffered heavy losses at the battle at Franklin, Tennessee. Everyone knew of the battle and the attack by General Hood's army of Tennessee against General Schofield's Union army. Now they heard that the Florida boys had attacked the left flank of the Union army and had successfully beaten the defenders, but the attack had not been properly coordinated with other units, and unsupported, the Floridians were forced to give way and return the way they had come. They left a field covered with dead and wounded forms in grey.

The men of Dickinson's command were aware that their Captain had again been turned down for promotion. The high command received the recommendations for promotion, all of these with favorable endorsements, but yet these papers would be returned acknowledging Captain Dickison's skill and success, but each time the promotion would be turned down because there was no opening for the rank, or no regiment available for him to command.

As the men of the entire Second Florida Cavalry put it, "Goddamn politics, yet you see some asshole promoted that doesn't know his ass from hole in the ground!"

Meanwhile, away from the war, another tragedy takes place.

Colorado militia under the command of Colonel John Chivington, attack the Cheyenne village at Sand Creek, Colorado Territory, and kill almost one third of the Indians, and torturing and mutilating many of their victims. Many of the dead are women and children. The Cheyenne, under Chief Black Kettle, deny being involved in any raids were supposed to be under the protection of the garrison at Fort Lyon. The massacre is later condemned by the Federal government.

34

"Well!" exclaimed Ralph. "I reckon the wedding's postponed indefinitely. General Sherman has surrounded Savannah with over sixty thousand blue-bellies. General Hardee only has eighteen thousand to defend the trenches."

"Yea, I saw the telegrams, too. Looks like Sherman has cut the South from the west to the east. We'd already been cut in half when Vicksburg and the Mississippi was taken. You're lucky, you could be in Savannah now with Flora."

The December chill crept into the South, and Florida, although not to the extent of the other states, still suffered the cold of the winter.

Food and supplies, although not in great abundance, were still adequate for the Florida rebels. Medicine was in demand and many home remedies were used for the different maladies. Turpentine and sulphur were used for almost everything, and a poultice of the painful Stinging Nettle plant mixed with salt, helped relieve sprains and arthritis symptoms.

Other remedies were: The Aloe plants for burns and insect

bites, the Poke Weed Plant (root was used to induce vomiting), and the bark of the Prickly Ash was chewed to produce numbness in the mouth at the time of toothaches. Also, Sassafras tea was always good (fer what ailes ya).

Cutler thought of Dr. Algernon Speer's orange grove. He certainly had some sweet oranges in that grove. He wished he had a few now to munch on. He could still remember as a boy, walking home along the sandy Fort Read road, carrying a sack of oranges and eating several on his way home. His father always knew he had consumed several, probably by the telltale juice stains alongside his mouth and down his chin. Sam had used quite a few of those sprigs to start his own trees. Some of Sam's planting techniques had been used by the old Timucuan Indians. Planting and the cultivation of crops had been a very important means of food supply in addition to their hunting and fishing.

Fort Read was a one-story block house that had been built during the Seminole Indian war. This now abandoned block house, still stood about a mile from Fort Mellen. Cutler remembered Fort Mellen. As a child he would go there with his father and Blue Waters. He would sit on the wharf and watch the steamboat arrive, smoke pouring from its tall black stacks, water spraying, and steam hissing from its valves. The hustle of the rivermen fascinated him, and toil of the slaves as they struggled to unload the supplies, was just a way of life. The supplies would eventually be trudged across narrow trails by braying, stubborn, mule teams, westward, to the small settlements beginning to grow in Florida's interior. Few supplies stayed at the eight, log, two-story buildings that composed Fort Mellen. The fort had been for Indian fighting, and now was being used as a trading center and warehouse.

The closest settlement was across the lake, Enterprise. The Garnett plantation was almost two miles south of Fort Mellon. Their neighbors were a few scattered planters on the west side of the lake and the slightly more populous area at Enterprise.

J.J. Jed, the poor farmer that had lost a foot to a hungry alligator, still fished in Lake Monroe, the Saint Johns River, and some of the weed-choked streams surrounding the area. J.J. still plowed and tended to a small field, but this handicap made the work hard and painful. Besides, his wife, who loved to complain,

171

could plow further, deeper, and straighter than he, and as he said, "she's happier when she's complainin, and I'm plumb tickled to make her happy." He always had several barrels of salted fish ready for the steamboat returning north, and that made a clear profit of almost seven dollars, not counting the cost of the salt and the barrels.

Cutler could not contain his joy upon reading the first lines of Cora's letter.

Mrs. Cutler Garnett
Mellonville, Florida

10 December 1864

My Dearest,

I am rushing this letter to you. Therefore, be not disappointed, dear heart, of its brevity, for the news I have to give you should more than make up for any discomforts that you are now suffering.

After confering with dear Ernestine, and sweet Mara, in embarrassing details, certain facts concerning my physical conditions, I have the most welcome honor of informing you, my wonderful husband, that this spring you will become the father of our love and affection.

I wish I could tell you in person, but alas, you are forced to learn of this blessed event by humble writings.

I must give this poor letter to Jeffrey to rush it to the boat that it is about to leave the wharf in less than an hour.

We, here, are all well, and send you our undying love.

Your loving wife,
Cora

172

"Whoopee! Hot damn, I'm gonna be a daddy," shouted Cutler, as he jumped up and down in the dust, waving his letter around his head.

"Slow down, partner," said Ralph, as he patted Cutler on the back. "How'm I gonna shake your hand when you're twirlin around circles like a tot's top?"

The two friends talked late that night while snoring sounds were heard from the surrounding tents.

The following day, news arrived that much of the Army of Tennessee had been destroyed by General Thomas' Union army at Nashville. General Lee was still short of men and supplies in the trenches around Petersburg, and General Hardee was powerless against General Sherman at Savannah.

"You know, ole man, the noose is gettin tighter," mumbled Cutler. He was thoughtful over this depressing news. Now that he was about to have a family, he suddenly realized that things were changing. No more fun and adventure and taking chances. He was going to be a father and had the future to think about. Since his marriage, he had already become somewhat more cautious and concerned for his own well being. And, except for his one, almost-fling, he had been completely faithful to Cora. But now, all of a sudden, he was having second thoughts. The war was not going well at all. Would he be stupid to stick it out, or do as some had done already in other units, quit. "Quit? What would Pa think? How about the Capt'n? Quitting...that's a nice way of saying deserting. No way! I've helped capture deserters, and despised the scum all the while, even while a few, that really didn't look that mean, looked at me with big, pleading eyes. I guess I never thought of why they deserted. I can just see my son now. Of course it's going to be a son! I can see him now looking up at me and asking me, "Pa, where were you during the war? You said you were with Captain Dickison, but your name isn't on his Honor Roll, and whenever the veterans get together, you never go. Why, Pa?" I guess I'll just stick around and see what happens. it might even get interesting!"

Ralph—had looked up at Cutler's first few words but then said nothing, realizing that his partner was really talking to himself and was, again, in deep thought.

"Well, I've learned something," thought Cutler. "Civilians and politicians starts wars, soldiers fight 'em."

173

35

Christmas and New Years had come and gone, and except for best wishes for a prosperous year by Captain Dickison, a few goodies brought by the ladies in the vicinity, and some seasonal songs, sung for a few evenings, nothing changed. To most, the holidays were a mournful, thoughtful time of year, instigated by the war and frustration of not being at home with friends and relatives. The War for Southern Independence, as some still called it, was trying men's souls. Thomas Paine had known what he was writing those years ago, but these men had also endured for almost four years. These were no Sunshine Patriots!

At sunset, on the 2nd of February, 1865, Captain Dickison, Lieutenants McCardell, McEady McLeod, Haile and Haynes, with one hundred twenty-five men, traveled to the now, deserted city of Palatka.

The Captain formed his men and told them he intended crossing the mile-wide St. Johns River, into strongly occupied enemy territory. Understanding the risk, he could understand anyone not wishing to continue. Dickison had never done this before, but the results were the same, every man present was willing to cross.

The one flatboat could carry but twelve men and horses. Therefore, it was ten o'clock the next morning before the entire command was safely on the eastern shore. Cutler and Ralph, being among the first to cross, were able to sleep for several hours while the river was still being crossed by the balance of the command.

The Confederate's target was the Fort at Picolata, now held by a garrison of U.S. Army troops. There was a small settlement there on the shores of a wide section of the St. Johns River. The settlement was connected by a stagecoach road eastward to St. Augustine.

As the tired men neared Picolata, Private Ernesto Hernandez was called forward. Hernandez' home was nearby, and his father was still living there.

The young man led the silent column to within one mile of the fort, then he continued on to his home. Within the hour

Hernandez returned with his father.

The information was crucial. The garrison had been reinforced that day with about three hundred Federals and several cannon, which were now positioned on the fort. Without artillery of his own, Dickison realized that an attack on such a strong position could be suicidal

Additional information was more encouraging.

There were several small detachments of Union cavalrymen throughout the area, some on patrol, some at outposts, and also several attending a dance close to St. Augustine.

The tireless Dickison awoke his men and they moved rapidly to the first outpost, a station twelve miles down the stagecoach road. The Confederates quickly and quietly surrounded the place and captured twelve Federals and their mounts.

Taking the prisoners, they continued until they reached the crossroads to Jacksonville and St. Augustine. Placing a detachment on each, the remainder of the command arrived at the house where the dance had been held.

Many of the merrymakers were just leaving when the trailworn men in grey swooped down on them from every side. Without a chance to resist, the surprised Federals, surrendered.

Meanwhile, the detachment stationed on the road to St. Augustine, captured a four-horse ambulance and twelve musicians. Dickison's command now had a total of forty prisoners, eighteen horses, and one fine ambulance. So far, not a shot had been fired.

Now Dickison divided his command, sending Lieutenants Haile, Haynes and McCardell, a detail of guards, and the prisoners, with orders to continue up Haw Creek and rendezvous near the Braddock farm, about seven miles east of the St. Johns river. Captain Dickison's command, with Lieutenant McEaddy and the advance guard, turned southward on the road towards Volusia.

The men ate in the saddle as the sunlight faded in the clear sky.

Cutler looked at the full moon as it slowly lifted above the black treeline. He and Ralph were among the advance guard. The two of them keeping their horses side by side, about thirty yards ahead of Lieutenant McEaddy and the rest of the detachment.

"I don't think I have a single spot on my body that isn't sore and tired," whispered Ralph.

"Me, too. I don't see how the Cap'n does it. I guess the Yankees don't see how he does it either. I hope I'll be like he is when I get that old," answered Cutler.

"Right now, all I want is to be allowed to get older."

"You're right there...Shhh, hey look up ahead. Isn't that a column coming towards us? Quick tell the Lieutenant."

Cutler stopped off the trail while Ralph hurried back to inform Lieutenant McEaddy that they were about to have company.

In less than five seconds the Lieutenant and the rest of the troop, charged the surprised Federals. Most of these quickly splashed into the swamp and hid, only one man and two horses being captured.

"Man, they disappeared quicker'n I ever did see. Well, let's go on for another hour, then we'll stop and rest for an hour," said Lieutenant McEaddy.

The men were asleep as soon as they lay down on the ground wrapped in their blankets. Unfortunately, an hour thus spent, passes quickly. Wearily, they remounted and continued on their way. Every few miles they would meet deserters on their way to St. Augustine. These would be questioned and then sent to the rear as prisoners.

From the deserters, Captain Dickison learned that Colonel Wilcoxson, the Union commander, was at that time at the Braddock farm preparing to leave with ten large wagons loaded with cotton. Realizing that he was outnumbered, Dickison arranged his command for attack to his advantage, as soon as the Federals came down a long hill with their wagon train.

Dickison and his two officers, Lieutenant McEaddy and Dr. Williams, the surgeon, prepared the men for the attack. Sergeant William Cox, dismounted the men and placed them along a stream, while the rest of the men waited along the road.

The Federals appeared through the trees. They moved along in no particular order alongside the wagons, having no advance guard to clear and check the way.

The wagons came to a halt and the advance, instead of waiting for orders, fired. Immediately, Dickison ordered a charge on the wagon train.

The Rebels charged among the startled Federals. Teamsters immediately put their hands in the air along with many of their escort. The road being narrow, the Federals had no room to maneuver, many falling off their well fed, well rested, spirited, and plunging horses. Others were knocked off the animals by the galloping, yelling, and wild-eyed Southerners.

Although Dickison's men were outnumbered, the shots from the thickets and the double file of rushing troopers, gave the impression that there were several hundred, instead of just fifty-two. The balance of the troop was with Lieutenant McCardell.

A number of the escort fell back into the woods, pursued by Ralph and Cutler. These shortly came to a halt and surrendered as their companions had.

The Federal commander, his staff, and the last detachment of twenty men charged down the hill towards the wagons and prisoners. Dr. Williams and Lieutenant McEaddy quickly called some men to meet this new threat. Cutler lined up with the officers, along with Sergeant Cox and half a dozen others. Ralph was holding his pistols on the prisoners, trying to watch in two directions.

The Southerners fired and eight saddles were emptied. The remaining Federals surrendered, except for their commander, Colonel Wilcoxson, who, after firing his last shot, threw his pistol at the Southerners.

With a shout of rage and frustration, Colonel Wilcoxson galloped toward the prisoners, possibly hoping to free them. There was but one way for him to do this—through Captain Dickison!

Seeing the Colonel approaching, and knowing who he was, he rode on to meet him, expecting a surrender. Instead, Wilcoxson drew his saber, yelled, and charged. The rest of the Federals and Confederates stopped all action, and turned to watch this last surprising drama unfold.

Dickison called, "Surrender, you fool!"

Finally , when only a few yards apart, Dickison fired, the shot hitting the Federal in the left side. Both horsemen turned again to face each other. Wilcoxson charged again, his saber flashing in the air. The Captain fired twice more, and the Colonel slumped in the saddle. Cutler jumped off his horse and caught the reins of the slowing animal, then he caught the wounded man as he slipped off the horse.

Colonel Wilcoxson opened his eyes and whispered, "Is that your commanding officer?"

"Yes sir, it is. That's Captain John Jackson Dickison."

"Of course, who else. Help me up. I must talk to him."

Captain Dickison turned as Cutler and the wounded Colonel approached, leaning on Cutler's arm.

"Captain, this is Colonel Wilcoxson. He wishes to talk with you," called Cutler.

Captain Dickison dismounted and walked toward the Federal officer. Seeing the seriousness of the wounds, he said, "Colonel, why did you throw your life away?"

"Don't blame yourself. You are only doing your duty as a soldier. I alone am to blame."

Dr. Williams came up and helped the wounded man lie down on a blanket under a tree. As he looked to his wounds, he found them to be mortal. He also saw him to be a Mason, which both the Doctor and Captain Dickison were. The three men; the dying Federal and two Confederates talked for several minutes, then suddenly Colonel Wilcoxson gasped and died. Dr. Williams closed the dead man's eyes as Captain Dickison stood up, and removed his hat, looking down at the dead man. "Too bad, he was a brave man." He stood for a moment, then turned to his duties.

The Federals had four dead and quite a few wounded, including seventy-five captured. Not a one of their command having escaped. The Southerners had a few minor wounds, but no other casualties. They now possessed a wagon train of ten wagons, each with six mules, all loaded with cotton.

The long column moved out slowly toward Horse Landing, but with darkness coming on and so many prisoners, Dickison called a halt for the night after only three miles. He sent a detachment of four men to the crossing to order the flatboat brought over so when they reach the landing the next morning they could begin crossing immediately.

Meanwhile, at the landing, Captain McGahaghan, and his Rebel infantry company of seventy reserves, was working on the wreck of the gunboat Columbine in order to remove what machinery that was still usable.

Still no word had been received from Lieutenant McCardell

and his command.

The exhausted men chewed on dry crackers and, wrapped in their blankets, fell asleep quickly. The cool, dry night was still, and the men slept soundly. Insuring that each shift of guards remained alert, the tired men were assigned two-hour tours in pairs.

Well before dawn, Dickison had his troopers on the move, knowing that being on the east side of the St. Johns, in enemy occupied territory, and outnumberd at least fifty to one, he was in a most perilous situation. He knew that at this time, the Federals had to be aware of his raid and would have patrols searching the countryside.

The Confederates reached the landing at ten in the morning and immediately began the crossing. Dickison maintained a heavy vigilance in a semicircle to his rear, as the crossings began. Twenty-five hours later, the last load, bearing Captain Dickison finally landed on the western shore, accompanied by shouts of welcome by his men.

Lieutenant McCardell and his men arrived while the crossing was being made.

The single flatboat had crossed and recrossed the wide river and carried over two hundred and fifty men (including prisoners), ten heavily loaded wagons, two ambulances, sixty mules, and almost three hundred horses.

Private David Ambler was immediately sent to Waldo to announce the success of the expedition. Telegrams were sent from there to all points, the news greeted with joy.

St. Augustine, Fla., March 23, 1865

Captain J. J. Dickison:

Sir, I have heard that you are a most kind and honorable gentlemen and a Free Mason. Believing this to be a fact, I, as the widow of an honored Mason and brave soldier, appeal to you for a great favor.

179

The sword which my husband, the late Lieutenant-Colonel Wilcoxson, wore at the time of his capture by you, was presented to him by his brothers of the "Mystic Tie," members of St. John's lodge, of Norwalk, Conn., in token of the high esteem in which they held him. If you are a Mason, you will understand the value which is placed upon the gift, and why I so strongly desire to possess it in order that I may re-present it to the lodge.

It is possible for you to return it to me? Or, if it has passed out of your immediate possession, can you in anyway effect the restoration of it to me? The centennial celebration of the St. John's lodge takes place in May next. Earnest have béen the entreaties from the brotherhood that the Colonel would make an effort to be with them at that time. He will be present with them at that time in spirit, without doubt. What would I not give to be able to place in their hands the sword which, though it passed from my husband's hands in such a manner, has never been dishonored!

Yours respectfully,

Mrs. Albert H. Wilcoxson

Camp Baker, Waldo, Fla., March 31, 1865

Mrs. Albert H. Wilcoxson, St. Augustine, Fla:

Madam, I have the honor to acknowledge the receipt of your letter of the 23rd instant, which reached me a few days ago by flat of truce.

Previous to the receipt of your letter, at the request of your husband, I had concluded to send you the sword which was worn by him at the time of his capture. It is unusual, in time of war, to return captures of this description, but, in this instance, I will deviate from that course, on account of the feelings I entertained for your husband as a brave officer. With this, I send you his sword, trusting that it may reach you safely.

I am, Madam, yours respectfully,

J. J. Dickison
Captain, Commanding Forces

Cutler now learned that the most effective strike force was most often a small, highly mobile, self-sufficient, well-informed unit.

Obviously, Stuart, Mosby, Hampton, Forrest, Dickison and a few others realized this already.

36

"Oh, I'm gonna sleep for a week..." groaned Ralph, as he stretched out on his bed of pine needles and blankets.

"Me too," answered Cutler. "My eyes burn, my neck's stiff, and my ass is sore; I think it's pounded all the way up into my throat."

"Yea, I know all about it, that's why you've got a shitty taste in your mouth, ha!"

Dickison's men returned from the very succesful, but tiring raid against the Federals. They were gone ten days. Ten days of little sleep, little to eat, and many hours in the saddle. The raid culminated with the fight at the Braddock farm and then the long crossing across the St. Johns river.

Upon their final return to their headquarters at Waldo, the men bathed themselves and their horses in a nearby lake. They all cavorted gleefully for a short time in the cool waters and crisp air. After finishing with the care for their animals and weapons, they ate quickly and almost everyone was asleep by dark.

Captain Dickison was wide awake. On his return that day, February 9th, 1864, he found dispatches from Captain E. Sutterloh, waiting for him.

Captain Sutterloh was on outpost near Cedar Key. He had telegraphed urgent news. The Yankees, under cover of their gunboats, were advancing eastward from Cedar Key.

That evening, another telegram arrived stressing the urgency of the situation. Captain Dickison telegraphed this news to headquarters at Tallahassee. He informed his officers of the situation and then retired to his tent.

In the back of his mind, he felt that his men would have to be contented with one night's rest. At least they had plenty of the latest weapons and sufficient ammunition for a quick action. The men would be sleepy and sore, but he would allow them to leave their own horses and take the well-rested and well-fed, captured U.S. Army horses. This was all in case they did have to move out to confront this new threat. It was, after all, unusual for his unit, to fight in the western part of the state, leaving the areas immediately adjacent to the St. Johns River and the heavily occupied eastern shores, practically unguarded.

Sure enough, he was awakened around midnight. The guard apologized for waking him but lit two candles on his desk and handed him a telegram.

The enemy had penetrated the interior on the Levyville road, raided the surrounding areas and needed to be stopped. Dickison was to take his force and advance rapidly toward the west. He was to harass the Federals with his small cavalry force until General Millar could reach the area with his brigade, by train, from Lake City.

Dickison blew out the candles and went back to his bed. He knew that he and his men would be useless without some rest.

At dawn a bugle called the men to formation. They were told to be ready to leave in one hour.

The men groaned, but as soon as they were informed that the Yankees had penetrated the interior from Cedar Key, the groaning stopped.

Within the hour, the fresh horses were saddled, ammunition issued, and dried food and water loaded. There was no time to cook rations for the trip.

Ready to leave, Ralph and Cutler were among the fifty-two men from Company H, Second Florida Cavalry under Lieutenants

McCardell and McEaddy. Joining the column were eighteen men from Company B under Lieutenant McLeod, twenty men from the Fifth Battalion, Company H, commanded by Lieutenants Haile and Haynes, and one twelve pound howitzer, commanded by Lieutenant Bruton, in all, ninety men.

As this cavalry force left Waldo, another detachment also left for Tallahassee with the prisoners.

The remaining force knew that, while Captain Dickison was away, they would have to remain active and alert, not allowing the Union forces to realize the thinness of the Confederate defenders.

Dickison allowed little time for rest, and by the thirteenth, the little force reached the "No. 4" station from Cedar Key. They had ridden through woods, on narrow trails, along the railroad tracks, and over some wider sandy roads. Cutler remembered the route very well. He had come this very way with dispatches a year ago. It was just before the battle at Olustee.

A year ago? It didn't seem possible! So much had happened since then. He wasn't even married then, and now he had a wife, a pregnant wife at that. Even his father was now remarried.

The men cleaned their weapons on their first day while on the trail. At that time it was realized that although the new Spencers were going to be effective firepower, for the small force, it was also realized that the cylindrical tubes that were inserted forward from a circular opening in the buttplates, would be useless if not loaded with seven jacketed shells. There was a shortage of shells, and there was also a shortage of spare tubes. Although all the men had their ball, and cap pistols and sabers; thoughtfully, a few also brought their older ball and cap rifles.

Not knowing the exact whereabouts and size of the enemy forces, Captain Dickison slowed the column's advance that afternoon. He did realize that the Federals were only a few miles distant, and judging from his scout's reports, they outnumbered him.

A halt was ordered at nightfall, no fires allowed, and a strong picket put out around the camp. The horses were cared for and haltered nearby in small groups, bridles and saddles ready.

"I think tomorrow's the day," said Ralph.

"Yea, I think so, too. We're only a few miles from them, but they must know we've arrived, 'cause they're gathering in their patrols and consolidating, and according to the last scouting report, the Yanks are returning back toward Cedar Key." Cutler had hoped to be among the scouts that day, but having rotated with some of the other men during the trip, he was back in the column. Scouting, although more dangerous, was what Cutler preferred. He had more freedom and felt more secure in his own wood-lore experience. Besides, who wanted to ride along with a bunch of sweaty men and horses, inhaling dust, being splashed on from the horses in front, and adjusting your pace to the guys in front? Slow down...speed up...slow down...catch up, what a pain in the ass!

Early the next morning, Captain Sutterloh and eighteen men from the outpost, and Captains King, Price, Waterson, and Dudley, and their thirty-seven man militia company, arrived. Captain Dickison learned from Sutterloh that the enemy's force consisted of two regiments of troops, six to seven hundred strong. They now occupied a solid position on the high embankment of the railroad.

A courier arrived from General Millar and informed them that he was advancing as quickly as possible on the road from Lake City.

Dickison held a short council and decided to attack the larger force as soon as possible. He felt that by attacking he could possibly hold them long enough for his reinforcements to arrive. If, instead, the enemy retreated to the island, their gunboats would render an engagement impossible. Allowing them to simply retreat without attempting to fight them was simply unthinkable!

Dickison sent out his skirmishers and then moved the column toward the position of the entrenched Union regiments.

At the first sounds of firing, Dickison commanded the entire unit forward to within range of the enemy. The woods were sparse with scattered pines and oaks, the underbrush was barely a foot high.

The men dismounted quickly and then charged forward on foot. The quick dash, so startled the Federals that they fired a scattered unorganized volley and then turned and ran when the Southerners fired in return. In just a few minutes, Dickison's men captured the road and were lying down firing over the top of the rails, into the unorganized Federals.

"Quick, give us a hand," shouted Lieutenant Bruton.

Cutler, Sergeant Crews and several others turned and joined the struggling cannoneers in rolling the heavy howitzer into position. The caisson was placed several yards to the rear of the unlimbered gun, the horses unhitched and led to the rear behind a small clump of cypress trees in a low area.

"Thanks men, this ground is sure soggy, and it sure makes this little bugger hard to roll. Stay close, we may need you again."

As the men returned to their positions, Joseph Crews grunted, fell to his knees, clutching his stomach. As Cutler turned to help him, he felt a tug at his sleeve.

Helping Crews into a more comfortable position, he saw the blood stain spread over the front of the man's jacket.

I'll take care of him now," said Dr. Williams, as he crouched over the wounded man. "Let me see your arm," he then said to Cutler.

Cutler looked down and saw blood dripping from his sleeve; he hadn't felt any pain, but remembered the tug at his sleeve.

A bullet had nicked him in the fleshy part of the arm, just below the elbow. It didn't seem to be serious, but he was bleeding like a stuck pig.

Dr. Williams sprinkled some powder on the wound and quickly wrapped it. "You're as good as new, for now. I'll look at it better later." Then he turned back to Sergeant Crews, who was lying quietly on his back, gritting his teeth, one hand on his stomach.

"Well, Sergeant, that's a nasty one, just try to lie quietly while I poke around."

The firing increased as the Federals prepared to retake the lost ground, but the well handled artillery piece, kept them at bay. Lieutenant Bruton alternated solid shot, exploding shells and cannister, changing the field of fire from left to right, not allowing the Federals to take cover before each next shot.

Showers of pine branches, bark and cones, sprayed over the men as the minie balls hit the surrounding trees. The Yankees were obviously firing too high, for some reason, therefore, little damage being done to the Confederates.

A column in blue was seen advancing over the railroad trestle from the island. Dickison directed the gun crew to turn towards this new threat. Lieutenant Bruton and his men with a help of a few others, rolled the cannon and caisson to a position facing the water.

The cannon was first loaded with a solid shot then aimed just ahead of the advancing column, almost three hundred yards distant. When the Federals reached that point, Bruton put his fire to the touch hole.

The solid ball struck the head of the column, knocking men down as pins, pieces of bodies flying in the air.

"Nothing discourages more than seeing pieces of meat where your buddies just were," commented Ralph, dryly.

Cutler looked in the direction of the trestle and shuddered. He remembered the grizzled old fighter he had met briefly at Smyrna and thought of the words he had spoken to a young soldier that day. You never forget the death and suffering, and although occasionally you can harden to it, by seeing so much of it, you never get used to it. The man had fought Englishmen, Mexicans, Indians and then Americans, and he had said how easy it was to kill but how difficult it was to live with it. Cutler wondered whether he would be plagued with these thoughts and nightmares when he got older. If he got older! He also wondered what happened to the old man. Where he was? Was he still alive?

With only four shells left, the little howitzer was returned to the center of the line. Then, with his last shot, Bruton waited until the enemy made a desperate charge. When they were just a short distance he showered them with grape. The men in blue, still able to walk, returned as quickly as possible to their cover.

The little cannon was pulled to the rear. Lieutenant McEaddy, with ten men, moved to hold the trestle as long as possible.

The fight continued until the Captain learned that most of his men had shot their last cartridges. He passed among his men distributing whatever ammunition he had, then ordered the unit to fall back slowly, taking all casualties and weapons.

The little command withdrew about six hundred yards into the woods, then waited, preparing to make every shot count. Instead, the Federals did not renew the attack.

"Now what? We're in deep shit now," commented Ralph. He had five shots remaining in his pistols, his empty rifle slung on his back. "I guess if they get close enough we can use our pig

186

stickers," he continued, indicating his saber.

"Not much choice, but I don't think it'll come to that. The Captain's not goin to let us get slaughtered or captured. We'll probably retreat towards our advancing forces. They can't be too far away," answered Cutler.

At that time a courier came up and reported the ammunition wagons within six or eight miles and loaded with ample small arms and artillery ammunition.

Lieutenant Bruton brightened up, "Well, I'm sure tickled to hear that. All I need is powder. We can put anything in the barrel for short range work—stones, pieces of iron, nails. I don't care what. Can you imagine one of those Yanks going home to his momma saying, "I was sent home—the Rebs hit me with a rock.""

The men chuckled. Knowing they would shortly have ammunition certainly helped their dispositions. "Nothin more helpless than sitten thar with an empty gun. Might as well have a pea-shooter."

Cutler had his wound attended to by Dr. Williams, who found it to be not serious, although probably painful. Sergeant Crews and five others were severely wounded and were placed in wagons that were returning immediately to Lake City with a light guard. Crews winced as the wagon began its long bumpy return trip.

The next day, the well armed Confederates anxiously moved forward to the attack. Instead, they found many of the enemy dead and wounded, some captured slaves, many horses, and several hundred cattle. The Federals had evacuated the area and returned to their gunboats! Several stragglers were still trying to escape by wading up to their necks or trying to swim across the bay to the island. Some drowned in the process.

The Federals had lost over seventy casualties. This had been a very costly raid for them!

Dickison's command stopped at Gainesville on the way back to Waldo. As the column entered the little city, Cutler wondered uneasily whether he would see Lydia. He hoped not. He had finally gotten smart and realized what a stupid thing he had almost done.

The town's people were waiting for the soldiers, couriers having already preceded them with the news. Even people from around the countryside, lined the main street shouting and clapping as the tired, ragged column passed through town. The troopers, straightened their backs as they rode proudly passed the joyous crowds. Several young boys ran alongside the horses, now and then touching a stirrup, or the sweaty flank of a cavalry horse. They would have much to tell their envious friends in days to come.

The women of Gainesville had prepared a feast, and this was brought to the men at their campsite just outside of town.

The Captain had decided that, although there was still plenty of daylight for traveling, it would be a definite morale booster for the men to have a good hot meal and some praise from their grateful country folks.

As in most areas of Florida, city, town, or countryside, there were those who said nothing, but looked at the proceedings with bitterness. There were still many Union supporters in the South, especially in Florida, being such a newly settled state.

Although there were families that had been in the state since the early Spanish occupation, the majority had arrived since 1845, the year Florida was first admitted to the Union.

These Floridians' loyalties had not changed over to the Confederacy, and although many did not fight against the South, they certainly did not sympathize with her.

They definitely knew how to keep their mouths shut.

Cutler did not speak to Lydia Taylor, although he did see her in the distance as she brought some covered dishes to the officers. He made himself as inconspicuous as possible in case she came looking for him.

She didn't and he wasn't sure whether he was relieved or disappointed.

The State troops were once again disbanded now that the present emergency had passed. They would be called again when needed.

The following morning, Captain Dickison's command returned to Waldo.

Now that the immediate emergency had passed, the men joked on their way back to camp.

Their favorite subject was an incident that had happened to their Captain on the previous raid toward the Braddock farm.

188

The detachment had stopped at a small farmhouse and the heavyset lady of the house, had mistaken the Captain and his men as Union soldiers.

Before the Captain could say anything, the lady assured him that she was a staunch Union supporter, that she had two sons that had deserted from the Confederate army and were concealed in the swamp, and would remain hidden until they heard that that terrible man, Dickison, had rerossed the river.

Pretending to be a Union Colonel, he and his men wearing blue overcoats, Dickison was able to get accurate information as to the whereabouts of Colonel Wilcoxon and his men.

Just then, more of Company H rode up and dismounted. These were not dressed in blue overcoats. Not wanting to be found out, Dickison called her attention to them and said, "See, those are some of Dickison's men we have captured."

At the time, he called out to his men in blue to guard the prisoners well.

The lady exclaimed, "God bless you, Colonel," and all two hundred pounds of her hugged slender Captain Dickison tightly.

Before leaving, he told her that he would send his wagons to her to furnish her supplies of coffee and flour for the fodder his men had taken. Having only Confederate money, he certainly couldn't pay with that!

She hugged him again as he was about to leave, his men doing their utmost not to smile.

This episode was a subject of much laughter and lightheartedness for many years to come.

The Union lady? She soon found out that she had hugged her most hated enemy, Captain J. J. Dickison, C.S.A.

37

Cutler and Ralph gathered the wood for their cooking fire during the cool, frosty, early morning hours. The light mist seemed to penetrate straight through their clothing. The men wore over-coats and, additionally, had blankets draped over their shoulders.

"My fingers feel like they're goin' to fall off," muttered Ralph.

"Yea, me too, and I think my teeth are goin to chatter off. I'll get the lighter pine and some shavings. You get some coals from another fire and let's get some coffee a boiling," answered Cutler.

Shortly, the men had a crackling fire radiating heat in the immediate area. The greasy pine smoke was shortly replaced by a smokeless hot oak fire.

"Well, what's going to happen with you and Flora? Made any decision?" asked Cutler.

"As you know, I got a letter today and she agreed to just wait until we can get to Savannah to get married. We do want to take you up on your offer to move to the plantation and start up the lumber mill," Ralph answered after a light sip of scalding coffee. He always burned his mouth, no matter how careful he was.

"Good, we'll need all the help we can get. I hope Orin joins us at the plantation, too, although we haven't heard from him since the Florida was taken in Brazil. We don't know where he is. No matter how this war turns out, you know that things are going to be tough."

"Yeah, I can imagine. There sure isn't goin to be much money around...whatever type it is!"

"I guess there's no real decisions we can make at this time. Just keep our ears and eyes open."

Ralph spat in the fire and watched it sizzle.

In Northwest Florida, another one-sided battle was fought at a place called Natural Bridge.

Early on the morning of March 6, 1865, began the first of a series of assaults by nine hundred Union troops, against well entrenched Confederates.

During that entire day, General Miller's collection of Confederate soldiers, militia, scattered cavalry, old men, wounded, and young boys from the West Florida Seminary at Tallahassee, held off the Federal assaults.

The Federals had landed from gunboats at Apalachee Bay, and had intended to capture Tallahassee. The gunboats had attempted the navigation of the St. Marks river, but they had run aground. General Miller had blocked the way of the Union infantry at the

Newport Bridge on the St. Marks. The Federal commander, General John Newton, tried to flank the Rebel force at Natural Bridge, but instead, found them waiting for him.

By late afternoon, Newton realized that it was pointless to continue attacking, so began the long retreat to the protection of the gunboats and then return to Key West.

To prevent the pursuit by the Confederate forces, trees were felled along the road of retreat.

The Union losses were twenty-one killed, eighty-nine wounded, thirty-eight captured, and one hundred and forty-eight missing.

The Rebels had three dead, twenty-two wounded.

Although this was another Confederate victory, and the papers praised the deed, the men were losing their enthusiasm. The Yankees just kept coming, no matter how many were killed or taken prisoner. They just kept coming, and everyone of them had new guns, new clothes, new shoes, new haversacks...and full ones, too. It was disgusting!

Dickison's forces continued skirmishing with the Federals in the St. Johns area.

Then on April 10, 1865, the dreaded news arrived.

Somberly, Captain Dickison read the telegram to his assembled troops:

"Sunday, April 9, 1865, Appomattox Courthouse, Virginia, General Robert E. Lee, Commander Army of Northern Virginia, surrendered his army to General Ulysses S. Grant."

The following days are hectic and confusing. Lincoln's death on April 15th is met with mixed feelings. Surprisingly, the men do not feel that rejoicing is in order. On April 17th, General Johnson surrenders to General Sherman, although the terms are controversial to the two governments.

Many individual units find Federal bases and surrender and apply for parole. Others continue the fight.

Captain Dickison, who now receives appointment to be Colonel of Cavalry, respects the truce that is now in Florida and finally on May 5, 1865, the Second Florida is paroled and is no more.

The Federal officer who paroles the Florida men at Waldo says that he has never witnessed "such devotion from soldiers to their commanding officer."

After many goodbyes, and exchanging of addresses, sorrowfully, the men leave the camp in small groups. Cutler, Ralph, and half a dozen others, start on the road to Ocala. On the way they encounter citizens who ask them to confirm the news. There are many tears from this defeated population.

Vito Forselli, footsore, tired, dirty, and hungry, is walking home from Virginia. What was left of the Fifth, Eighth, and Eleventh Florida Regiments, were captured by General Armstrong Custer's cavalry. Many of the Rebel officers, including a Major Burns, are sent to Johnson's Island and held as prisoners for many months.

Cutler Garnett and Ralph Jacobs arrive in Ocala. Flora practically flies out of the store and into Ralph's arms. Cutler stays for just an hour and then continues to Mellonville.

On a lonely road he sees a body swinging slowly from a tree. The negro man is dressed in a pair of old ragged trousers, and is barefoot. His hands are tied behind his back, and his back and shoulders are raw with whip marks, the dried blood on his back covered with flies. The man's head is forced to one side to accommodate the heavy rope stretching his neck. The swollen tongue is purple and protrudes from the mouth.

Cutler stares in disgust at the dead man, and he looks at the eyes that gaze upward into the skies. The eyes have frozen the fear, torture, and pain the man felt during his last minutes of life.

Cutler cuts down the body and lays it carefully at the foot of the tree, also cutting the wrists free and placing the hands over the chest.

He looks down at the dead man and shakes his head. "You were probably killed by some good, loyal, frustrated, God-fearing citizens. You never knew why your good masters killed you....I'm sorry, but you should feel sorry for us. For generations, the South will be paying."

Cutler unrolls one of his blankets and covers the figure, remounts and rides southward. Later that afternoon, the man's wife finds him this way...covered with a Confederate grey blanket.

Cutler does not delay any longer. He has a wife to hold, a son to meet, and a life to start.